OTHER BOOKS BY MARY LOGUE

Novels

Red Lake of the Heart
Still Explosion

Claire Watkins Mysteries

Blood Country
Dark Coulee
Glare Ice
Bone Harvest

Poetry

Discriminating Evidence
Settling

POISON HEART

A NOVEL OF SUSPENSE

Mary Logue

BALLANTINE BOOKS NEW YORK

Poison Heart is a work of fiction. Names, characters, places, and incidents are the products of the author's imagination or are used fictitiously. Any resemblance to actual events, locales, or persons, living or dead, is entirely coincidental.

Published in the United States by Ballantine Books, an imprint of The Random House Publishing Group, a division of Random House, Inc., New York.

Ballantine and colophon are registered trademarks of Random House, Inc.

Library of Congress Cataloging-in-Publication Data is available from the publisher upon request.

ISBN 0-345-46224-6

Printed in the United States of America

Ballantine Books website address: www.ballantinebooks.com

2 4 6 8 9 7 5 3 1

First Edition

Text design by Julie Schroeder

For Sharon Hendry

POISON
HEART

WHEN PATTY JO TILDE HEARD HER HUSBAND HOLLER her name, she was inside the house, sitting at the kitchen table, looking at *People* magazine and wondering when Cher's face was going to split wide open from all the plastic surgery she'd had done. Patty Jo had considered a neck tuck. Nothing drastic. She figured she might lose ten years or so. She had turned sixty in May and wouldn't mind being able to pass for fifty.

Walter hollered again, and she could tell the sound was coming from the barn. She thought of ignoring him. Who knew what stupid thing he wanted to show her? When was he going to realize that she didn't need to see every little thing he discovered?

She stood up and walked to the screen door. It was warm out. The wind spun a dust devil in the farmyard.

"Hey," Walter yelled.

She wondered what he needed. After strolling out the door, she walked slowly toward the barn.

When she looked in through the large rolling door, she saw Walter seated on a hay bale, bent over like the old man he was, his hand to his head. She could hear his ragged breathing all the way across the barn. She didn't say anything, just stood and watched.

"Help," he hollered, and bent over as if he had been hit by some force. Then he lifted his head and saw her.

"Patty Jo," he whispered.

She didn't answer him. She had been waiting for this moment for months. She had married hoping it would not be for too long.

"Call." He pointed at his head. He knew what was happening. Walter had suffered a couple of small strokes in the last year. The doctor had told him the next one could be bad.

The stupid old man would take his shirt off when he worked. At eighty, his ribs curved in over his sad belly.

"You'll be fine, Walter. Just take some deep breaths. Told you not to work so hard in this heat."

"I need . . ." He paused and breathed. "Help."

Patty Jo walked over to the shirt and picked it up. Then she handed it to Walter. "Put your shirt on, Walter. I'll go call the doctor."

At her words, he slumped over farther. The shirt slipped from his fingers, then he fell to the barn floor.

Patty Jo stood over him and said, "Don't worry. I'll be right back. You take it easy. I just have to go call the ambulance."

She walked back to the house. She was pretty sure this was it, but she didn't want to take any chances. The doctor had told her that to make sure Walter survived the next stroke, he needed to get to the hospital within the first three hours.

Patty Jo stepped into the kitchen and looked at the clock over the sink. A little after noon. She could say she hadn't found him until close to supper.

She sat back down at the table and picked up the magazine. She heard no more shouts coming from the barn. The dust danced for another moment in the yard, then settled.

CHAPTER 1

Claire Watkins sat on the steps of her new home watching the bluff line as the sky filled with light. A little over a month ago, right before school started, she and Meg had moved in with Rich Haggard in his family homestead, an old farmhouse along Highway 35 about half a mile from the center of Fort St. Antoine. The farm was the last house in the village to the south.

Since moving to the Wisconsin countryside, Claire had grown familiar with the movements of the sun and the moon. She knew when each celestial sphere came up, and where, and she knew how their orbits changed with the seasons. The sun would crest the top of the bluffs around seven-thirty on this cool September morning.

The hot cup of coffee in her hands sent up a warm cloud of steam. She breathed in the aroma of freshly ground beans. Rich knew how to make good coffee. He had spoiled her for the rotgut stuff that was brewed at the sheriff's department.

Although most of the summer flowers were done, she could still see drifts of purple asters blooming in the sandy fields along the highway. Their color was startling and alive in the early morning air. The last flowers of the season. Soon the leaves would start to turn.

She felt awfully happy, and it scared her.

Claire knew the fragility of such happiness, knew it could be lost with the next breath. She scarcely dared breathe. She could hear Rich out in the barn, feeding his small flock of pheasants. Meg was upstairs sleeping in on this Saturday morning. They were coming together as a new sort of family.

She went over a mental list of what she had to do today. She needed to put an ad in the shopper to rent out her house. Rich had told her not to worry about it until she was settled. She was starting to feel settled. She should take a walk down along the railroad tracks and pick a bouquet of asters. Her uniforms needed cleaning this weekend. She still found it odd to think of herself as back in uniform.

Four years ago, she had left her job with the Minneapolis Police Department, taken a job as deputy sheriff for Pepin County, and moved down to the small town of Fort St. Antoine. The latest census had said there were 142 residents, which didn't include the weekenders. Half the town's homes were owned by part-timers who lived in the Twin Cities.

The first two years working in Pepin County had been hard: Claire had missed the Cities, missed the police department, missed working with other women officers. But she was starting to feel comfortable in this small community, an hour and a half from the Twin Cities, on the banks of the Mississippi River.

She had left the Cities because her husband had been killed. At that time, she'd had little thought of finding another man to take his place. Then Rich Haggard had walked into her life. She still remembered the first time he had come over to her house and brought her some morels. She was such a city slicker she hadn't even known what to do with the freshly gathered mushrooms. Now that didn't really matter, because Rich was a much better cook than she was.

They were very officially a couple. Marriage had been talked about, but she wanted to see how they worked as partners first. So far the only thing about Rich that really bugged her was that he often felt the need to tell her how to do things.

Last night while she was loading the dishwasher, he reached in and rearranged the plates. She set down the glass she was holding and left the room.

He came after her. "Aren't you going to finish loading the dishes?" he asked. "I thought I'd run it."

"I don't seem to be able to do it correctly."

"It's better if you put the large dishes at the edges. That way the sprayer works better."

Claire just looked at him.

"Only a suggestion."

"No," she corrected him. "It wasn't a suggestion. You were in there moving the dishes around. If you want me to load the dishwasher, you need to let me do it."

Claire had finished loading the dishwasher and then started it herself, even though she knew that Rich liked to check it and then start it before he went to bed. Claire had a feeling that they would be fighting about how to load the dishwasher for many years to come. She looked forward to it.

She sipped her coffee. Rich walked out of the barn, and her heart filled with love. Life could be so good.

The phone rang, and she ran into the house to get it.

Ruth, a friend who lived in Fort St. Antoine, asked, "Are you guys going to the Pain Perdu for coffee?"

"Yeah."

"Good. I'll talk to you there. A friend of mine needs some help."

Something pinched her foot. Meg gasped and grabbed at the sheets.

"Meggy, didn't mean to startle you. It's time to wake up." Her mother's voice spoke firmly.

Meg turned to see her mother standing in the doorway on the wrong side of the bed. She still wasn't used to this small room tucked under the eaves of Rich's house—a room that didn't get the morning sun like her old room had in her mom's house.

"We're leaving. Time for you to get up."

Meg snuggled down in her bed. Luxurious. Sleep seemed to weigh on her eyelids and her arms, urging her deeper into the bed, but then her stomach grumbled.

Under her mother's watchful eye, Meg sat up. She was not one of those people who could jump out of bed. She needed to ease herself into the daylight world the same way she walked into a lake—slowly and carefully, letting the water slide up her body as she got used to it.

She put her feet on the floor. Her mom continued to watch her.

"I'm up," Meg told her.

"Almost."

"Mom, I'm up."

"Claire," Rich's voice shouted up the stairs.

"I'm coming," her mom hollered back. Then to Meg: "I'll be downstairs."

Meg shook her head. Sometimes her mom bugged her. She hovered. Part of the problem was that her mom was a deputy sheriff, and it made her more cautious about everything. But she didn't seem to get that Meg was a sixth grader who had moved on to middle school and had different classes for each of her subjects. If Meg could handle all that, she could certainly get herself up in the morning. Or not. Why couldn't she sleep in?

She heard her mom and Rich talking downstairs as she pulled on her bathrobe and slippers. After taking a couple of running steps, she slid down the hallway. Her mom hated when she did that. Rich didn't seem to care, and it was his house. Then Meg trotted down the stairs, pretending she was on a horse. She had been bugging her mom for a horse. Aunt Bridget said she would give her riding lessons.

Rich looked up and smiled at her. "There she is."

Meg walked over and burrowed into his flannel shirt. He smelled like wood smoke and cold air. A brisk, good smell.

"How about some coffee?" Rich asked her.

Without looking at her mom, Meg nodded. Her mom didn't approve of Rich letting her drink coffee, but it was hardly any coffee at all, just mostly heated milk that he foamed and topped with sugar and cinnamon. She loved her special coffee. Besides, he only made it for her on the weekends.

As Rich set the coffee in front of her, her mother pulled on her coat. "We're off, Meg. You're going to be all right?"

"Of course, Mom."

"Try to be out of your pajamas by the time we get home."

"Maybe."

Her mom came over and took her face in her hands, wiped the sleep out of her eyes, and kissed her on the forehead. "See you later. We'll be at the Pain Perdu."

"Bye."

They left. Meg couldn't believe it. She had the whole house to herself. She put on her new CD—the Dixie Chicks—and turned the volume up loud. Just the way she liked it. As the first song came on, she danced back into the kitchen and put a piece of bread into the toaster.

Meg lifted her cup of coffee to her lips and toasted her newfound freedom.

The next hour was heaven. She thought about school and how it felt to be in her new grade. She thought about the boy who sat in front of her in two of her classes. Ted Thompson was his name. She wasn't sure, but she thought she might be in major like with him. All day long she dreamed about the cowlick on the back of his head and wanted to touch it.

She knew his telephone number by heart. Without thinking, she walked to the phone and dialed it. It rang three times, then a woman's voice answered. As soon as the woman said hello, Meg hung up. She was covered with goose bumps. She wondered if Ted had heard the phone ring. She wondered what he was doing today.

After putting her dishes in the sink, she went and stood by the kitchen window. The sun fell down through the trees, making the ground look like the dappled coat of an animal. *It would be a good day to go for a walk in the woods,* she thought, and ran upstairs to dress.

As Meg sat on the edge of her bed putting on her shoes, she heard an odd sound out in the driveway—like a car tire squealing, or maybe one of the pheasants stuck in the fence. The sound pulled deep in her stomach and worried her. She looked out her bedroom window.

Standing in the middle of the driveway facing the house was the largest animal she had ever seen.

Whatever it was, it was bigger than she was. Gargantuan. It looked as big as a small elephant. It must be either a deer, a moose, an elk, or a reindeer. Its legs were set wide and its head drooped down.

What she had heard was its breathing, the sound a bellows might make, rasping and shrill.

Where had it come from? Escaped from a circus, come down from the far north, a hybrid of a horse and an elephant? Meg wanted to know what its story was.

She ran downstairs and opened the back door to get a better look. The animal heard the door open and picked its head up a bit. Huge antlers balanced on top of its head like a candelabra. It made Meg's neck ache just to think of the weight of it.

Meg tried to read its deep brown eyes but could not see their bottoms. She felt as though it had something to tell her. Then she saw something dripping off its neck. Meg stared at the ground. At first she thought she was seeing oil from one of the cars, then realized the creature was bleeding from a gash on its neck.

She wanted to comfort it but knew it could be dangerous. As the wind picked up for a moment, a rich, dank smell wafted toward her from the animal. It had carried the scent of the forest with it. She took a step toward it, and the side door closed behind her.

Meg stopped herself. She knew if she got too close, the animal might run away, and that would be bad. It needed help. Rich would know what to do.

Meg turned slowly back toward the house to call Rich, but when she tried the door she found she was locked out. She walked as calmly as she could around the side of the house. When she got out of sight, she peeked back at the animal. It was still standing there and didn't look like it was going to move. She started to run.

Patty Jo stared out the front window.

The farmhouse stood right in the middle of the fields with only a paltry row of shade trees to the south along the driveway and another row of pines to the north for a windbreak. Nothing imaginative about the plantings, but then this was a working farm. Patty Jo couldn't wait to be rid of it.

From the front window of the house, she could see the soybean field Walter had planted. Soy was all the rage these days. Just a stroll through the supermarket told you soy was in everything. Read any health column—they claimed it was a cure-all. Walter had even suggested she cook up a plate of beans for them one night. Told her it might help her arthritis. She told him regular canned beans were good enough for her.

Walter had been pleased with the market price for soybeans and had been counting his money in advance this summer. He had the other fields planted in alfalfa and cover crops, but he was tickled about his soybeans. She saw the plant as a runty, weedy crop, looking like vetch run amok over the countryside. Patty Jo didn't have much time for soybeans.

She was going to be out of this godforsaken place as soon as she could. She had a fantastic offer for the land, and she'd sell off everything in the house for what she could get. Other than a few of her own family pieces, she wasn't taking a stick of furniture with her.

When she had married him, she'd hoped Walter would be her ticket out of Pepin County. Walter had survived his stroke, but just barely. Now it wouldn't be long. Just so long as Walter or his whiny daughter didn't get in her way. But she knew she could take care of Walter if she had to. Then nothing could stop her.

Patty Jo wanted to move to the Cities. It wasn't too late for her to start a new life. Someplace in St. Paul, a small condo. Minneapolis scared her. Just too darn big. But St. Paul wasn't bad. Maybe near the fairgrounds, because she knew how to get there.

Looking out the front picture window, she scanned a soybean field that stretched all the way to the road, a twisted sea of stalks and leaves. Edwin Sandstrom had called last week and said he'd harvest them for a percentage of the yield. Patty Jo had figured how much she'd clear from the deal, and it came out to about $2,000. She could use the cash. She was on a roll at the casino, but it was a bad roll—Lady Luck was taking a break. She'd told Edwin she'd let him know.

Patty Jo walked to the phone.

Edwin picked up on the second ring.

Something turned in Patty Jo, and she changed her mind—maybe it was Edwin's sober voice on the phone, maybe the thought of watching those blasted soybeans rot, maybe just plain orneriness—but instead of telling him to go ahead she found herself saying, "Edwin, I thought about your offer for my soybean crop, and I've decided that I'll pass."

He was a slow talker and didn't say anything for a moment. "Someone give you a better offer?"

"No. I don't think I'll harvest those beans."

She thought he'd argue, but he just said, "Suit yourself." Then he hung up without another word. Edwin wasn't one for talking, period.

Patty Jo stood staring out the window with the silent phone receiver in her hand. She would watch, day by day, as the crop overripened, then frosted to black, then sank into the ground. Someone else would plow them under. As far as she was concerned, it was all those soybeans were good for. Walter wasn't in a position to stop her.

CHAPTER 2

Claire smoothed her dark hair while looking in the rearview mirror. She had pulled it back in a low ponytail, but it did want to go into wisps around her face. She shouldn't look too closely either; she was starting to see a few gray hairs. Rich tapped on the window.

She pulled her light sweater around her and got out of the pickup truck in front of the bakery. The "sink," as she called it, had begun. She could see evidence of the sink in the flower gardens outside the bakery.

Actually, the sink was in full force.

Since moving to the country, Claire watched for that time in the late summer when the plants reversed themselves. It came when they had grown to their fullest, stretched out and up as far as they could. One day, it seemed, all together, the plants began their retreat. The leaves pulled in on their edges, the petals fell, the trees lost their vitality. Seed pods formed. Everything diminished and went back to its skeletal form.

Rich grabbed her hand, then sniffed the air. "It smells fallish."

"That sounds like something I would say."

"Not surprising. You've definitely had an influence on me," he said, steering her toward the bakery.

The main street of Fort St. Antoine, starting at Highway 35 and winding up the bluff, was empty except for a cluster of cars and pickup trucks in front of the bakery. But within a couple of hours, the streets would be lined with cars from the Twin Cities, folks out for a drive in the country.

Before the tourists arrived, the kaffeeklatsch gathered every Saturday morning at Le Pain Perdu. The owner, Stuart Lewis, reserved the big table next to the window for them. Every week he put out a basket of French doughnuts, everyone's favorites. The loosely knit group was made up of folks from the area—newcomers and old-timers alike—and it ebbed and flowed with the seasons.

Claire loved having coffee with them. Rich had been doing it for years before she met him. As far as she knew, the group had coalesced on its own. There was no organization, no hierarchy, no structure, no purpose. They drank coffee, ate whatever sweets appealed to them that morning, and talked about their small community and the world at large. They hardly ever agreed on much, yet they didn't seem to fight. Not that there weren't occasionally snits and huffs and contretemps, but there was a lot of room to move in the group. Usually between five and ten people gathered at the bakery, but sometimes the group could number up to fifteen.

This morning they were a smaller group. Ruth and Jake had grabbed the window seats—the luxury of the first comers. An artist from the Cities, Ruth had bought a farm on the outskirts of town and was growing herbs. Jake's wife had run off, leaving him with their young daughter. He had started working for Ruth, and then they had moved in together. They made a very handsome couple, she with freckles and strawberry blond hair, he with dark eyes and broad shoulders.

Lucas, the bookstore owner, was sitting next to them. He probably wouldn't stay long; he opened his store at eleven o'clock.

Claire was glad to see that Edwin Sandstrom, an older farmer from on top of the bluff, had come and brought Ella Gunderson with him. Ella had helped Claire with a case a couple of years ago, and Claire loved talking to her. The older woman had been a schoolteacher and still read the *Christian Science Monitor* every week—online, in 48-point type, because her macular degeneration had gotten so bad.

Ella poured Edwin a cup of coffee and managed to get most of it in his cup. Edwin took a sip and smacked his lips. "Too thick to drink and too thin to plow."

Ruth said in a loud voice, "I can't stand it. We've got to do something to stop this guy."

Claire sat down next to Ella and touched her hand to say hello. "Who are we stopping today, Ruth?"

Ruth and Jake said hello, then Ruth added, "That son of a bitch."

Ella tsked. Edwin chuckled.

Rich said, "Don't tell me you guys are already talking about Reiner. Let me get a cup of coffee so I can join in. Claire?"

Claire nodded, then turned back to the table to get the latest news. Daniel Reiner was one of the newest part-time residents of Pepin County. He had bought an old farmstead up on Lost Creek when its elderly owner had been forced to go into a nursing home by his kids, who wanted to sell the farm. It had been a nasty deal from the get-go.

The first thing Reiner had done was tear down the old farmhouse and the barn. He had saved some of the lumber to use in his new structures. He'd put up one of those new "not-so-big" houses, which were a laugh as far as Claire was concerned. Admittedly, a six-thousand-square-foot house might be smallish by the standards of the fashionable suburbs of the Twin Cities, but it was four times as big as any farmhouse in Pepin County.

Since his first purchase, Reiner had been buying up as much acreage around him as he could get his hands on. He was offering so much over market value that even the longtime farmers were having a hard time resisting. Claire felt as if they were watching a small fiefdom come into existence. Claire had never met him, so she hadn't formed an opinion of the man. This same factor had not stopped other members of the group from feeling very strongly about him. As far as she knew, Reiner was oblivious to all the talk. He didn't really want to have anything to do with the community along the river, which irked everyone. He just wanted his grand estate.

Claire asked, "What did he do now?"

Ruth flung her hair back behind her shoulder and said, "It's hard to know where to start with that guy. . . ."

Jake turned to Ruth. "Let me tell it. You get a little too emotional."

After shooting him a dirty look, Ruth picked out a French doughnut and ceremoniously took a bite. Claire thought that looked like a good idea and grabbed one too.

"Reiner's talking about putting in an airstrip," Jake explained.

Rich slid in next to Claire, handing her a mug of coffee. "An airstrip? How can he do that down in the valley?"

"Not right next to his place," Jake said. "He's been buying land on top of the bluff."

"Then, of course, he'll need a funicular to cart his guests down to his manor in the vale," Ruth added with a snap in her voice.

"Funicular?" Jake asked.

"A fancy way of saying tram," Ruth explained.

Edwin stirred his coffee and said, "I don't care for that man myself. I've had some dealings with Reiner, and I don't trust him as far as I could heave him, and that's not very far anymore."

"What about the zoning for an airstrip? Can't the township board rein him in?" Claire asked.

Ruth laughed. "The board. There's nothing in place. No zoning to speak of. All the board sees is dollar signs in the form of more taxes on all Reiner's buildings. They won't stop him from doing a thing."

Everyone fell silent at the table. Holding his spoon in the air as if it were a small bird, Lucas remarked, "I'd like to ride in a funicular."

"I think that mode of travel would suit you," Claire told him.

"I could see getting a special outfit for it. Maybe something iridescent and glittery, with wings."

Stuart walked up with another plate of French doughnuts. "If you start wearing wings, Lucas, you're eighty-sixed."

"Have you ever met Daniel Reiner?" Claire asked Stuart.

"Yeah, he comes in for bread sometimes. His wife has a sweet tooth, so she'll buy a bag of cookies."

"At least he's supporting the local economy," Ella said. She liked to see the best in everyone.

"Only because he didn't make it to some fancy bakery on his way out of town," Ruth snapped.

"What's got you so dead set against him?" Rich asked Ruth.

"Oh, I guess it's that feeling the poor, starving artists have when they discover a place and then the rich businessmen come in and buy up the town so that everything that made it charming is gone and nobody with character can afford to live there anymore."

Claire was reading Ruth and didn't feel that this was the whole story. "What else?"

Ruth took a sip of coffee. "In order to build his airstrip, he's made an offer on some land that should be going to a friend of mine, Margaret Underwood. Do you know her?"

Claire shook her head.

"She and her husband live up top. She helps me out with my garden sometimes. They raise goats. It's a long story."

Everyone at the table waited, so Ruth continued. "Some of you know what happened. Edwin, I think you know Margaret and Mark. They were both born and raised here. Margaret's dad had a bad stroke about two months ago, and the new stepmother has been spending up a storm. Margaret just heard that Reiner has made an offer on her father's farm. Her father always told her the farm would go to her. She's been counting on inheriting it. She grew up on it. Actually, Claire, I've been meaning to ask if you could help her out with something."

Claire said, "Sure," before she even knew what she was getting into. She had to learn not to do that. Just as she was about to ask, Rich turned quickly and stood up as he saw someone come in the door.

When Claire looked to see who had caught his eye, she saw her daughter barging into the bakery in a state of distress. Meg looked as though she had run the whole way to town. Claire stood and tipped her chair over.

"Meggy, what is it?"

But Meg continued straight toward Rich. She flung herself at him and said, "You've got to come right now. It's bleeding—it might be dying. You have to save it. You can't let it die."

Margaret sat in her car outside the Lakeside Manor and cried. She cried every day. Sometimes it was just a small dribbling sniffle. Once in a while it erupted into wholehearted sobbing. However it overtook her, she tried to hide it from Mark. He couldn't stand to see her cry. It affected him the way puppies got to her—he went weak in the knees and could barely talk.

When the crying jags had first hit her, she'd thought she was going crazy. She had never behaved so erratically in all her life—the weeping, the crabbiness. Anxiety racked her body. She had considered going to a therapist. Then one night, her whole body flushed with heat and woke her up. As soon as she felt it and identified it, she was relieved. A hot flash. At least now she knew what was going on.

Since then she had read many books on menopause. At first the books made her feel better, let her know that she wasn't the only one feeling strange, that other women had gone through this and survived. After she read a couple more, she felt sick about what she was learning. You went through this horrible withdrawal from estrogen, and when you finally made it to the other side, you were old.

One night she had tried to describe menopause to Mark. She told him it was like going cold turkey off any addictive substance. "My body," she said, "has been on this estrogen for close to forty years, and now I'm in withdrawal."

Her bones ached, she woke up at three in the morning and couldn't go back to sleep, she was crabby, she cried every day. She wished her mom were still alive so she could talk to her about how to get through this period of her life.

Mark suggested that she take something.

"You mean like hormones?" she asked.

He nodded.

She guessed he wanted her to take a pill and be her old self again. She tried to placate him. When he got impatient with her, his anger would lash out on chairs and doors.

"I might," she said.

Before she had time to consider her husband's suggestion, she got the news that her father was in the hospital after having a bad stroke. They weren't sure he would make it. For two long weeks he had been on the brink of leaving the world. Now she thought it might have been better if he had died.

It was time to go see her father. Margaret wiped her face with the Kleenex she kept in the glove compartment, then looked at herself in the rearview mirror. Her eyes were a little red, but she didn't think her dad would notice. He noticed very little these days.

She entered the nursing home, hoping that her father was having one of his better days. She tried to visit him in the morning so that she wouldn't run into Patty Jo, her stepmother. Patty Jo came in the late afternoon because she liked to play bingo with the patients.

Margaret peeked into her father's room. He was sitting in his wheelchair, facing the window. She couldn't see if he was awake. His head hung down between his shoulders and his bad hand dangled toward the floor. She hated to see his hand hang so lifelessly. Her father had been a strong man all his life, but as he lost weight, his muscles melted like old snow. An IV pole was set up next to him with the feeding bag almost empty: the remains of his breakfast.

After pulling a chair up to his good side, Margaret sat down facing him. He was asleep, his lips parted in slow breathing, his flannel shirt buttoned crooked, and two-day stubble on his face. She knew being well groomed didn't matter to him anymore, but it hurt her to see him like this. He had always been a dapper dresser for a farmer, insisting on ironed shirts and, if needed, two shaves a day.

"Dad," she said gently, lifting up his dangling hand and holding it in her lap. She and her father had never touched much while she was growing up. They were not a demonstrative family. But after his stroke, she had taken to touching him more, since he couldn't talk to her. It made her feel like she connected with him.

He roused, stretching his head up. His eyes blinked open. He reminded her of a baby bird peering out of the nest, hoping for food. He looked so vulnerable.

He grunted. It was his form of hello.

"Hi, just thought I'd stop by for a few minutes." Margaret tended not to stay long. It was too hard to stay when they couldn't talk to each other. There was nothing for her to do. "It's a nice fall day."

He nodded. He seemed to understand what she was saying.

"How're you today?" she asked.

He pressed his lips together and blew.

"Have you tried to eat today?"

He didn't respond. After the stroke, he hadn't been able to swallow, so a feeding tube had been inserted directly into his stomach. Therapists were still working with him, trying to get him to be able to eat soft foods such as ice cream or yogurt, but he choked on them.

As he woke up more, he got agitated. The fingers of his good hand picked at the blanket that covered his lap, and his lips mouthed words, but nothing came out. He shifted in his wheelchair and groaned.

"What, Dad?"

He looked at her with pleading in his eyes.

"What do you want?"

He moved his hand.

"Are you thirsty?"

He shook his head and moved his hand again. She knew he was trying to tell her something. What could he want?

"Do you want something?"

He nodded and held out his hand.

"Something you hold in your hand?"

He nodded again.

Margaret wanted to understand. He had never tried this hard to communicate with her before. "A comb?"

He groaned and shook his head. Then he looked down at his hand and moved it across the arm of his wheelchair. It looked like he was trying to write.

"Dad, do you want to write something?"

He quickly nodded.

Margaret opened her purse and pulled out a pen. She handed it to him, and he started to write on the wheelchair arm.

"Wait, Dad, wait. I'll get you a piece of paper." Margaret looked around the room and found a notice about activities left by the staff. The back was blank. She found the tray that they put over his wheelchair when they wanted him to work on something. When the tray was in place, she set the paper in the middle of it and took his hand and put it in the middle of the paper.

He started writing. She was so excited, she thought of running out in the hall to tell someone. Her dad could write. But when she looked at what he had written, she couldn't make any sense out of it. If it was a word, all the letters were written one on top of the other, making it illegible.

"Dad, you need to keep moving your hand when you write. Let me try to help you." She took his hand, but he pulled it away and went back to writing in a very tight space. Then he looked up at her.

It still was a small mound of scribbles.

She took his hand. "Let's try this. Go."

As soon as he formed a letter, she gently moved his hand, giving him room to form the next.

Margaret could tell the first letter was *f.* The next letter looked like an *o,* and the next letter looked like an *n,* and the final letter she couldn't read at all.

He looked up at her, expectantly.

"I can't quite make out the word, Dad. Is the first letter *f*?"

He nodded, and his hand started writing again without her help.

This time she could make out the first two letters: *f-a.*

Margaret was afraid she knew what he was writing. But she wanted to be sure. "Dad, let me help you one more time."

She held his hand and guided him and he wrote out *f-a-r-m.* She could read the *m,* although it looked more like an *n.* She had said nothing to him when she heard that Patty Jo was thinking about selling the farm. She didn't want to worry him.

"Farm?" she asked.

He nodded, happy.

"Are you worried about the farm?" she asked.

He nodded again.

Margaret didn't want to lie to her dad. She hardly knew how to do it. "I think it's fine, Dad. Everything's going to be fine."

Now she needed to make sure that was true.

CHAPTER 3

Rich's heart sank when he saw the elk standing at the top of his driveway. Its large, antlered head hung between its legs in a stance he recognized. Years ago, when he had shot a deer and it finally stopped running, it had stood like that, an arrow in its chest, waiting for what was to come. He had never gone hunting again.

There were two elk farms in the area—the nearest was on the Reiner estate, and he figured that had to be where this animal came from. He wanted to see how close he could get to the animal. The fewer people around, the better. A bull elk could be dangerous. But he needed to get closer to assess the animal's problem. Slowly and evenly, he walked toward the elk.

When he was about ten yards away, Rich stopped. The smell of the animal wafted toward him—rank, musky, a bit of the swamp in it. He could see the wound on the elk's neck and hear its labored breathing.

The tan-and-black bull elk was one of the biggest he had ever seen. He guessed it weighed in at over eight hundred pounds. The rack was a good eight-pointer, which probably meant the elk had been around for at least eight years.

He turned and walked back down the driveway to the car. Leaning into the car, he answered Claire and Meg's questions before they were asked.

"Yes, it's still there. It's still alive, Meg. Claire, call Kate Jenkins. She works out of the Wabasha vet clinic. And then call our friend Mr. Reiner and ask him if he knows where his elk stud is. If it's missing, ask him how tame the animal is and has it ever been haltered. And ask him what could have happened to it."

"What are you going to do?" asked Meg.

Claire looked at him, cell phone in her hand.

"I'm going to go sit quietly near the elk and watch him. If he takes off for the woods, I'll probably follow him. You two stay here and wait for the vet."

Claire grabbed his sleeve. "Wait for me to make these calls. Then take the phone with you. That way you can call and tell us where you are."

"Good idea."

Kate Jenkins was available and said she'd be right over. A minor miracle. Rich had reason to hope.

Mrs. Reiner said she didn't know anything about the elk. They were her husband's thing, she explained, and he wasn't home. Claire asked her to have him call, and handed the phone to Rich.

"Be careful."

"As careful as you always are," he said.

"Can we go inside?"

"Yes, but use the back door. We don't want to spook this guy. But would you wait until the vet shows up? Then bring her in through the house."

Rich walked back up the driveway, as cautiously as before, no sudden movements. The bleeding appeared to have stopped, but if the elk started running again, it might reopen its wound.

Rich sat on the bottom step of his front stairs, about fifteen yards from the elk, and watched it. The elk raised its head high enough to take a look at Rich. It didn't seem afraid, but Rich did not take that for a good sign. It could mean that the animal was past the point of fear.

Then the animal did an extraordinary thing—it took a step toward Rich. He couldn't believe it and stopped breathing. The elk kept looking at him. If Rich hadn't known better, he would have guessed it was trying to ask something of him. He didn't know how tame elk could be. He had never been around one before. Maybe it wasn't afraid of humans. That would make tending to it a lot easier.

From where he sat, Rich had a good view of the neck wound. It was possible that the animal had run into something and hurt itself, but it looked like someone had intended to bring down this animal. The neck was a vital area, and if a shot hit the neck bone or struck an artery, it would kill quickly. What he couldn't figure was why anyone would shoot this elk. It had to be a captive animal. The last native elk in Wisconsin had been killed off about a hundred years ago. Didn't make much sense that someone would shoot at it.

After that one step toward him, the elk stopped moving. It hung its head again, and Rich waited with it, worrying that if it fell to its knees, it would never get up again. Rich felt as though he was meditating—breathing with the animal, willing it to stay on its feet. For a while, he forgot that he existed as a human.

After half an hour, he felt a hand on his shoulder. When he turned he saw the vet, Kate Jenkins.

"You've found Harvey," she said.

"Harvey?"

The elk lifted his head at his name.

Jenkins went on. "Reiner's stud elk. Tame as a dog. Bottle-fed. Probably just standing there waiting for something to eat. You got an apple?"

Rich walked into the house to get one.

Bridget picked up the phone to call her sister, Claire. She was hesitant to make the call because it would seem so final. Just as she was about to punch in the number, she saw her daughter, Rachel, holding on to the table leg.

Rachel looked over at Bridget, let go of the table leg, and took a step all by herself. Her first step. Bridget hung up the phone to watch her daughter. What an amazing creature this just-turned-one-year-old girl was. And, as usual, her father was not there to see it happen.

For the last year, Chuck had been gone more than he was around. Bridget knew he was busy with his work. These were not new problems, but they had gotten worse since Rachel was born. Sometimes he seemed afraid of Rachel, especially when she cried.

Watching her smiling baby totter toward her, Bridget didn't understand how anyone could help but love her to death.

About three months ago, Bridget had sat Chuck down and had a long talk with him. She'd told him how his behavior made her feel, and she'd suggested some things they could do to try to make him more comfortable. He was reluctant even to talk about it. He seemed to think it was her job to take care of the kid. She was starting to pick up more hours at the pharmacy again, and she needed help.

Two months ago, Bridget had set up an appointment with a marriage counselor. Chuck hadn't shown up. Bridget had gone to the counselor for four sessions, then stopped. The marriage counselor had wished her luck.

A month ago, she had screamed at Chuck in the middle of their front yard. He had stayed out until after midnight, and she'd gone outside to meet him when he drove his truck into the yard. He'd been drunk, but not outrageously so. He had even been in a good mood. Bridget had surprised herself when she told him to go find someplace else to stay for the night. She said that anytime he didn't make it home until after midnight, not to bother coming home. She meant it. For a week, he got home before midnight; then, three nights in a row, she didn't see him. What was really sad was she didn't even care where he had been.

Rachel stopped halfway across the room. She tottered, looking as though she might fall, then put out her foot and took another step.

A week ago, Bridget had hired a babysitter for Rachel. She and Chuck went to a fish fry in Nelson. After two beers, she told Chuck she didn't think it was working anymore. He nodded in agreement. She asked him what he wanted to do.

"We'll get through this, Bridge," he said. "It's just a phase. You know, new baby and all."

"New baby?" Bridget found her voice rising. "Rachel is almost a year old. She's hardly a baby anymore. In case you haven't noticed."

"Oh." He seemed surprised. "Why do you have to talk to me like that? You sound like my mom."

"Just what I don't want to be. Your mom."

"Speaking of my mom, she'd like to come by and see Rachel this weekend."

"Do you hear me when I talk? Don't you think we have a problem?"

"If you'd just calm down."

That was when she lost it. She looked at this man she had loved so dearly, who had been such fun to be with, who had called her his little chickadee. They couldn't even talk to each other anymore. She had married him believing he was the man she would grow old with. She didn't want him to see her cry, and she didn't have anything else to say. She stood up and walked out, leaving the waitress balancing her plate of walleye and fries in her hand.

The next day she called Chuck at work and said that she would be moving out of the house, asked him to stay away until then. He agreed, but said he had to come home to get some clothes while she was at work.

Rachel, her dark hair flying around her head like a feathery halo, fell into Bridget's arms at the end of her first steps.

Bridget held her close. "My big girl. You are the best. You are the best walker and the best child anyone could ever want. I'll love you enough for two. That's all there is to it."

After she set her child down on the floor, she walked to the couch and picked up the phone. She dialed her sister's new number. When Claire picked up the phone, Bridget asked her, "Have you rented out your house yet?"

Claire said no.

"Good," Bridget said, "I'd like to move in."

Later that afternoon, Claire got a call from Margaret Underwood, asking for her help. Halfway through their conversation, Margaret started to cry. Even though Claire didn't know the woman, she felt horrible for her. After listening to her concerns, Claire called the sheriff, got his okay to check out the situation, and drove right out to the Underwood farm.

The leaves fluttered off the hood of her car as they flew down from the trees in the autumn wind. The sun was shining as though it would never go away, not even in the darkest of winter days. Claire knew that was a lie, but she still enjoyed it.

Margaret must have been watching for her, because she walked out of the house as soon as Claire pulled up. She was a large woman with honey-gold hair lightly sprayed with gray. She had beautifully shaped eyes, deep blue. Close to Claire's age, she guessed. She could see why Margaret and Ruth were friends. They were both good examples of the back-to-the-land, earth mother type.

"Do you want me to drive?" Margaret asked as she came up to the car.

"No, I might as well. After all, this is official business." Claire didn't mention that it would be better to have someone less emotional behind the wheel. "Hop in."

Margaret's husband came to the door of the house and waved goodbye. A wiry man, he looked about the same size as Margaret.

Margaret pointed him out to Claire. "That's Mark. I couldn't ask him to do this with me because I'm afraid if he was in the same room with my stepmother, he'd kill her." Margaret gave a nervous laugh and went on. "Not really. He doesn't have a mean bone in his body, but it would be hard on him to stay civil."

"Do you both work at home?" Claire asked, steering them to a safer topic.

"Yes, we raise goats. We make goat cheese and sell their milk. If you'd like to try it, I could give you some cheese when we get back to my house. We've got some new feta that's just ready."

"I'd love that. Ruth raves about your cheeses." Claire had turned back down the road. "I'm not sure where your stepmother's house is. Tell me where to go."

"It's not far. Just on the other side of the church. It was so nice to be close to Dad. But now I try not to drive by the home place. I don't like to see Patty Jo if I can help it. And the soybean fields are a disgrace."

"I gather your stepmother's difficult?"

Margaret sighed. "She can be."

"Was she always?"

"No, not really. At first, I was glad she was friends with Mom and Dad. She helped them out a lot. Now I can see she made it so they couldn't live without her. She made herself indispensable. Dad really depended on her after Mom died. They married within a month. Maybe I should have stepped in, but I wanted him to be happy."

"Sounds like a good decision."

"I don't know. I can't help thinking about how different things might have been if Patty Jo hadn't come along." She grew silent as they drove past the church, then she pointed. "There's the house."

Claire turned into the driveway. The house looked like many of the farmhouses in the county, a big white four-square—four rooms up and four rooms down, with a screened-in front porch that ran the width of the house.

"Does she know we're coming?" Claire asked.

Margaret nodded. "Yes, I called. I wanted to be sure she'd be there. I told her I had something to ask her, but I didn't tell her what. I didn't want her to have a chance to think of an excuse."

"So she's not expecting me?"

"All I said was that I was bringing a friend. I didn't tell her you were a deputy. She wouldn't have liked that."

"That's fine, but she'll find out soon enough." Claire had put on her uniform per protocol. The sheriff always wanted them dressed in uniform on any department business.

As they walked up to the house, a plump woman with frizzy blond hair came to the screen door in the porch. She was wearing jeans and a sweatshirt. Claire was surprised by how young the woman was, maybe sixty. And by how much makeup she was wearing. Especially the bright pink lipstick. Farm women seldom wore lipstick unless they were going to town.

"Hello, Patty Jo," Margaret said when they reached the bottom of the steps.

"Margaret, who is this?" Patty Jo's voice had an edge to it as she looked at Claire.

"Claire Watkins. I asked her to come along. She works for the sheriff's department."

"Obviously. Why ever did you feel it necessary to bring a police . . . person with you?"

"Patty Jo, we need to talk."

"Come on into the porch, but don't let the flies in." Patty Jo held the door open.

At one end of the porch was a swing filled with striped pillows. It looked like the place to be on a summer night. A small table was set up with wicker chairs around it, but Patty Jo didn't invite them to sit. They all stood by the front door.

"This is very nice," Claire said, thinking how convenient it would be to have a screened-in porch like this when the mosquitos got bad. "You must spend a lot of time out here. Especially on a day like today."

"It's all too big for me," Patty Jo said. "Now that Walter is in the nursing home, I can't keep it up. I'm selling the place. Margaret, I hope you heard about that and the auction."

"Yes, Patty Jo. That's why I wanted to come by."

"Well, I'm glad you have. I've decided to give you the trunk. I think your father always wanted you to have it. As long as you were coming over, I thought you could take it with you."

"Thanks, I'll be glad to have that."

"Let's get it into your car before we all get comfortable. It's in the barn. Maybe you could back right up to it and we could lift it in."

Margaret looked at Claire. "Is it okay?"

"Sure, I'm here to help."

Margaret and Patty Jo walked out to the barn, and Claire backed the squad car up to it. The trunk was old, made of a blond wood with beautiful scrollwork on it and the words *Stockholm, Wisc.* written on it. It was a tall trunk that narrowed at the base and was lighter than it looked. The two leather handles on the sides were in good shape. The three women were able to load it into the trunk of the car. By tipping it on its side, they could make the trunk lid close over it.

As they walked back to the house, Margaret said to Patty Jo, "I can't believe you would think about selling the farm. I wish you had talked it over with me."

Patty Jo pursed her pink lips, then said, "I didn't want to bother you, Margaret. I know you and Mark have a full plate."

"It would have been no bother. If you're having trouble keeping this place up, Mark and I can help out."

"Margaret, you have your own life. Your father's illness has been a terrible blow to us all. Your father left me in charge, and I think it's time the farm is sold." Patty Jo's voice broke. "You know he'll never be able to come back here. I've got a very good offer for it. We will need that money to keep your father in the home."

They walked back into the porch, and this time Patty Jo offered them chairs. They all sat down. Even though the two women were being civil to each other, Claire could feel the tension.

"What about his stocks and bonds? What about his money market?" Margaret asked.

From the look on Patty Jo's face, Claire guessed that she hadn't thought Margaret knew about those assets.

"How much time have you been spending at the casino?" Margaret pushed her stepmother.

"None of your business." Patty Jo's voice grew louder. "You have to face facts, Margaret. Your father will need constant care the rest of his life. I can't manage the farm, and neither can you."

"But I think we can manage it. Mark and I had always thought the farm would come to us. We had planned on it. It's in Dad's will."

"Well, that was a big mistake. Things happen. You should never have counted on the farm."

"Maybe if we sat down and went over everything we could figure out a way of keeping it," Margaret said hopefully.

Patty Jo shook her head. "I'm afraid not, dear. There's simply no other way."

"What about his insurance?"

"Doesn't come close to covering it."

Margaret drew herself up. "I would like to go over all Dad's assets with you and see exactly where we stand."

"You don't need to worry about this. It's not your problem. I've had someone I trust go over everything."

"I think I have a say."

"Margaret, I'm your father's wife. I think you know I do not need your permission to do what I want to do." Patty Jo paused and then announced, "You do understand that your father signed over power of attorney to me. Durable power of attorney. That means that I have the right to do anything I want with our assets."

"Well, that's why I called the sheriff's department. I don't want you to sell the farm. I don't think you are taking care of my father's best interests."

"Margaret, how can you say that? Your father would not be happy with you."

Margaret snapped, "My father loves me. He was always happy with me until you came along. Now he's worried sick about the farm."

Patty Jo stared at her. "How do you know what your father's worried about?"

Margaret said, "Because he told me."

"That's impossible."

"He can write things down."

Patty Jo shook her head as if flies were bothering her. "He can?"

"He tries," Margaret explained, then added, "I won't let you sell this farm. I'll get a court order stopping you."

"I'm sorry, Margaret, but I will do what I think best. You try for your court order if you must, but I know they will listen to me. I'm his wife."

Margaret stood up and said, "Well, I'm his daughter. I've loved him a lot longer than you." Then she slammed out the door, leaving Claire standing on the porch.

Patty Jo turned to Claire. "I'm sorry you had to witness that. Margaret is a little unstable. She and her father had a falling-out not long before his stroke. I don't think she's forgiven herself. I know this is hard for her. I'd hate for her to take this to court. It would be a terrible waste of money."

Claire found Margaret sitting in the front seat of the squad car, clutching at her dress, tears streaming down her face. "Don't mind me. I cry all the time. It's the change. You know."

"Menopause?"

"Perimenopause, that's what my doctor calls it. That's when all the hard stuff happens. I get real sensitive and cry at any little thing."

"Your father's stroke is no little thing," Claire said as she started the car. "Especially if you had a falling-out right before he got sick."

Margaret sat very still. "Is that what she said?"

"Isn't it true?"

"No. My father and I always got along. Until Patty Jo . . ."

Claire didn't know what to think. She started the car and headed down the driveway.

Margaret turned to her and asked, "So what do I have to do to stop her? Take her to court?"

Claire didn't want to get her hopes up. "Let me talk to the county attorney."

"Would you?" Margaret's voice lifted. "I'm sure my father doesn't want her to sell the farm. I'm supposed to inherit it."

"If he can write, can you get him to write down what he wants to do?"

"I could try."

CHAPTER 4

"You have to let me pay rent, just like anyone else." Bridget had known Claire might pull this on her, telling her she could stay in the house for next to nothing. It was the day after she had asked Claire if she could rent her house, and Claire was giving her the grand tour. Bridget set Rachel's car seat down on the floor in the living room of the old house.

Claire turned in a circle in the nearly empty room. "You don't even know how long you'll stay."

"Claire, this is really happening. Chuck and I are breaking up. Rachel and I will not live with him again."

Claire sat down in one of the chairs she had left at her house. Bridget watched her stare at the windows. Claire ran her finger across one, and it left a clean streak. "How did it happen?"

Bridget looked at her darling daughter, Rachel, and then said what she had just recently figured out. "Chuck wanted to be an only child."

Claire lifted her head to look at Bridget, and then a small laugh burst out of her. "You're terrible."

That set Bridget off. She started laughing, and Rachel joined in, clapping her hands at the good joke. Bridget collapsed on the floor next to her baby and laughed until she was exhausted.

Claire looked at her. "What are you going to do?"

Bridget rolled over onto her back and stared up at the beadboard ceiling. She loved this old house. It would be a pleasure to live in it. "First, find a good babysitter. Move into this house. Cut back my hours at work. Get ready for winter."

"Sounds like a plan."

"I want to chop up a whole cord of wood. I think that would be a good way for me to work out my anger. I'll move my horse into the field."

Claire sat on the floor next to her and Rachel. "I still don't understand. Where did Chuck go?"

"I'm sorry I didn't tell you more as it was happening, but it was just too hard. He just went away. Started staying out later and later, and then not even coming home."

"Another woman?"

"I hope so. That way he won't be so apt to come running back to me."

"How're you feeling?"

"Glad Mom and Dad aren't alive to see this. Isn't that funny? I think it would be harder for me to get a divorce if they were still around."

"I understand." Claire looked at Bridget. "A divorce?"

Bridget decided not to tell her she had already started to check out lawyers. She needed to break things to Claire slowly. "I think we're headed that way."

"Are you going to be okay?"

Bridget pulled Rachel out of her car seat and had her stand up. "That's what you have to stop doing—you have to stop worrying about me. It's not your duty, even if you are my big sister."

"I'll try."

"Now, Rachel has something she wants to show you. Hold out your arms." Bridget aimed Rachel in Claire's direction and let go of her hands. One sturdy foot in front of another, Rachel stepped across the floor to her aunt's waiting arms.

"Wow!" Claire hoisted Rachel up in the air. "You're amazing. I think you beat out Meg by about a month. She didn't start to walk until she was nearly fourteen months."

"I think crawling frustrated Rachel—simply not fast enough."

"Not much of a view either." Claire looked around at the house. "I can get in here and give it a good cleaning."

"Let's hire someone. You don't have the time and neither do I."

"When are you planning on moving in?"

"Within the week. I'm ready."

"Oh, I didn't tell you. We've got company at our house."

"Who?"

"His name is Harvey."

Bridget felt her heart stir. "Is he as cute as Rich?"

"Cuter."

What Claire would always remember about the Reiner house was its front entrance. Where most houses in Pepin County were thought to be the bee's knees if they had a mudroom for your boots, the entrance to the Reiner estate was more like the lobby of a grand hotel. It seemed especially incongruous after driving down a winding dirt road that meandered around cornfields and over trout streams. The neighboring houses were old white farmhouses. One already had bales of hay tucked up against the foundation as additional insulation against the coming winter. The Reiner house looked as though it belonged in Edina, the richest suburb of the Twin Cities, not in the depths of this rural county.

After Mrs. Reiner let her in, the first thing to greet Claire was a bronze statue of Hiawatha, much larger than either woman. Two landscapes of the Mississippi River hung on each side of the statue. The landscapes were old and lovely, with a quaint, romantic air. Other than the somber colors of the landscapes, the entrance was done in white:

glass chandelier in the middle of the room, white marble floors with white walls that went up two stories. No dirt ever dared cross the threshold, Claire figured.

Mrs. Reiner looked out of place in this museum of a room. She was dressed like a normal suburban housewife in jeans and a big sweatshirt that said *Minnesota Twins* on it. Dark brown hair in a bob and moccasins on her feet. A pretty woman in a bouncy sort of way. Claire figured she was probably in her late thirties. Claire explained who she was and why she was there.

"I'm Candy. Come on in. Daniel's anxious to talk to you. He's on the phone. I'll let him know you're here."

She led Claire into the living room and offered her a seat on a couch that was so white Claire automatically swiped at her pants seat before she sat down.

"Can I get you something to drink?"

"No, thanks."

"I didn't know they had women cops down here."

"Well, we're a little behind the times, but we're trying to catch up."

"I'll try to wrench Dan away from the phone."

"Great."

The room that Claire was left sitting in was bigger than the main floor of Rich's house. She had to admit that someone had a sense of quirkiness. Above the mantel of the floor-to-ceiling two-story limestone fireplace was an old wagon wheel. It looked genuine, showing the wear of several decades.

"Where'd the wheel come from?" Claire asked when Candy came back.

"We found that in the back of the barn when we were tearing it down. Dan wanted it on the mantel. I told him it could stay there until I found the right piece of art. But I've grown fond of it. The old place . . . you just gotta love the history of a place like this."

Claire wondered why, if they loved the history so much, they had so completely destroyed it.

"He should be with you in a moment. I hope you don't mind if I leave you alone. We're getting ready to go back to the Cities."

"Don't worry about me. I'll just catch up on *Architectural Digest.*"

The woman gave a quick laugh, then left the room.

Claire picked up a magazine and was looking at apartments on Central Park with leather and chrome interiors when Daniel Reiner came in the room. He was a short, stocky man with a shock of tawny hair that made him look like a beaver, and one that, at the moment, wanted to chew on something.

She stood up and told him who she was and that his elk was boarding at her house.

"So you're a deputy and our animal happened to wander over to your house. How convenient."

Claire wasn't sure if he was kidding. Then he smiled.

"That's right."

"And you're the one who's going to find out who did this?" Reiner asked.

"That's my job," Claire assured him. "Would you like to know how Harvey is doing?"

"Harvey?"

"Oh. I thought that was his name."

"You're probably right. I'm not on a first-name basis with him. My caretaker is in charge of the herd. Do you know how much that animal is worth?"

"No, sir." Claire was curious.

"The going rate for a bull elk his size is about fifty thousand dollars."

Claire nodded. No surprise that money was important to this man. "I wonder why someone shot him. They wouldn't be able to get fifty thousand dollars for him when he was dead."

"It's senseless."

"Do you have any enemies down here?"

"No, we don't even know anybody."

Claire realized the guy had no idea how much animosity he had stirred up in the farm country around his estate. "What about the men who worked on your house? Any trouble there?"

"Oh, no. I'm still working with most of them. We brought them all down from the Cities."

That wasn't such a good idea, Claire thought. Bringing in more-expensive labor from the Cities when there were contractors begging for work in Pepin County.

"I know you've been buying up a lot of land. Any chance this could be tied to one of your deals?"

"I doubt it. I'm offering over market value. Everyone seems real happy to work with me."

"Well, I'll keep checking into it. The vet said the elk could be moved anytime. The wound is superficial."

"Why don't you talk to the caretaker, Jim Bartlett? Set it up with him when he can come and get the animal. That's what I pay him for. He can show you where the elk was when he was injured. What do I owe you for keeping the elk?"

"Not a thing. We've enjoyed having Harvey, once we knew he wasn't going to die on us. The vet said she'd just send you the bill."

Reiner pulled out his checkbook. "I insist on giving you a little something."

Claire shook her head again. "Just being neighborly."

"I hate to be in your debt."

Claire looked at him, wondering. "Why is that so awful?"

"Just doesn't feel right."

"Well, if you'd like, you could bake us a cherry pie."

Claire drove back down the long winding driveway to the caretaker's house. She parked, and at the sound of her car, a stout tree trunk of a man came out of the garage. He wiped his hands on his jeans as he walked toward her.

Claire introduced herself and told him that Reiner had said she should talk to him.

The first words out of his mouth were what she had expected to hear from Reiner. "How's the elk?"

"Good. The vet said he doesn't have an infection in the wound and didn't lose that much blood."

"Scared the shit out of me."

"What?"

"Come and see what I walked into." He turned and led the way around the back of the garage and over to a pen. "We keep Harvey in here, separate from the females. Until he's needed."

"Not much fun for him."

"I know. He gets everything he needs—food, shelter, even a harem. But not a lot of excitement, no reason to use his antlers."

Claire looked into the enclosure and saw that the two trees that stood inside of it were rubbed barkless at about Harvey's head height. "He's been using them on the trees instead."

"Yeah, it looks like it feels good. An itch satisfied." Jim pointed. "I walked out to feed the herd and saw the fence line was broken. I can't figure why they would cut the fence when they were going to shoot him."

The strands of barbed wire flopped free, three strands cut through and hoof marks leading out of the pen.

"They also cut the wires into the fence that held the whole herd. When I first walked out, I saw the cut fence, I saw Harvey was gone, and then I saw the other fence was cut too. I couldn't see the herd, so I wasn't sure if they had discovered the break and taken off. I walked back over the hill and there they were, grazing. But Harvey was gone."

"Any ideas who might have done this?"

"Not really. I'd say just some prank a kid would play, but there really aren't that many kids around here."

Claire looked at the big guy. "Anybody mad at you?"

"Oh, I suppose. But not mad enough to do this. And I don't know how they think this would hurt me. Harvey's not my elk."

"You'd be blamed?"

"Is that what's happening? Does Reiner think I did this?"

Claire hurried to reassure him. "I didn't get that impression at all."

"To tell you the truth, I think he's getting a little bored with the elk. At first when he bought the herd, he'd come visit them most every time he was here. Now he hardly ever stops by, and he's been complaining about their feed bills. Says the market has not been good to him. He's no longer worth a hundred million, just seventy-five."

Claire walked around and checked the barbed wire. Not much to see, but it was obvious the wires had been cut. The breaks were clean and right on top of one another, and the wires weren't pulled away from the fence. "Did whoever did this leave anything here?"

"I didn't find a thing. Not even a footprint. They were plenty careful."

"When did it happen?"

"Must have been late Friday night, early Saturday morning."

"Did you hear anything?"

"I was gone Friday night—didn't get home till late and didn't check on the animals before I went to bed. I had settled them before I went out. It wasn't until Saturday morning that I noticed the elk was gone. I called Reiner, but he was up in the Cities. I was thinking of calling the sheriff when you called Mrs. Reiner and she called me."

"All the other elk okay?"

"Yeah, I went out and counted heads right after the call. They all appear fine."

Claire looked around. "Not everyone in this community is real happy about what Mr. Reiner is doing here. This whole setup. Buying up all this land."

"Sure, people are jealous."

"You think that's all?"

A little anger showed in his face. "What do I know? It's not my business to think about it. It's just my job. A man's gotta make a living."

"Sure. I know."

He looked at her, then reflected. "You know what's weird, though?

There's no blood anywhere. Not in the pen, not outside the pen. You said it was dripping off his neck. Whoever shot him didn't do it here."

Walter couldn't see very well anymore. He looked and looked out the window, but all he could make out were lumps of color floating in a sea of light. The lumps moved sometimes, and he followed them with his eyes—if he wasn't sleeping. What he did was not really even sleeping; it was not being awake. When he went deep, sometimes it felt like not being alive.

A nurse came in and talked to him. "Hi, Walter. How're you feeling?"

He could hear her words, he could even understand them. But he couldn't make any words himself. When he tried, his tongue tripped him up, and the sounds that came out of his mouth were garbage. He had quit trying. He knew the words, but they didn't travel through him the way they used to.

He nodded, and the nurse stuck a thermometer in his mouth. He had never been sick a day in his life. That's what good hard work did for you. Until this complete disintegration of his body. Now nothing worked right. His one hand tried to keep at it, but the rest of his body had gone kaflooey.

She pulled the thermometer out of his mouth and looked at it. "Normal." Then she leaned in close to him, and he could see that she was young and pretty. "Do you want anything?"

He wanted so much. But he shook his head. Better not to try.

"Oh, look who's here. Your wife."

For a crazy moment, he thought Florence had finally come to get him. He felt as though he was waiting so hard for her. But then he saw that it was Patty Jo. Could get a little snappy sometimes, but she had been there for him.

"Hi, Walter." She sat down in front of him and talked loud. Patty Jo had always had a voice on her, and since his stroke, she insisted on shouting at him.

He nodded to her.

"I had a visitor yesterday. That daughter of yours."

Margaret and Patty Jo had never gotten along. Or at least not after he had married Patty Jo. He wasn't sure why. Patty Jo had explained to him that Margaret was jealous, thought she could keep her dad to herself. "You spoiled her, Walter. It's your own fault."

Somehow so much was his fault. Patty Jo delighted in pointing out his mistakes. But she had helped him out so much when Florence died. He didn't know what he would do without her.

Patty Jo tapped him on the knee. "Margaret is trying to tell me what to do, Walter, and I don't care for her tone. She seems to think she knows better than me. I'm your wife, after all. I make the decisions. She can't seem to understand that."

Walter felt very tired. The world seemed to twist and tilt on its own. Then he wanted to close his eyes and make it go away.

"But she said you could write, Walter. That's such good news. Can you show me how you can write? Would you write your name for me?"

She put a pen in his good hand.

"Can you sign your name, Walter?"

He nodded.

"Let's try a practice run." She put a paper under the pen and he wrote his name. He couldn't see it, but he remembered how to do it. You don't forget how to write your own name.

She looked at it and said, "Walter, you have to concentrate. That looks like a kid in kindergarten did it. Just a big, jumbled mess."

He tried again. He was doing the best he could. Margaret knew how to help him do it.

Patty Jo looked at his signature. "Not good enough. I guess I shouldn't have believed Margaret when she said you could write. She thinks you know what's going on, but you don't. I can go ahead and sell the farm without your signature. She won't be able to stop me."

Walter was so worried about the farm. His old friend Edwin had come in and told him that Patty Jo was going to sell the farm. Now she'd said it too. She shouldn't do that. They needed to keep the farm.

The farm was his. He would be going back to the farm as soon as he could. He had lived there all his life.

He grabbed Patty Jo's arm and tried to ask her about the farm. His mouth moved and sound came out, but it was as bad as his writing, all jumbled.

She took his hand off her arm. "I know, Walter. I've asked the nurses to keep Margaret away from you. I think she upsets you too much."

His Margaret. The sweetest girl in the world. She had such beautiful blue eyes. Like her mother. He needed to close his eyes.

Patty Jo leaned in and whispered to him, "You won't be in here much longer. I'll take care of you."

He hoped she was right. All he wanted to do was go home.

CHAPTER 5

After school, Meg ran to the barn and sat on the top bar of one of the old stalls. Harvey watched her from his stall as she watched him. It was a comfortable viewing, each of them patient and curious. Meg felt as though she were drinking the animal in.

Harvey would be going home tomorrow, and she might never be friends with an elk again. From the first moment she had seen the elk, there had been a connection between them.

She had a cut-up apple in her pocket. She watched him wrinkle his nose as she offered him a piece.

"Do you smell it?" She hopped down and came closer to him. He was safe in the stall, so she didn't need to worry about him running away, but she did move as slowly and carefully as she could so as not to spook him. She could smell him. He gave off a forest odor that was a mixture of goodness and grossness: rotting leaves, wild plums, muck stewed in tree hollows.

Meg had cut the apple into six pieces. She knew he was fully capable of eating the whole apple by himself, probably in one big bite, but she wanted to dole it out so that she could watch him and so that he really knew where the apple came from. That it came from her. Maybe he would always remember her when he ate apples.

She held the first piece up to his nose to allow him to sniff it. She held her hand flat. She didn't want Harvey to accidentally nibble at her fingers. He lifted his lips back, if that's what they were called—the rim of his mouth around his teeth. He had big teeth. They looked like petrified wood, but lighter. He pulled at the apple section with his lips and sucked it into his mouth.

In school she had told her friends that they had an elk staying at their house.

"Aren't you scared of it?" Miranda Wales asked.

"No," Meg explained, remembering what the vet had told her. "Elks that have been bottle-fed are one of the tamest animals there are."

"You going to kill it and eat it?" Ted Thompson asked. He thought he was so smart.

He actually was pretty smart. That was one of the things she liked about him. And she liked the way he wore his watch. He wore it turned over, so the face was on the underside of his wrist. When he looked at it, he had to turn his wrist. Then time seemed his very own secret.

"No way," she said.

"But you kill and eat all those pheasants."

"That's different."

"How?"

"They were raised for that."

Meg wondered what Harvey had been raised for, why the Reiners had elk. She knew that sometimes people raised animals just to let them loose and hunt them. The English did things like that on their grand estates.

She fed Harvey his next piece of apple. He sucked it up faster than the first. Maybe they hadn't been feeding him enough.

"Harvey, who shot you?" she said out loud.

Harvey shook his head.

Meg laughed. "You don't know? You didn't get a chance to see them?" She gave him another slice of apple. "My mom will find out."

Harvey stood still, then looked over her shoulder.

Meg whirled around and saw her mother standing by the barn door. "How's he doing?"

"Good," Meg said. "You want to feed him some apple?"

"No, but I'll watch you do it. Then you need to come in for dinner." Her mother walked up closer but stayed behind Meg.

"I'm going to miss him, Mom."

"I think I will too."

"We need to have either a new kid in this family or a dog."

Her mother gave a yelp of a laugh. "You don't want all the attention focused on you?"

"Not particularly. I want someone else for me to think about and worry about and fuss over."

"Well, Rachel will be just up the street."

"That is so cool, I can hardly believe it."

"Will that do for the moment?"

Meg felt as though it was a trick question. "How about a horse? To keep Aunt Bridget's horse company."

"We'll see."

"Did you find out who shot Harvey?"

"No."

"Then how can we send him back there? What if they do it again, only this time they don't miss?"

"It's not up to us. Mr. Reiner, his owner, is willing to take that risk. I'll keep a close eye on him and that property."

"Mom, because you're a deputy sheriff, I always know all the bad things happening in this county."

"I guess that's right."

"Sometimes I wish I didn't know."

"Sometimes I wish you didn't too. Do you want me to stop telling you?"

"No. I guess I just wish they would stop happening."

Her mom picked up a slice of apple. "Okay. Let me try." She held it out and tensed up as the elk's nose came down and sniffed her hand.

"Don't drop it, Mom."

Then Harvey gently picked the apple slice off her hand.

"Bad things won't stop happening, Meg. But things really aren't so bad. You never know how they're going to turn out. If Harvey hadn't been shot, you never would have met him."

Meg nodded. "I never would have had the chance to feed a real elk a piece of apple."

Claire sat outside on the front porch and watched the sun set. She could hear Rich banging around in the kitchen. On her way home from work she had stopped and bought a pizza. A farming couple baked them in an outdoor wood-fired oven, and she had ordered one covered with end-of-the-season tomatoes and grilled peppers. Stopping to get the pizza counted as having made dinner, so according to their home-management agreement, Rich had to do the dishes. Meg had emptied the dishwasher and then run upstairs to do her homework.

But now Claire wanted Rich to stop fussing around in the kitchen and come sit next to her to watch the sun slip away. She felt incredible happiness, tinged with sadness. Sadness that this sliver of time would not last, that this moment of her life too would end.

As if he'd read her mind, Rich slammed open the door with his hip and brought out the garbage.

"Come and watch the sun set," she said.

"Let me put this in the garbage can."

"This is only going to last another moment. Can't you stop and watch it?"

He must have heard something in her voice because he threw the garbage bag down the stairs and came and sat next to her, leaning into her side.

"The days are getting shorter," Claire said, as if it explained her need for him.

"It happens every year."

"I know, but every year I regret it." She reached out and took his hand. "I'm happy."

He smiled over at her. "I'm glad. So am I."

"It scares me."

"You, the big tough cop?"

"I'm a marshmallow."

He dipped his head and kissed her lightly. "I like marshmallows."

"We've been living together for over a month."

"Yeah, it's been great." Rich squeezed her shoulder.

"We haven't had a fight yet."

"Do you think we're overdue?"

"I just wonder what it will be about."

"The dishwasher disagreement doesn't count?"

She laughed and shook her head.

"The pizza was great," he said.

"Changing the subject?"

"I don't feel like we need to rehearse our first fight. It will come in its own good time."

"How was your day?" Claire asked.

"Busy. Loaded up another truckful of pheasants. Three more to go. How about you?"

"We haven't gotten anywhere on what happened to the elk. It's frustrating. The crime scene doesn't make sense. No blood. Makes me wonder if they let him loose, then followed him and shot him in the woods. Not very logical, but criminals often aren't that smart. All I can figure is it was intended as a message to Reiner."

"Not a very clear one."

"No. Not yet. And that's what worries me. I'm afraid we haven't seen the last of this."

"Did you do any checking on Margaret's situation with her stepmother and Walter's farm?"

Claire knew Rich was fond of Walter Tilde. They were in a wood-carving group that met every Wednesday night. "I made some calls. It's hard to know where she stands legally. Because Patty Jo has power of attorney, Margaret has to prove that Patty Jo doesn't have her husband's best interest at heart. How do you prove that? And in the meantime, Patty Jo is going to sell the farm. Margaret might not have anything to claim if she doesn't try to fight this woman soon. I'm going to call her first thing tomorrow and get her moving."

"Sounds like you worked hard."

"Running in place is what it felt like."

The phone rang, and Rich rolled over to look at the clock. Two in the morning. Must be for Claire. He nudged her. She moaned.

"Claire. Phone."

She uncurled and sat on the edge of the bed. The phone rang again. "Hello?" Her voice sounded full of sleep. "Huh? Rich? Wait a minute."

Rich sat up and turned on the light. Claire covered the receiver with her hand. "It's for you. Some woman. She sounds drunk or something."

Rich took the phone, totally puzzled at who it could be. A drunk woman? He hoped it wasn't his ex-wife, but they hadn't spoken in years. "Hello?"

"Rich, it's your mother." The voice that was saying this was one he had never heard before. So slowly and flatly was this woman talking that it sounded like a record that someone was playing at the wrong speed.

"My mother?" He couldn't keep the disbelief out of his voice.

"I know it's late."

He started to recognize his mother's voice as his mind sped up the voice of the speaker. "Mom? What happened? Why are you talking so slow?"

"That's why I'm calling. I don't know, Rich. I don't feel so good."

"What's the matter? Tell me."

"I woke up and I couldn't move my arm. I'm drooling. I never drool."

He was afraid he knew what had happened to her. The knowledge shot through him like a jolt of electricity. He was an hour away from his mother. She needed help immediately. He had to get her off the phone. "Mom, you need to hang up so I can call 911. Then I'll call Mrs. Swanson."

"No, don't bother her. It's too late. I'm fine."

"No, you need help. Can you hang up, Mom?"

"Yes, I can do that. But . . ." Her voice quavered in a way he had never heard before. "Rich, I wish you would come. I'm scared."

"I'm on my way. Let me make these two phone calls, then I'll meet you at the hospital."

"I'm hanging up."

"Good, I'll see you soon." He hung up the phone.

Claire whispered, "Rich, what's going on?"

"It's my mother. Let me do this." He dialed 911. "This is for Rochester, Minnesota. My mother lives there. Can you connect me?"

The call went through, and a woman answered. He gave his mother's name and address. Then added, "I think she's had a stroke."

Claire stood up and pulled her bathrobe on. She went downstairs, and he heard her starting coffee.

Rich called Mrs. Swanson. She was an eighty-year-old woman who lived next door to his mother in an apartment. She answered the phone after three rings. No hello, just "Yes, who is this?"

He told her who he was. "My mother's not feeling very good. I'm worried she's had a stroke. I called the ambulance. Can you go sit with her?"

"Of course. I'll go right over. Those strokes are nasty things. I'll just walk right over in my bathrobe."

"Thank you. I'll go right to the hospital."

"Don't worry."

After he hung up the phone, he shucked off his pajamas and

grabbed the jeans he had worn the day before. A clean flannel shirt and socks and he was down the stairs.

Claire handed him coffee in his thermos cup. "Piece of toast?"

He waved her off. "I'm not hungry. Thanks."

"Do you want me to go with you?"

"No, you've got a full day. You'll have to get Meg off to school."

"Call me as soon as you know anything."

"I will."

"I'm so sorry, Rich. I hope she's okay."

"I do too. She won't be able to stand it if she isn't."

Claire laughed, then looked like she might cry. She put the back of her hand to her mouth. "Be careful. If a cop stops you, tell them what's happened and they might escort you part of the way there."

He kissed her and grabbed his jacket and was out the door.

The cool September air hit his face. No moon showed, and the stars were smeared across the sky. He wiped the dew off his car window with the back of his sleeve. He climbed in, started the motor, took a sip of coffee, and pulled out of the driveway. There would be no traffic at this time of night.

The dashboard clock read 2:20.

As Rich turned onto Highway 35 and headed south, he wondered what had happened inside his mother's brain. How would he find her when he arrived?

CHAPTER 6

Claire heard buzzing all around her. There seemed to be a point in the middle of the morning when the sheriff's department exploded—phones ringing, people coming and going, the fax machine printing, the computer beeping—and then, shortly after that, the quiet of lunch settled in.

She didn't leave for lunch. She hadn't heard from Rich yet. It was making her antsy. She hadn't been able to focus on any of the minor cases she had in front of her. One of the reports on her desk needed to go to the county attorney by tomorrow. Being the investigator for the Pepin County sheriff's department meant that she didn't get out on the street as much as she used to. She missed patrolling.

The phone rang, and she snatched it up. "Watkins."

"It's me."

Rich sounded exhausted, his voice over the phone thin and distant. She was scared to ask the question. "How is she?"

"Stroke."

"I'm so sorry, Rich. How's she doing?"

"You know, when I first saw her she looked pretty good. She could talk and she could move both arms and legs, although her left side was definitely weak. But since then, she's gone downhill. The doctors are watching her carefully."

"Oh, Rich . . ."

"Claire, she can't talk anymore. She can wave her left arm, but that's about it."

"What's going on? Did she have another stroke?"

"No. Her doctor says it's swelling in the brain. They're going to start her on medication for it, but it might be a day or so before we see results. He says she just has to ride this out. There's nothing more they can do."

The discouragement in his voice was palpable. She wished she could touch him. "Do you want me to come to the hospital?"

"No, I'm not going to stay here much longer myself. They don't think she's in any immediate danger. I'm going to see her settled in her new room and then I'll come home. Reiner's guy is coming to get Harvey today. I should be there."

"Don't worry about that."

Rich fell silent. Claire held the phone, waiting for something more.

Finally he said, "You know what my mother asked for as soon as she saw me in emergency?"

"What?"

"The newspaper. She wanted to do the crossword puzzle. I got it for her, but by then she was getting worse." He paused, then he said, "Her voice sounds so flat. Like she has lost all emotion."

"She's a fighter, Rich."

"Yes, I know, but how is she going to come through this? What will she have left of herself?"

After they hung up, Claire looked at her desk and decided to chuck it all. She needed to get out of the office. She decided to drive out and talk to Margaret Underwood. It was on her way home.

She called Margaret and let her know that she was coming, then she stuck her head in the sheriff's office. She explained what had happened to Rich's mom, then said, "I'm going to run over to Margaret Underwood's."

Claire had talked to the sheriff about Margaret's claim that her stepmother was trying to raid her father's estate.

He nodded and said, "Yeah, go talk to her. I'm not sure we can stop her stepmother, but it might make her feel better."

"Then I'm going to go home. Reiner's guy is coming to take the elk home today. I want to be there."

"How are you going to move the elk?"

"We won't make him walk home. Although that might be easier. Caretaker said he'd send a big trailer. Will be interesting to see them try to load him up—not my problem. My daughter's going to miss him."

"He has that much personality?"

"He does. And he has big brown eyes. You know what that does to the girls. He's amazingly tame for such a large animal."

"Speaking of which . . ." The sheriff tapped a pencil on his desk and said, "I got another call from Reiner."

"Yeah?"

"He wants us to find out who shot his elk. He's all torqued up about it, wants to know why we don't have the perpetrator in hand." The sheriff paused for a moment, then launched into a speech. "What is it with these townsfolk? They come down here, and if anything doesn't go their way, they threaten to sue everyone in sight the way we offer coffee to our neighbors. Don't they realize they've got to live with us the rest of their lives?"

"These are people who don't know their next-door neighbor's name in town, let alone their problems." Claire laughed. "I should know, I was one of them."

"This Reiner seems particularly obnoxious. Where does he get off?"

"He runs a big business. Used to everyone jumping when he demands it. Gets a lot done that way. I know he came from money, but I bet he earns his income now."

"All I know about the guy is he pays his taxes, and they are nothing to sneeze at. A couple months' salary of one of our deputies. I suppose he's an asset to this community."

"Yeah, but he should look at himself. I don't think he realizes how stirred up he's got people in this county over some of the things he's doing."

The sheriff swiveled back in his chair. "What're people stirred up about?"

"I think just who he is, what he represents. The thing is, he doesn't even see them. It's like they're just part of the local color."

"That'll make folks mad."

"But mad enough to walk on his land, cut his fence, and shoot one of his animals?"

"People have done worse with less reason."

Walking up to the Underwood house, Claire noticed a flower—a clematis vine had crawled up a trellis in front of the house, and a single fading purple blossom bobbed in the autumn breeze. Maybe the last flower of the season.

Claire knocked on the door, and Margaret yelled at her to come in. Opening the door, she found herself looking into the kitchen. An old woodstove stood next to the far wall, Margaret looking into it.

The floors were wide pine planks, polished to a shine. A large porcelain kitchen sink was placed right under a window with a row of plants—rosemary, scented geranium, thyme—lining the ledge. Under another window was the trunk that Claire had helped her carry into the house. There was nothing fancy about the room, but it was full of light and warmth and wonderful aromas.

"Something smells good."

"Have you had lunch?" Margaret asked, looking up from where she was squatting in front of the oven, checking on something she was baking. "I made some soup and corn bread."

Claire automatically was going to say no, but when she thought of her options, she changed her mind. "I'd love to join you. Better than a burger at the Fort. You have a great place here."

Margaret stood and smiled. Claire didn't think she had ever seen the woman smile before. It made her nearly beautiful, her cheeks full, her eyes lit up. "Thank you." Then Margaret's eyes fell and her smile crumbled. "I tried to go see my father this morning, but they wouldn't let me see him."

"What? Who?"

"Patty Jo told the nurses I was not to be allowed to see my father. I was standing in the hallway just outside his door, but I couldn't go in. What will he think when I don't show up?"

As she often did in her job, Claire felt amazed at how mean people were to each other. "Why would she do that?"

"She's afraid I'll talk to Dad about her selling the farm. I didn't bring it up the last time I saw him, because I didn't want to upset him. Now I wish I had. He has a right to know what's going on." Margaret set another place for Claire. "Can she do this to me? Can she stop me from seeing my dad?"

"I'm not sure. I'm not sure what her rights are. I'll check into it. You need to get a lawyer."

Margaret put her face in her hands. "I can't believe this. How can this be happening? It's bad enough that my father has had a stroke, but then to have this woman ripping him off and keeping me from seeing my own father . . ."

"I did talk to the county attorney about her selling the house. You need to get your own attorney and file a petition for an injunction. She said the best thing would be if you could prove undue influence."

"How am I going to do this all in time? I just found out that this Friday she's auctioning off the contents of the house. It was in the shopper. How do I prove anything before then?"

Claire thought the chances of her stopping the auction were slim. She knew how slowly the court usually moved. "Talk to your attorney immediately. Once you have filed the petition, we can freeze the assets. If you can do it fast enough, there's a chance we could stop the auction. You need to get right on that. And I wouldn't spread the word. I don't think you want Patty Jo to know what you're doing."

Mark walked in the kitchen door in time to hear the last few words. "What about Patty Jo?"

"Mark, take your boots off. Claire's been telling me what we need to do."

He slid them off on a piece of newspaper right by the door and walked in his stocking feet to the sink to wash his hands. He was a small man, maybe five-eight, but up close Claire could see that he was a solid block, muscles filling out his flannel shirt. He had thin brown hair tied back in a ponytail and deep wrinkles running down his cheeks, but he was handsome. Weathered, but attractive.

As he wiped his hands on a towel, he talked to Margaret. "I'm not happy with Letty's tit. It still looks swollen to me."

"I'll pack it again. Letty's one of our ewes." Margaret explained to Claire. "She's a good producer, but one of her teats has been impacted."

"Say no more," Claire said.

Mark reached out his big hand. "I don't think we've actually met." His handshake resembled his stature: firm and short.

"No, I just saw you that one day I picked up Margaret."

He sat down in a chair at the table. Claire got the impression he was holding a lot in, as if he might burst if he didn't control himself. "Patty Jo needs to be taught a lesson. She's going around like she owns that place. She doesn't. It's supposed to go to Margaret."

Margaret served big bowls of soup and then handed the corn bread around. "How do we prove that Patty Jo isn't acting with my dad's best interests in mind? She's his wife—how can she have undue influence?"

"From what I understand, you need to show that she took advantage of his situation. How did she persuade him to sign the power of attorney? I know it doesn't sound easy. Did your father ever complain about Patty Jo? How she was trying to take advantage of him?"

"I'll ask around. I doubt it. He was pretty tight-lipped. To tell you the truth, I don't think he talked to anyone about those sorts of things."

"Good luck."

They were all silent for a moment, then Margaret asked, "What if she had something to do with his stroke?"

Claire looked at her. "What do you mean?"

"I don't mean she brought it on, but she claims she didn't know anything had happened to my father until she called him for dinner. When I got to the hospital the doctor told me it looked like he had the stroke hours before the ambulance came. The damage was irreversible. Why didn't Patty Jo find him sooner? He was just out by the barn. What if she just let him lie there?"

This horrifying picture shot into Claire's mind: an old man on the ground, his wife in the house watching TV.

Meg had known they were coming to take Harvey away, but all day she tried to put it out of her mind, the way you try to keep a tongue away from a sore tooth. But there was no avoiding it when, a few minutes after the school bus dropped her off, two men arrived with a huge trailer. Meg saw them from the kitchen window.

They backed the trailer up to the barn and then went inside. Meg ran out from the house to see what they were doing and found them tying a rope around Harvey's neck. She could tell that he didn't like it and she tried to make them stop, but they wouldn't listen to her.

"You need to wait," Meg shouted at them. "Wait until my mom gets home. She needs to be here."

"Sweetie, get out of the way," one man said. "This animal is liable to buck, and you might lose your front teeth again."

Meg decided it would be best if she didn't watch them. She walked into the house and sat on the floor in her room and wondered how Rich's mom was doing. She knew Rich had left in the middle of the night and that he wasn't back yet. She felt like praying that Beatrice would be okay, but she didn't understand prayers. God had always felt so far away from her, even farther than the president of the United States. Older, but with his own tight agenda. God, if she thought he existed, scared her. When her worries about Beatrice started to overwhelm her, she decided maybe it would be better to see how Harvey was doing. He was here, and maybe she could help.

When she walked out of the house, the two men were standing on each side of Harvey, trying to lead him up the ramp and into the trailer. Harvey wasn't having any of it. He had planted his legs and wasn't moving. Meg was surprised by how badly it was going. She could see, right off the bat, so many things they were doing wrong. She could try to tell them, but she was sure they wouldn't listen to her.

Then her mother drove up the driveway.

As her mother stepped out of the car, Meg ran to her.

"Mom, they don't know what they're doing. Can't you stop them?"

Claire wrapped an arm around Meg's shoulders, and they walked up to the side of the trailer. "Hey, Jim. How's it going?" she said.

"Not so good. He's been in a trailer before, but he doesn't seem to want to budge today."

"I think I can make him get in the trailer," Meg told them all.

Her mother looked down at her. "You can?"

Jim said, "I'd like to see that. Do you want to give it a try?"

Claire squeezed her shoulders. "My daughter could get hurt."

"No, Mom, I won't get hurt. I know what I'm doing. I'll be very careful. Plus, Harvey's used to me. He's seen me every day for the last week. He knows me. Let me at least try."

The two men shrugged, and her mother said, "Okay, but we're going to stand here. If anything happens, these men will jump in."

"Fine, but stand back. I need Harvey to forget you're there. He doesn't trust those guys." Then Meg laid out her plan. "First let's take Harvey back into the barn and let him calm down."

They led him into the barn and tied him to his stall. Meg walked back out with the men and told them what she wanted them to do.

"You need to turn the truck off. That noise is bothering him. It's too much."

They turned the truck off.

"Now, open both doors at the end of the trailer. That way the whole trailer won't seem so claustrophobic to Harvey."

The two men walked around to the head of the truck and opened the doors on either side of the trailer.

"Wait for me. I'll be right back. Then I think we can load him." Meg ran into the house. She found an apple at the bottom of the refrigerator and cut it into four pieces. She stuffed it in her pocket and ran back outside.

Her mother and the two men were waiting. The men seemed impatient. Meg decided she had to do it all herself. The men would not be gentle enough. "I'll get him now," she said, and walked into the barn. She showed Harvey the apple, then led him out to the bottom of the ramp.

"I can do it, but why don't you move a little farther away? Walk away, but don't make any sudden moves." Meg stood at the bottom of the ramp and fed Harvey the first piece of apple. While he was eating, she talked to him. She told him he was a good elk. She told him where he was going and how happy he would be to see all his friends again. Then she walked halfway up the ramp and held out another piece.

Harvey took a step up the ramp and stretched out his neck to reach the apple. He ate the second piece. Meg backed up to the top of the ramp, and he followed. She fed him the third piece.

Facing him, she walked backward until she hit the back wall of the trailer. Harvey was watching her. She held out her hand with the last slice of apple. Meg could tell he was trying to decide what to do. But he was already up the ramp and didn't really want to go back down.

Harvey sniffed the air. Meg held the apple on the palm of her hand as if it were a diamond for him to inspect. She could see his eyes were on the apple slice. This was where patience came in—something she had learned in school when it got too boring. Minutes went by. There was one moment when he turned his head and she thought she had lost him, then she clucked her tongue and he looked at her and the apple again.

Finally he decided. She could tell by the way he shifted his weight on his legs even before he took the step. What he didn't like, she knew, was entering the enclosure of the trailer.

Suddenly he lunged forward, as if to get it over with, and stepped into the trailer, and she pulled the last piece of apple in closer to her chest. He came all the way into the trailer and put his muzzle on her hand, grabbing the apple.

After he had taken the last piece of apple, she tied his rope to the bar that was next to her head. The smell of the elk surrounded her. She whispered to him, "I won't forget you," and then she jumped out one of the doors at the head of the trailer.

Her mother was standing right there and said, "Good job, Meg."

"How'd you learn to do that?" Jim asked her.

"You need to think like an elk, that's all," Meg told him, and then left the men to secure the trailer. She didn't want to watch them drive away. She ran to the house and went inside.

She went to her room and sat on the floor. She would never have another elk in her life like Harvey. She hated it when she got left behind. A hole where the elk had stood in the barn every day for the last week grew in her mind until it sucked up the whole universe. Tears started leaking out of her eyes and running down her face. The sadness in her was like a stream that wouldn't stop.

Meg heard her mother come to her doorway. "Meggy, you were great."

"I was not." Meg couldn't keep the sob out of her voice.

Her mother knelt by her and put a hand on her shoulder. "What's the matter, honey?"

Meg pulled away from her mother's touch and wrapped her arms around herself. "I'm not honey, and you know what the matter is. Another thing gone. Everything I love goes away. I hate it." Meg couldn't help herself as the words tore out of her mouth in a mean way.

"It must seem like that sometimes."

"Mom, leave me alone. I don't need your words of wisdom. You don't understand. I need to be by myself right now and do it my own way."

CHAPTER 7

"I just picked up the injunction. I'll swing by and get you," Claire Watkins said to Margaret over the phone.

"Thank you so much. I'll be standing at the end of the driveway, waiting," Margaret said.

Margaret was finishing up the laundry—folding Mark's clothes—but all she could think about was the auction. It would have to stop. Margaret just hoped they got there before anything important had been sold.

She checked the clock again: 11:47. It was only two minutes later than the last time she'd looked. The auction was supposed to start at noon. The shirt in her hands was crumpled into a ball instead of folded to be put away. She snapped it out straight and then started to smooth it with her hands.

Having been to a couple of hundred farm auctions in her life, she knew the schedule by heart. The first two hours—from ten to noon—would be devoted to letting the crowd mill around all the stuff. The farm implements and machinery would be out in the barnyard, and some of the big pieces of furniture would be left in the house, but since it was a nice day a lot would have been carted outside. Most of the small items would be boxed and sold as a lot—the linens, the silver, the china, the geegaws.

She could picture it so clearly. Her neighbors would be walking around her parents' farm, poking and pawing all the trappings of her family's life together. Margaret wanted to throw up.

Mark was worrying her. He had gone out to the barn to finish milking the goats. He didn't even want to talk about what was going on. He seemed ready to snap at any moment.

She could tell the problems with Patty Jo were eating Mark up inside. He was drinking a bit more than she had ever noticed him doing before. During the day he threw himself into work, but at night he was restless. That's when he would start to drink. She wouldn't have minded so much if it would calm him down, but often it made him worse. He would get belligerent with her and then often leave. She didn't know where he was going at night.

She tried to push Mark out of her head. He would be fine when they got this situation resolved.

Margaret couldn't help thinking about all the little things of her mother's she would like to have: her sewing kit, the quilt she had made, the old doll that sat in the china cabinet. Come to that, the china cabinet.

She bent the sleeves of the shirt in toward the middle and then folded the shirt in half. She wasn't half the housekeeper her mother, Florence, had been. Her mother hadn't made a wasted movement, and she put things back where she found them as soon as she was done with them. Her pies had been the best in the county, and she had the blue ribbons to prove it. She'd sewed a tidy stitch and set a perfect table. Margaret had tried to learn all these important country lessons, but her mind often strayed.

Since she'd begun struggling with menopause, she found it harder than ever to stay constant. In the midst of a chore, she would find herself a million miles away.

Margaret remembered how her mother would say to her when she was young, "Come back here, Margie, before I send the dog to fetch you."

Now she felt as if she had failed her mother. Not because she couldn't keep a house as clean, but because she had let all her mother's valuable keepsakes go to a stranger. She hadn't been able to save her mother; now she couldn't even save what was left of the remnants of her life.

Margaret remembered one of the last conversations she had with her mother after moving her to Lakeside Manor. Her mother hadn't taken to her new residence. Her level of paranoia increased. The doctor said that was part of the Alzheimer's. She was having trouble remembering who people were. Once or twice she had called Margaret "Angie," her aunt's name. Margaret didn't argue. It only made it worse.

On this particular morning, when Margaret walked into her room, her mother had thrown a carton of milk at her.

"Mom, what's the matter?"

Her mother looked right at her and said, "That woman is stealing my mind."

"What woman?" she had asked.

"The one that smiles all the time. The one that's really a deep monster."

"A deep monster?"

Her mother pointed out the window. "From the lake. She's come from the bottom of the lake."

At the time, Margaret had assumed her mother was fussing about one of the nurses. Now she wondered. Who had her mother meant? What had she thought was happening?

Claire would arrive any minute. Margaret took off her apron, slicked at her hair in the mirror, and ran outside carrying her purse in her arms like a baby. She hollered at Mark, "I'm leaving," not really caring if he heard.

Running to the end of the driveway, she saw, with relief, the squad car coming down the road, Claire Watkins behind the wheel. Claire slowed, and Margaret hopped in.

Claire handed her a large manila envelope. "You can have the pleasure of delivering it."

Maybe they'd get there before the auction started. Before one item of her parents' lives was lost.

Patty Jo had set up a chair for herself in a prime location, about fifteen feet in front of the auctioneer's podium. She wanted to be able to watch every item be sold. That way she could keep track of the money. She had planned a long time for this moment, and she was going to enjoy every second of it. As each piece of furniture and each lace doily was sold, she would feel herself become freer. Nothing to hold her down. More money to do what she wanted.

She had put her umbrella on a folding chair to save the seat for herself. It was a warm day for September, in the high seventies. While everyone else was looking around at all the stuff to be auctioned off, she had wandered around looking at the people. She found it easier to be pleasant to all her neighors since she knew she'd soon be leaving them behind.

Lucille Clowder stopped her by the floral-print sofa. "This looks like such a nice sofa, Patty Jo. Why are you selling it?"

"I want to start over."

"I suppose it has sad memories," Lucille murmured.

Patty Jo didn't bother to correct her. These last few months, she had played the dutiful wife with as much dignity as she could muster. Let them think what they would; she would be gone soon.

"I hear you already have an offer on the house?" Lucille pushed.

"It looks that way."

"I wonder what that Reiner man intends to do with your land. It'll be a shame if Walter's house gets torn down. Beautiful old place like this. One of the nicest houses in the county."

"That ain't saying much."

Lucille flinched at Patty Jo's words, and Patty Jo felt the impulse to tell her more, to really shake the old woman up. She knew damn well that Lucille was just at the auction to get all the latest gossip and visit with everyone. She would probably buy some old glass vase for fifty cents, worth about five dollars new. She'd be proud of her bargain, take it home and stick it in the back of a cupboard where it would gather dust until she died. She'd spend all day wandering around looking at everything and maybe have a cup of coffee and a piece of pie. It would be her entertainment for the day.

Patty Jo felt like telling Lucille a few things she wouldn't forget, but then shrugged it off. What was the use? Patty Jo was planning to enjoy the day, so why not let Lucille enjoy it too?

"You looking for anything special, Lucille?"

The older woman colored at the attention being paid her. "Oh, you know, I don't need much anymore. I only buy something if it catches my eye." Then the woman added, "I would like something to remember Florence by. I do miss her. She was such a good woman."

The highest accolade in this little county—to be a good woman. It had never been said of Patty Jo, and she never wanted it to be.

Holding her tongue, she moved away from Lucille. The auctioneer looked ready to start. She walked over to her chair, opened up the umbrella, and lifted it over her head.

After the auctioneer welcomed everyone and exclaimed how lucky they were to have an utterly perfect day, he lifted an old lamp and said, "Let's start with this. I'm looking for an opening bid of five dollars. Can anyone give me five dollar? I'm looking for five dollar. I got a hand there, five, do I see ten, do I see ten. . . ." The sound of the auctioneer's chant was a song in her ears. He rolled suggestive prices for the lamp off his tongue like the trillings of a bird.

Another hand flew in the air and the auctioneer spieled out more numbers. Patty Jo felt a glow in her stomach. She was on her way.

Then she noticed a commotion behind the auctioneer. A woman in a deputy's uniform was talking to a partner in the auction business.

Patty Jo recognized the woman. She was the deputy who had come to the house with Margaret. Why was she at the auction in uniform?

Patty Jo got a real bad feeling when she saw Margaret was there too, holding some sort of letter. She had been sure that Margaret would not come to the auction. She hadn't thought Margaret would be able to handle watching all her family heirlooms being sold out from under her. What was she doing here?

The lamp sold for $25 to Clarence Johnson's wife. What did she want with an old lamp? But $25 wasn't too bad. Twice what she would have paid for it. After the bid was accepted, the auctioneer turned and started talking to the deputy. He was shaking his head and waving his arm. Then he stepped down from the podium.

Patty Jo stood and snapped shut her umbrella. Whatever was happening, she would have to put a stop to it.

Claire described the scene at the auction to Rich as he stood outside, grilling chicken for their dinner. "You wouldn't have believed it. I've never seen anyone so mad. Patty Jo came walking up to the auctioneer and started screaming. Her face turned red. She took a lamp that had just sold and smashed it right there. Threw it on the ground and smashed it."

Meg sat on the porch railing and listened. Claire didn't know how her daughter could balance on there so easily, looking like a bird on a wire.

Meg piped in, "Did you arrest her?"

"Arrest her?"

"Because of the lamp. Destruction of property."

Claire resisted laughing at her daughter's use of cop jargon. "No, I couldn't. Since no money had changed hands, it was technically still her lamp. She could do with it what she wanted."

"Although, really technically, it wasn't her lamp anymore. It might have been Margaret's with this new injunction. According to you, Margaret inherits the farm, right?" Rich pointed out.

"That's true. But Margaret is aimed at bigger fish than suing Patty Jo for the value of a lamp. After her behavior today, I'm not even sure the woman should be allowed to stay on the farm. I don't trust her to leave everything alone. I'm afraid she might do something drastic. I'm thinking Margaret should push to have her asked to vacate the premises. What do you think?"

"Maybe the house will fall on her and her feet will curl up," Meg suggested.

"And Margaret will get the red shoes," Rich added. Then he looked at Claire and saw how serious she was. "Can Margaret do that? It sounds awful drastic. Where would the poor woman stay?"

"Patty Jo is no poor woman. You should have seen her this afternoon. She's not afraid to create a scene. The woman went ballistic. I'm afraid if she'd had a gun, I wouldn't be here right now."

"Mom, don't say things like that. Not when I'm listening," Meg said, jumping down off the railing. She leaned over the grill to peer at the meat, poking at it with her finger. Rich gently rapped her hand with his tongs.

"Little pitchers have big ears. Why don't you go in and set the table?" Claire pushed her daughter toward the house so she could talk with Rich.

Rich leaned back against the railing. "I still say it seems a little drastic, asking Patty Jo to leave her own home."

"I suppose. I just have a bad feeling about that woman."

"Don't get so involved, Claire. Margaret needs to figure this out."

"I'm already involved. The one good thing is, because of the auction, we have a complete list of all the items in the house. So Patty Jo can't sell anything without us knowing about it. I don't trust her at all."

"What ended up happening with the auction? Did Patty Jo have to pay them for their time?"

"I'm not sure how that's going to settle out. I can tell you the auctioneers were not happy. Nobody was happy. All the people who were there were ready to buy things, and they were pretty upset, although most of them have a lot of sympathy for what Margaret's going through."

"How did she take it?"

"Margaret? She's an odd one. I can't imagine what she's feeling. When my dad died, my sister and I had to divvy up all the family stuff, but we did it very easily. This is like the worst thing that could happen. Having all the family stuff yanked away. And her father isn't even dead yet."

"How did you leave the place?"

"Well, that turned out okay. The auctioneer said they weren't going to put any of the furniture or other things back into the house. They said they'd already done enough work for no money. They took off in a huff. Patty Jo said the stuff could sit out for as long as the judgment took. She didn't care what happened to any of it. Margaret asked me to help her start to put some of it back into the house. A couple of guys who had come for the auction helped us haul a bunch of the bigger pieces inside."

"Well, Patty Jo might be doing herself in. If she doesn't take care of the furniture, it makes it easy to prove that she isn't watching out for Walter's best interests."

"Right. I like the way your mind works."

"Isn't she legally bound to take care of the estate?"

"Probably. She got into her car and drove off. Actually, that was the best thing that happened. Margaret's husband, Mark, arrived, and we got most everything back into the house."

"What does Margaret want to do? Or Mark?"

"They seem shell-shocked. I think they still can't believe that they might lose the farm. They seemed uncomfortable even touching any of the furniture. As if someone would accuse them of something."

"I can understand that. Like they've been dispossessed in full view of the community." Rich started to pile the chicken onto the platter she held out for him. "Good thing you got there before anything was sold."

The smell of the grilled chicken made Claire realize how hungry she was. "It worked out."

"On a different subject, I had a long talk with the doctor about my mother." Rich put the last piece of chicken on the platter and looked up at Claire.

"What did he say?"

"The good news is that my mother has recovered better than they could have hoped. They have even had her up and walking a few steps. But the bad news is they want her to leave the hospital in the next couple of days. We have to talk about what we're going to do with her. She can't decide for herself."

Claire felt as though the platter of chicken had gotten very heavy. "What do you want to do?"

He continued to watch Claire. "She can't go home now, not in her condition. She can't take care of herself. She's too far away for us to be running back and forth to help her. And she's going to need therapy for a while."

Claire knew what she had to say, so she forced the words out of her mouth. "Do you want her to come and stay with us?"

He had his answer ready. "Not in a million years."

CHAPTER 8

A week after Beatrice's stroke, Rich picked her up at the hospital to take her to Lakeside Manor. As the pickup truck barreled down the freeway, Rich noticed that Beatrice was sitting crooked. The traffic on the freeway was so heavy, he couldn't stop to arrange her better. But then, everything about her was crooked. Even her smile seemed to slide off her face. At least she had smiled at him this morning when he came to pick her up.

"How're you doing, Mom?" he asked now.

She jolted a little at the sound of his voice, then turned her head slowly toward him. She still had a significant deficit on her left side, the doctors had told him; he wasn't even sure she could see him.

"I'm tired," she said.

"We're getting close."

"Where are we going?" she asked in her new flat voice.

He had told her three times already this morning and many times the previous days. But she didn't remember much. "I think I told you. You're going to go stay at Lakeside Manor, a very nice nursing home in Pepin, only a few miles from us. That way Claire and I can keep an eye on you."

"I want to go home."

"I know you do. Mrs. Swanson is watching your apartment. You'll be going back there soon."

"Don't lie to me, Rich."

"I'll try not to."

"She doesn't know how to water my African violets."

"I'll be checking on things. You can tell me how."

"It's not the same."

"I know."

There was silence. Her head nodded. She slept.

After driving through Wabasha, Minnesota, they crossed over the delta of the Mississippi and the Chippewa and into Wisconsin. He saw a lone fisherman far back in the sloughs, but the season was winding down. The sumac, the harbinger of fall, was starting to turn red on the lower edges of the woodlands.

Off to the right an egret lifted its head out of the muck and walked a few tilting steps. The walk reminded him of his mother's attempts at locomotion. She could stand up, but she was hard put to walk more than two or three steps.

He wondered how long she would have to stay at the nursing home. She would get some rehabiliation there, but he wasn't really sure she'd ever be fit to go home again. He could hardly stand to think about it. His feisty mother stuck so far from all she loved, from the good life she had created after her husband had died.

When they got to the nursing home, the director came out to greet them and sent out a nurse to help transfer Beatrice into a wheelchair.

The big blond girl looked like she was just out of high school. She carried her weight well and transferred Beatrice out of the car and into the chair as if the old woman weighed no more than a Chihuahua.

"That was slick," Rich commented.

"I'll teach you how to do the swivel transfer if you like."

Rich nodded but was nervous that if he tried such a manuever with his mother he might drop her. Rich got out her suitcase and followed behind the nurse and the wheelchair. He had had to pack the suitcase himself and had tried to put in it all the things she might need. They had given him a list of clothes to bring: seven nightgowns, seven of everything. It appeared they would take it a week at a time.

"I'm Bonnie," the young nurse told him. "I work every weekday. So I'll be helping with your mother on a regular basis. She seems like she's doing real well."

"I'm right here," said Beatrice.

Rich felt his heart lift. A little of her old spunk was a good sign.

Bonnie laughed and said, "Okay, then, where would you like to be? Would you like to sit up for a while?"

"No, I'm tired. Put me in bed."

"Certainly." The young woman restrapped the transfer belt around Beatrice's waist, cinched it, and hoisted Beatrice up and pivoted her until she was right next to the bed. Then she eased Rich's mother down until she was sitting on the edge of the bed. Grabbing Beatrice's feet, she picked them up and put them on the bed. Beatrice sprawled back onto a pile of two pillows.

"If you need anything, press your call button. I'll be right down the hall."

Bonnie walked out. Rich looked around the room. Two windows faced south and the sun came in through the Levolor blinds. The floor was a beige-speckled linoleum and reminded Rich of an Easter egg candy he had eaten when he was young. The only pieces of furniture in the room were a lounge chair and a battered chest of drawers. Why hadn't he thought to bring some personal items to soften the room?

"Tell me what you would like and I'll bring some of your things here to make this place more your own."

"I don't need anything."

"Mom, a few of your photographs, some books, your afghan . . ."

She kept shaking her head through his list of possibilities.

"I know—I'll bring some of your violets."

"Don't bring the violets."

"Mom."

"Don't bring the violets here." She sounded as if she was going to cry, which unnerved him more than anything else he had witnessed. His mother never cried.

"I won't bring the violets."

"Rich, I don't want to be like this."

He looked down at his mother, lying crookedly in the hospital bed, her bad arm in a sling. She reminded him of a poorly stuffed animal in an old diorama. He could even imagine the signage: SUPINE EIGHTY-YEAR-OLD FEMALE HOMO SAPIENS. NO LONGER QUITE RIGHT IN HER BODY. "I understand."

"Can you help me? Can you help me get out of here?"

He bent down close to her. Communicating with her now was like talking to a frightened animal. You had to get close enough to her so she could feel your presence, and then talk soft and low. He took her limp left hand and gently rocked it. "I can. But let's give it a few weeks. See how you do. I have great faith in you. I think you're stronger than you even know."

Beatrice looked around the empty room. "This isn't where I want to die."

Beatrice slept so hard that she felt she had dropped off the face of the earth and fallen—*splat*—on the sky. When she dragged her eyelids up, she could see that she was in a strange room and that there was light shining in from a doorway. She needed to know where she was. She found her glasses on a table by her bed and, with difficulty, set them on her nose.

A clock next to the bed indicated eight o'clock, but Beatrice wasn't sure if that meant morning or evening. When she looked out the window, she saw it was dark, so it must be evening.

She knew she was not in the hospital. It was too quiet for the hospital. But it wasn't her apartment; she knew that for sure.

Then she remembered where Rich had taken her. A nursing home. She couldn't believe she had ended up at one. She had hoped to die in her own bed one night without even knowing, to move gently from sleeping to nonexistence or whatever else came after. It was enough to make a person cry to find herself suddenly in a nursing home.

She knew she wasn't supposed to get out of bed by herself. If she could just get someone to help her . . . Through the crack in the door, she could see a woman coming down the hall. If she could get her attention . . .

Beatrice made a small noise, like a yelp. After she made it she felt ashamed. What kind of business was that, making yelping noises in the middle of the night? The woman stopped and looked toward her door but evidently couldn't see into the darkness of the room.

But Beatrice could see the woman. She didn't look like a nurse; she wasn't wearing a nurse's uniform. She had blond frizzy hair and was rather stout. She was carrying a large purse. She went into the room across the hallway from Beatrice's room.

Beatrice put her head back on her pillow. She was so tired. Even holding her head up made her tired. Even keeping her eyes open.

She remembered who was in the room across from her. She had met him in the hall when the nurse pushed her to dinner. His name was Walter. He made her situation look positive. He couldn't talk, he couldn't eat, he couldn't walk. He had a tube in his stomach. His head bobbled on the end of his neck like a flower blowing in the breeze.

She wondered why the woman was visiting him so late. She wondered why she was staying in this strange hotel. But these thoughts were like swallows flitting, skimming over the surface of her brain, picking up insects and flying on. They didn't rest until they slept. She slept.

So many people were visiting Walter these days. They would stand at the edges of the room and nod and wave to him. They didn't say anything. He recognized a few of them: his third-grade schoolteacher,

Miss Lillehelm; Mr. Ramstead, the postman; Howard Levy, who had fought next to him in World War II. They came and went like ripples on a pond. They comforted him with their presence.

He was staring at them when Patty Jo came into the room. He could tell it was her even though she didn't turn the light on because she had a heavy walk and she swore when she bumped into a chair.

He had tried to please Patty Jo, but he didn't think she was very happy with him. She could be mean if she didn't get what she wanted. He had learned not to oppose her on anything. It just wasn't worth it. He went along with everything she wanted after what had happened to Florence.

She sat down next to the bed and reached out and took his hand.

Walter was surprised because she didn't tend to touch him much. He wished she would touch him more. He felt so adrift.

Patty Jo was holding his wrist like the nurses did. She was taking his pulse. He looked at her. She didn't say anything to him. He didn't bother to try to say anything to her. It was too frustrating.

He was lucky to have Patty Jo. She had promised to take care of everything for him. He was worried about the farm, but he was sure she would never sell it. She knew he wanted to go back there soon. Margaret would tell her.

He wondered where Margaret was. She hadn't come to see him in a few days. He tried to ask about Margaret. The noise he made sounded like a cow mooing.

Patty Jo put down his hand. "You know I can't understand you. I just want you to know I'm doing this because of Margaret. If she'd let things be the way I planned, I wouldn't be here right now."

The people lining the walls were waving again. He blinked his eyes at them. It was his code to tell them he could see them.

Patty Jo sat down next to him and leaned in close. "It's time to go to sleep, Walter."

He could fall asleep so easily these days. All he had to do was close his eyes. But then he couldn't see Patty Jo or his friends.

He blinked his eyes at her.

"Don't look at me like that, Walter. I'm doing this for your own good."

Patty Jo had always reminded him of his mother. That had been a favorite phrase of his mother's: "doing this for your own good." It usually meant something bad was going to happen.

CHAPTER 9

The Moravian Church was tucked down a winding road on the bluff top. Claire had always loved spotting the belfry of the small white church in the distance, but she had never seen the interior. As she turned onto the dirt road that led to the church, she scared up a flock of turkeys. The birds looked prehistoric to her, walking in their awkward, stilted manner. After they scattered off the road, she parked about a block from the church. The parking lot was full, and cars and pickup trucks lined the road.

When Claire walked into the church, she saw that it had raked seating with built-in stadium chairs that reminded her of an old movie theater. All the chairs were filled—there looked to be about one hundred of them—and people were lined up along the walls. She found Rich standing near the entrance waiting for her.

"What a funny old church," she whispered in his ear when he dipped his head.

"It won't be here much longer," he whispered back.

She looked questioningly at him.

"The congregation has dwindled to the point that they can't keep it going. They're about to desanctify the church."

"How sad," Claire murmured.

She looked over the people in the seats—most of them were over sixty years old—and recognized many.

Down front she could see three people sitting in the first row: Margaret and Mark Underwood, and Patty Jo Tilde. Margaret was dressed in a black dress, Mark had on a dark suit, and Patty Jo was wearing a red-flowered top with her blond hair pulled back and long dangling earrings.

Margaret had called Claire with the news of her father's death. She said that should take care of the problems with the estate. Margaret was quite sure that her father's will left most of her father's money to Patty Jo, but the farm would go to Margaret and Mark.

"I'm sorry to hear about your father," Claire told her.

"Yes, I'm sad that he's gone." Margaret paused, then said, "But I'm so glad he isn't trapped in that worthless body anymore. He hated what had happened to him. He was frustrated all the time."

"Of course."

"Thank you for helping me."

"It's my job."

"You went beyond your job."

"If I did, don't tell the sheriff."

Margaret chuckled, then gave Claire the information about the funeral.

A mahogany casket sat at the front of the church with Walter Tilde laid out in its white interior. His eyes were closed and his thin white hair was slicked back. His forehead still bore the signs of the tan mark from his feed cap.

"Did you pay your respects to Walter?" Claire asked Rich.

He nodded.

The pastor came in the side door, and everyone stood to sing the first hymn. Claire listened to the song and watched the three people in the front row. Mark and Margaret were leaning into each other, sharing a hymnal and singing. Patty Jo was standing alone, holding no hymnal, silent.

Claire wondered what made the woman tick. What had possessed her to try to take the farm away from Walter's daughter? How had she persuaded him to sign over power of attorney to her in the first place? She hoped for Margaret's sake that Patty Jo would take her share of Walter's estate and leave the county. She hoped it for her own sake. She didn't like the woman.

Margaret had decided not to argue with Patty Jo about cremating her father. She didn't think it was what her father wanted, but she didn't see how it could matter. Patty Jo seemed fine with Walter's ashes being buried next to Florence, and that was all that really was important to Margaret. She wanted her parents to be united again.

The day after the funeral she was surprised how relieved she felt. Mark had told her not to bother with milking the goats in the morning. He would do it. He wanted her to take it easy and relax. He patted her on the shoulder as he left to do the chores.

"It's all over, Margie," he said. "Your father's at peace."

"Yes, I think he is."

Mark stopped at the door. "You know the first thing I'm going to do with your father's farm?"

"What?"

"Plow under that field of soybeans. It's about composted by now. Be good for the soil."

Margaret smiled. Having the farm would be so good for Mark.

Five minutes later, the phone rang.

It was her father's attorney, Mr. Matthews. "I'm afraid I have bad news, Margaret."

Margaret's mind went blank. What more could possibly happen? She asked, "What now?"

"Well, it appears that Patty Jo has her own lawyer, which is news to me. He called me this morning to say that Walter had written out another will. It postdates the one your father signed with me."

"What does this mean?" She knew, but she had to ask.

"The new will takes precedence, I'm afraid," Mr. Matthews paused, then tried again, "Margaret, I'm sorry to have to tell you that everything in your father's estate goes to Patty Jo."

Margaret looked at the table and noticed that Mark had spilled coffee on the tablecloth. A dark stain spread out from his coffee cup.

"Margaret?"

"Everything?" she asked.

"Yes."

"Does that mean the farm? Does she get the farm?"

"Yes, I'm afraid she gets it all."

"But that isn't what my father wanted."

He sighed. Mr. Matthews had known her father a long time. "I know."

"Is there anything I can do?"

"I'm afraid not. I had this lawyer fax over the new will before I called you. It looks legitimate to me. I checked and it was dated a week before your father's stroke, so we have to assume he was competent." Mr. Matthews stopped, then added, "I'm sorry, Margaret. I'd like to be able to help."

"These things happen," she said, because she knew she had to say something. She couldn't blame Mr. Matthews. The only person to blame was herself. She should have known. She should have talked things over with her father after he married Patty Jo. But she had never guessed there was any need.

The lawyer said he'd send her a copy of the will and that she should call him if she had any questions. She thanked him and was glad when he said goodbye.

She was still wearing her bathrobe. It was going to be such a nice morning. She got a sponge out of the sink and ran hot water on it and squirted some dish soap on it. Then she tried to get the stain out of the tablecloth. Coffee was a bad stain. It faded but never really went away.

Then she stopped scrubbing. She looked down at her hands and started to cry. She didn't want to have to tell Mark the bad news.

CHAPTER 10

The nurse had left Beatrice sitting in her wheelchair in the hallway by the door to her room. She guessed it was the equivalent to the front stoop. She was supposed to make pleasant conversation with everyone who wandered by.

There were many things Beatrice didn't care for about this nursing home. But her pet peeve was all the senile people. How could one keep up one's brainpower with such a low level of intellectual activity going on around one?

She looked up when she heard someone coming down the hall. Walter's wife, the woman with frizzy blond hair, approached her. Her feet slapped the floor as she walked. What was she doing in the nursing home now that Walter had died?

The woman stopped in front of Beatrice's wheelchair.

"Are you going to play bingo?" she asked.

"I wasn't planning on it."

"I'm Patty Jo."

"Nice to meet you. I'm Beatrice."

Patty Jo looked her over as she sat in the wheelchair. "Why are you here?"

Beatrice told her, ashamed of the way her body had let her down.

Patty Jo tilted her head toward the community room, where people were getting ready for the afternoon bingo game. "What else have you got to do?"

"Not much. I'd like to do a crossword puzzle."

"You're good at those?"

"Yes. At least I used to be," Beatrice added, "before."

Patty Jo started pushing Beatrice's wheelchair down the hall. "Bingo'll be a good warm-up for you. Then you can move on to the crossword when it's done."

Beatrice decided not to argue. One game of bingo wouldn't hurt.

Patty Jo pushed her wheelchair up to one of the long tables and sat down next to her. All the old, slumped people around them said hi. Beatrice gave a general nod to the table.

A card was placed in front of her and then the woman at the front of the room started calling out the squares. "B-fourteen . . . N-six." Beatrice found it harder than she might have imagined to cover the squares that she had before the next one was called. Twice Patty Jo leaned over and pointed out one that she had missed. Beatrice didn't seem to be able to notice the squares on the left side of her card. She had to force herself to look all the way over there.

How stupid she felt that bingo had become a difficult game for her. She was relieved when an older gentleman at her table waved his hand in the air and rasped out, "Bingo."

While they were handing out new cards, Patty Jo said, "I play bingo at the casino in Red Wing. It's only about a half an hour away. You see some real action there. I try to get up there a couple of times a week."

"Do you make any money?" Beatrice had never been to a casino in her life.

"Sometimes. Had a streak of bad luck lately."

They started the next card, and Beatrice focused as hard as she could. She started on the left side of the card, and that seemed to help her see those squares. When bingo was called, she was one square away from it herself.

"Condolences on your husband's death," Beatrice said to Patty Jo as the next cards were distributed.

"Yes, it was sad. But Walter was ready to go."

"He wasn't in very good shape, was he?"

Patty Jo shook her head.

"Why are you still coming here?"

Patty Jo smiled. "I like to play bingo."

By the end of the hour, Beatrice was exhausted. She felt as though she had never worked so hard, even playing bridge for an afternoon with life masters. Patty Jo pushed her back to her room.

"Thanks," Beatrice said.

"You got the hang of it."

Without saying anything more, Patty Jo left her sitting in her wheelchair. Beatrice wanted to crawl into bed, although it wasn't even four in the afternoon. Then Patty Jo appeared in front of her and put a newspaper and a pencil into her lap. "The crossword."

Patty Jo looked at the balance in the checkbook. Her lawyer told her that it would take a couple of months to move the estate through probate. In the meantime she couldn't sell anything. She had spent the last of Walter's ready cash at the casino last Friday. She could run a tab at the grocery store in town, but she needed to get some money to pay the bills. She knew what she needed to do.

The kerosene was kept in the pantry. They had used it to fill the lamps they lit when the storms took the power away. It was back behind the shoe polish and the candles. Patty Jo pulled out the bottle and then bent over and grabbed a handful of old rags. Walter had used them to polish his tools. He'd never let her throw anything away. "Save it," he would say, "save it. It will come in handy for something."

These rags would be plenty handy for what she had in mind. The sun would set in an hour or so. She probably should wait until after dark, but she wanted to get it over with. She would get her money out of this farm one way or another.

The stupid barn wasn't worth the land it was built on, but Walter had insured it to the maximum.

Patty Jo kicked at the dirt as she walked to the barn. The soybean fields looked scorched. Interesting how quickly things decayed when they weren't attended to. The overgrown lawn had been trampled down at the auction. She sure wasn't going to pay someone to mow it. She wasn't going to put another penny into this place.

Once inside the barn, she walked to the far corner, where Walter had kept his tools. He had a big bucket of sand that he would plunge them in after he used them, and then in the fall he would oil them for winter. He'd taken better care of his tools than he had of himself.

It would look like an accident. She stuffed the rags next to the kerosene can and then set up a tall candle in the middle of the kerosene-soaked rags. Patty Jo stood and watched the little spurt of flame light up the top of the candle, then pulled herself away. That should give her enough time to be long gone when the rags caught on fire. At least a good hour.

The car was parked right in front of the house, and her purse was already in it. She got in, started the car, and spun out of the driveway. As she turned the corner to go to town, she couldn't resist taking one more backward glance. Nothing. No thin trail of smoke. Not yet.

She would be buying her groceries as the barn caught on fire. She would make sure everyone saw her all over town. After she had been gone a good hour, she'd drive back up the hill. She would be horrified by what she saw. The fire truck would be there. Her neighbors would all be gathered around. No one liked to miss a good fire. They would all witness how horrified she was.

She would call her insurance agent later today. She needed the money. She had been counting on the farm sale to Reiner, but now probate was tying everything up. The insurance money would have to tide her over.

The barn stood across a large open area from the house. A little wind was all it would take. If the house caught on fire too, so much the better.

* * *

Edwin Sandstrom liked Ella Gunderson. He was driving over to her house and thinking about how much he liked her. He had known her all his life. He could remember what she looked like when she was three years old and he was ten. She had been cute as a button then, and she was still cute as a button even if she was nearly seventy years old. His wife had died ten years ago, and she had liked Ella too.

The last year or two Ella and he had started to get serious. He didn't know how it had happened. Maybe it was her biscuits. No, it was her rhubarb pie that had put a spell on him. He couldn't get enough of those pies. He had told her he would mow her lawn if she would just bake him a rhubarb pie. The next thing he knew, he had asked her to go with him to the Friday night fish fry at the Bay Bar. Soon it became a weekly date, the two of them riding down the hill for the fish fry.

They didn't see each other every night. Two or three times a week seemed to be what kept them happy. They hadn't talked about living together or marriage or anything. Ella's eyes weren't working real well. She had that macular degeneration. She had tried to explain it to him, something about the middle part of her eye being blind, but she could see all around the edges. At night, he'd read to her. She loved listening to him, even though he read kind of slow and didn't always know how to pronounce the words.

He wondered if he should bring up a more permanent-type relationship. See what she said. Hard to tell with Ella. She had never wanted to live with anyone. "The old spinster teacher" is what she called herself. Said that life suited her. He wasn't sure they needed to live together. Maybe they should get married but both keep their own homes. Wouldn't that set tongues wagging. The kids could do it the other way around, but maybe the old folks needed to stay put. That way, if once in a while he was too tired to drive home, he could stay at her house and not worry about what the neighbors thought.

As Edwin drove past Walter Tilde's place, he shook his head. Poor Walter. What had he been thinking, marrying that Patty Jo? The soybeans were a damned disgrace. He had a mind to come over and plow them under just so he wouldn't have to look at that sorry field all winter long.

He had just pulled up to the corner and was turning to go down to Ella's place when he saw something out of the corner of his eye. A flash, he would say later, like from the wing of a plane or a mirror. A bright light of some sort, and it struck him as odd. He didn't like it. He stopped the car and turned around in his seat. His head didn't turn as easily as it used to, so he had to twist his whole body. He didn't see anything and almost continued on his way, but something tugged at him. He couldn't leave it. He circled the car around the intersection and headed back toward the Tilde farm.

Then he saw smoke rising from the edge of the barn. He felt relieved. Maybe that good-for-nothing Patty Jo was doing some raking and burning leaves. That would surprise him, but miracles never ceased. He wanted to see this for himself, so he kept going and turned again so he could see the back of the barn.

He was about to turn his attention back to the road and drive on when a flame burst through the side of the barn and crawled up the wooden battens. Edwin gasped. The flames danced up and down, tearing a black hole in the side of the barn.

His first thought was to drive in and rouse Patty Jo. He parked in front of the house and went and banged on the door. No one was home. He'd just go in and use the phone. But when he tried the door, he found it locked. That dumb sow. What a piece of work she was. The only person in the county to lock her door. Whatever happened now served her right.

Edwin moved as quickly as he could back to the car and tore back down her driveway. He needed to get help. The closest place was Ella's, so he drove like a maniac there. As he was driving he was thinking about how his oldest daughter wanted him to get a cell phone. He had always pooh-poohed her, but this was one time when he could have used it.

He found Ella sitting by the radio.

"Gotta use your phone," he said.

"Sure, go ahead."

As he dialed the firehouse's number, he thought about how that was one of the things he liked about Ella. She wasn't always asking questions about why you were doing something. She let you go ahead and do it and explain afterward, if you needed to.

"Fire at the Tilde farm. Corner of Double E and Pleasant Valley. The barn is up in flames." He gave his name and the number at Ella's and hung up the phone.

"Lord, Edwin. A fire?"

"Yes, I saw it as I drove by."

"What about Patty Jo?"

"She's not there. I tried the house. She had the door locked."

"Oh, that's Patty Jo. She's never trusted anybody."

"That's because she's so damn sneaky herself."

"Edwin."

"Sorry about the swearing, but you know it's true about Patty Jo."

"I suppose we better go over there."

This was the other thing he liked about Ella. She might be going blind, but she still saw so clearly.

CHAPTER 11

There's a fire. Thought you should know."

"Ella?" Claire recognized the voice. Meg looked up at her as she talked. They had been going over her social studies homework. "Are you all right?"

"We're fine."

"Where's the fire?"

"It's not here. The Tilde barn. Edwin's just saw it. He called it in. We're heading down there. He says Patty Jo's not around. Wonder where she is?"

"I'll see you there."

Meg closed her social studies book. "Can I come?"

Claire hated to leave her daughter. Not that she didn't think her precious child could be on her own, but they were having a nice quiet moment together, which happened less and less often these days.

"Yes, you can come. But when I tell you to stay in the car, I want you to do it. It could be dangerous."

Claire wrote a note to tell Rich where they had gone. They grabbed jackets and ran to the car.

As they were driving up the hill, Meg said, "Hope no one gets hurt."

"It's in a barn."

Meg went wide-eyed. "What about the animals?" she screeched.

"There aren't any that I know of. Don't worry. But you stay right where I tell you to."

"Mom, I'm not dumb. I know this is dangerous. I'm not like some stupid boy who plays with matches. I don't even like fires very much."

"Okay."

"I like candles."

Claire knew there was no particular reason she needed to go to this blaze, but she didn't like the sound of Patty Jo being involved with it. The woman had definitely gotten under her skin. At first she'd listened to Margaret's fears about her with a grain of salt, but the more she was around the woman, the more she thought her capable of evil.

Once on top of the bluff, she could smell the smoke. The sky opened up above them, and Claire could see a band of clouds to the west. But they were merely for decoration; it didn't look as though they were carrying any rain. Sometimes she drove up onto the bluff just to see the sky, especially in the evening when the sun was setting, spreading a soft glow across the rolling land.

She curved around several fields and then came in view of the Tilde farm. The sun was setting on the western horizon and silhouetted the dark barn with plumes of smoke rising out of it.

"There it is, Mom," Meg yelled.

"Yes, I see."

The fire pitched out of the hayloft like a crackling piece of foil. A fire truck was pulling up, and she parked on the edge of the road a good block from the farm, right behind Edwin and Ella. The two older people stood outside Edwin's car, leaning on it and watching the fire.

"I wonder if Margaret knows," Claire said to herself as she got out of the car.

"Who?" Meg asked, scrambling out behind her.

"Oh, the woman who grew up here. This was her father's farm."

"Is she the one who got it stolen from her?"

"Yes, that's a good way to put it."

As Claire watched, the fire traveled up to the peak of the barn roof. The wind played with the fire and made it seem alive. Golden orange flames danced along the roofline. The firemen unrolled the hose from the side of the fire truck. They aimed it toward the edge of the barn facing the house.

Claire realized the house was what they would try to save. The barn was gone. The fire had gutted it, and there was only the structure left. But if the wind shifted at all, the fire could jump to the house.

She walked up to Edwin and Ella, Meg tagging along behind her. "Hey," she said.

Edwin turned and said, "The barn's a goner."

Claire nodded. "That's what it looks like."

"At first I thought it might have been started by a brush fire," Edwin told Claire. "But it seemed to come from the inside."

Claire nodded again. "What do you think?"

"Nothing good."

Margaret and Mark pulled into the driveway, next to the fire truck. They jumped out and stood watching the blaze. Mark put his arm around his wife's shoulders as she folded toward him and buried her face in his shirt.

The blaze seemed to be dying down as part of the wall of the barn gave way. The water had made a considerable dent on it on the side toward the house.

Now that that wall was saturated, the firemen started to play a stream of water up and down the remains of the barn. The golden flames turned to smoldering smoke, and an acrid wind blew their way.

Meg blinked and scrunched up her face, then held her hand to her face and coughed.

Claire patted her on the shoulder. "Time for you to go sit in the car. Roll the windows up."

"I don't want to," Meg said.

Claire turned to her daughter. "What was our agreement?"

"I never agreed to it. You just said it. I won't do anything dumb. I want to see what happens."

"You can see from the car."

Meg folded her arms over her belly and humphed at her mother.

"Meggy, this isn't up for discussion."

"I never—"

Claire cut her off short. "You get in that car, young lady, or I'm never bringing you anywhere again." As soon as the words were out of her mouth, she almost laughed. What a stupid thing to say. So untrue. But it had an effect on Meg. She turned and marched to the car and climbed in.

Claire walked toward the barn, but before she could get to Margaret and Mark, they got into their truck and drove away. She saw the head fireman, Nick Chovsky. He had a farm a few miles out of Pepin. She didn't know him well, but they had been introduced at a couple of pancake breakfasts to raise money for the fire department.

When he saw her, he walked over. The two men on the hose were still playing water along the top of the barn ridge.

"I think we got here in time," he said.

"Not for the barn."

"That was gone from the get-go. These old structures are tinderboxes. I'm surprised any of 'em are left in the county. But the house—that's what I wanted to save."

"What do you think caused it?" Claire asked.

"I'd guess the usual—bad electrical wiring. These old barns were built fifty to sixty years ago. Nothing up to any kind of code. Most people redo their houses, but they never bother with their barns." He looked up in the sky. "Or thunderstorms. But wouldn't be that today. Not a cloud in the sky."

* * *

It was hard for Patty Jo to take her time in town. She finished her shopping after a half an hour. How long can you walk around a grocery store when you're shopping for one person? Then she ran to the bank and the post office. She bought a roll of stamps even though she didn't need them. She never wrote to anyone. Just used them to pay bills. She made it a point to have a pleasant conversation with everyone she saw. But they kept bringing up Walter's death.

Judy at the post office said as she was handing Patty Jo her roll of stamps, "You going to have another auction?"

Patty Jo thought, *What's it to you, you old vulture?* but answered civilly. "Oh, when probate's settled. That'll happen soon enough. Makes me sad for Margaret, though. The way she and her dad fought at the end. There was nothing I could do. Walter made me promise not to let her have a thing."

Judy nodded. "Terrible when a family ruptures like that."

"You can say that again." Patty Jo dropped the roll of stamps in her purse and marched out of the post office. She decided it was time to drive up the hill and see what was left of Walter's farm.

As soon as she got on top of the bluff, she could smell the fire. A good fall smell, like burning leaves. She was disappointed, as she neared the house, to see they had the fire under control. Black smoke rose from the wreckage of the barn, but the house was still standing. She wished she could have seen how high the flames climbed into the heavens.

She increased her speed and pulled into her driveway with a roar. As she got out of her car, everyone's eyes turned to her. A woman was talking to the fire chief. Patty Jo saw it was that woman deputy again. What the hell was she doing here? She seemed to be sticking her nose into everything.

Patty Jo ran up to Nick Chovsky. "Oh, my lord. What happened?"

"You had yourself a little fire here."

"How did it happen? Everything was fine when I left."

Nick shook his head. "Can't tell. I'm guessing electric."

Patty Jo jumped on that. "Yes, the electical wiring in the barn was terrible. I was always telling Walter we should have it redone. But his motto was, if it's not broke, don't fix it."

The woman deputy spoke to her. "I'm so sorry. You've had a rough time of it recently. We're trying to figure out when the fire might have started. How long have you been gone?"

"Well, I don't know. A couple of hours," Patty Jo stretched the time. No one would remember exactly. "I went to get groceries and then ran errands."

"Just lucky we got here as quick as we did. You've got Edwin to thank for that. Your house was close to going up too."

"Oh, my." Patty Jo stood and stared at the barn. "What should I do now?"

"Well, you'll want to knock that structure down. It's not safe. And call your insurance man."

"Yes, that's what I'll do. I'll call my insurance company. That's what they're for." She was sure everyone was watching her. She looked at the barn and shook her head. Then she headed toward the house.

She had left the number conveniently right next to the phone. It was good to be prepared for tragedies.

The clean sheets Claire had put on the bed earlier felt good against her skin. She loved the feel of the stiff fabric, fresh from the clothesline. She was happy in bed, reading Elizabeth George's latest mystery. She loved reading the dark British procedurals and was glad nothing that bad happened in her neck of the woods. Next to her, Rich was flipping through some farming magazine.

Suddenly, he tossed the magazine to the floor and rolled over and switched off his light. Claire turned her head and looked at the clock. Eleven. She needed to go to sleep. She reluctantly set her book on the nightstand and turned off her light too.

Rich's hand snaked through the covers and found her hip to rest on. She liked the way he needed to touch her in sleep.

"I know she did it," Claire said.

"The fire?"

"Yes."

"Patty Jo?"

"Yes."

"What're you going to do about it?"

"What else—try to prove it."

"What did the fire chief say?"

"Not much. Too early to tell. But he guessed it was electrical. I'll talk to the insurance company tomorrow."

His hand moved again, across her stomach now, the slight weight of it pinning her to the bed.

"Are you going to sleep?" she asked.

"Headed that way." His voice reached her in the dark, a deep whisper. She could hear the fatigue in his voice. He was busy these days shipping out the pheasants.

She turned toward him and reached out to touch his mouth with her hand. He let her finger smooth his lips, then he nipped at it.

She pulled her finger away. "I don't like her."

"It doesn't sound like anyone cares for her a great deal."

"Deep down inside I think she's awful."

"That's no crime."

"No, but I think she's capable of awful things."

He turned toward her and whispered, "Prove it."

She moved closer, and he bent his head and kissed her.

"How tired are you tonight?" she asked.

"Medium."

She kissed him back. "I'm medium too."

"That doesn't sound encouraging," he said.

She laid her head on his chest. "Margaret thinks Patty Jo had something to do with her father's stroke."

"How could that be?"

"Left him out there to die."

Rich put his arms around Claire and pulled her close to him under the covers so that their bodies touched all the length of them, down to their toes. "I think I'm glad you like me and that you don't think I killed anyone."

"No. I like you a lot."

"Prove it."

CHAPTER 12

Boxes lined the walls in every room. The couch was where Bridget wanted it to be—right in front of the fireplace. Last night she had hung two of her favorite paintings—horses coming out of mist—in the living room before she fell into bed. But the house was a disaster.

Bridget watched her big sister look around. She knew seeing all of someone else's stuff in her house would be hard on her. Claire always liked to be in control.

"I can't believe you're all moved in." Claire turned and stared at the big ficus tree in the front window where her old rocking chair had been. "You even moved that big old tree."

"Hired three big strapping college guys, and they did just what I told them to do." Bridget wondered if she should have asked Claire and Rich to help. She hadn't wanted to. She'd felt as though they were doing enough, that she should do this on her own. Now she wasn't sure. "Everything is in the right room even though it's not unpacked."

"It's going to look good."

"Really? You think so?"

"I like what you've done with it already. It looks like you."

"I didn't take much from our old place. I like a spare house. Not so cluttery. I've never been much of a housekeeper."

"It'll be easier without a guy to mess it all up."

Bridget had set Rachel on the floor, and the little girl was busy tearing up the cardboard tube from a roll of toilet paper. Bridget felt she had to explain her daughter's behavior to Claire. "I haven't found her toys yet."

"Poor baby."

Claire swooped her niece up. Bridget watched her kiss her daughter on the top of her head, right in the middle of her frothy dark hair.

"I have a question for you . . ." Claire started.

Bridget hoped it wouldn't be about Chuck. She didn't think she could talk about what was happening without breaking down, and she didn't feel like doing that in front of Claire. Not today. Not when she had so much to do.

Chuck had been gone most of the day that Bridget had moved. Then, right at the end, he walked in when she had just about emptied it of all she had wanted to take. The guys were busy tucking the smaller boxes in around the big pieces of furniture. Chuck sat down in his old lounger and didn't even look at her. He stared out the window. He didn't say anything. He acted like she was already gone. Bridget was afraid for him.

Claire said, "Let's say someone had some small strokes. . . ."

"Oh, this is for work." Bridget shifted into her pharmacist mode.

"Yeah, nothing that did any damage."

"Sounds like TIAs."

"What?"

"Transient ischemic attacks—otherwise known as light strokes. They don't tend to leave the brain damaged, but they are certainly precursors of what the patient has to look forward to."

"A major stroke?" Claire sat down on the couch with Rachel on her lap.

Bridget sat at the other end of the couch. "As you well know, that's impossible to say for sure. But yes, probably."

"Anything anyone can take to prevent it?"

It had always bugged Bridget how people wanted to know what exactly would happen if they took a certain medication or if they didn't take it. It wasn't like that. Everyone reacted differently to medicine. That's the only thing she could say for sure. Claire knew that, but she would still ask the questions and expect a concrete answer.

"Well, this person probably has high blood pressure, and certainly taking medication for that would be vitally important. Then the usual: quit smoking, ease up on the alcohol, and do steady exercise."

"Blood pressure medication? I'll check into that. Do the Tildes come to your pharmacy for their prescriptions?"

"Claire."

"I'm asking for their daughter."

"Have the daughter call me." Bridget watched Claire. "Why?"

"Walter Tilde died recently. He had a massive stroke after a series of TIAs. His daughter, Margaret, suspects his new wife of not getting him to the hospital fast enough."

"It makes a big difference. There are new medicines that they can administer within the first three hours that can almost reverse the effects of a stroke."

"That's what they tried for Beatrice. She's recovering, but never fast enough for her. One of the reasons I'm questioning what happened to this man is that his wife has inherited everything. She was a good twenty years younger than him, and they had only been married for a few months."

"I can't tell you anything more, Claire. I'll check into it. Have the daughter call me."

"So not taking the blood pressure medication could bring on a stroke."

"Yes, but everyone's different. Would it be murder if the wife kept him from taking his medication?"

"If it was done with malicious intent."

"How else could it have been done?"

Claire shrugged as if to say, *That's the point.* "The problem is it might be impossible to prove."

Rachel grabbed a hank of Claire's hair and pulled, causing Claire to yelp. Rachel started crying. Bridget took the child from Claire as they both laughed.

Claire stayed a while longer and helped Bridget unpack some boxes. They got most of the kitchen unpacked. They played music, Rachel danced for them, and they didn't talk about anything important.

Just as Claire was leaving, she caught the front screen door with her knee as it was swinging shut. She turned and really looked at Bridget. Then she asked, "How are you doing with everything? With Chuck?"

The question took Bridget by suprise, even though she had been waiting for her sister to ask. She looked down at Rachel and then answered, "Claire, I'm afraid this is all my fault."

"The doctor told me I shouldn't drink so much coffee," Sheriff Talbert told Claire, then took a sip from his ever-present coffee mug.

"How much does he want you to cut back?" Claire asked.

"It's a she, and no cups a day."

"That's definitely cutting back. What have you been averaging?" Claire knew he was a heavy coffee drinker, as she ran into him many times a day going to the communal urn.

"I count pots, not cups."

"How many pots?"

"I feel good on two to three."

"Why'd you have to cut back?"

"Not sleeping so good."

"I wouldn't go cold turkey," Claire advised him.

"I don't plan on doing that." Talbert drained his coffee mug. "Got a call from Patty Jo Tilde."

"What about—the fire?"

"Yes, she called to say she wouldn't be needing any help from the sheriff's department. She assured me that it was an accident."

Claire rolled her eyes. "Methinks the lady doth protest too much."

"Whatever you said, I think I agree."

"What'd she say about the fire?"

"She said the barn burned down."

"She speculate on how it happened?"

Talbert raised his eyebrows. "Something about electrical wiring. Why?"

"I got a bad feeling. I happened to be up there when it burned down. A neighbor called and told me about it."

"How so a bad feeling?"

Claire sat in a chair. "First, Patty Jo wasn't there when it started. She happened to be in town. Second, nothing of particular value was in the barn. Third, she comes back just as the fire is put out. Fourth, without asking many questions, or even really wanting to see what had happened, she goes in to call her insurance guy. And fifth, I don't trust her as far as I could throw her."

Talbert folded his arms across his chest. It was his prove-it-to-me stance. Claire recognized it easily after working with him for years. "Was Chovsky there?"

"Yeah."

"What'd he have to say?"

"He was the one who told her it was probably electrical. But he didn't really look around much. It was more like an educated guess," Claire explained. "I thought I'd give the insurance company a call. See if they're going to check into it."

"Well, I suppose you could do that. It's kinda putting the cart before the horse."

Claire stayed silent.

"We usually wait for the insurance companies to call us. Plus, many of them have their own investigators."

Claire had called Margaret last night and asked who her father had used as an insurance company. "Fort St. Antoine Mutual?"

"I don't know about them. I guess it can't hurt to call." The sheriff fussed for a moment, then said, "Claire, I trust you not to step over any lines here. I know you don't like this woman much, but you're not going vigilante on me?"

"No way. I'll watch it. I'll keep a tight rein on my feelings about Patty Jo. But that's not why I'm pursuing this. There's something there."

It was the end of the day, so Claire decided to swing by the insurance office on the way home. When she called the number she got a recording telling her they were open only two days a week. One of those days was tomorrow. Soon enough.

She packed her stuff and decided this was the day she would stop and check on Beatrice. She had gone over to the nursing home with Rich, but she had promised herself she would stop by on her own once or twice a week. Beatrice was the only parent she and Rich had left. Claire didn't always know what to say around Beatrice and she didn't always feel she pleased the older woman very much, but she would keep on trying.

Claire drove down along the Chippewa and then cut up through the backwaters to Pepin. Once a great blue heron had lifted off from the slough and flown right across the road. She had barely avoided hitting it. The size of the bird had stunned her. For a moment, it had completely filled her windshield. Since then, she always slowed down and kept a careful eye out for animals.

Another perfect fall day. In the high sixties. Not even cold yet. How long would it last? The end of September had been known to produce snow if it turned blustery. Claire rolled down the window to smell the leaves in the air.

It took her a few minutes to locate Beatrice at Lakeside Manor. She wasn't in her room, so Claire went to the activity room, thinking she might be involved in some bingo game. But Beatrice was not there either. Claire tried the lounge and found a small sea of white heads facing a TV set where a group of women were talking about how their boyfriends had impregnated other women. Beatrice was sitting at the back, slumped over in her wheelchair, sleeping.

Claire walked up behind her and gently roused her.

"Help," Beatrice yelped.

Claire got in close so that the older woman could see her face and said, "It's me, Beatrice. Let's go back to your room."

"Have you come to take me home?"

"Not yet." Claire felt sorry for Beatrice. She knew the older woman hated being in the nursing home. "Do you want to go to your room?"

"Better than here."

Claire pushed Beatrice back toward her room, but as she approached the door, she had a better idea. "Let's go outside."

"Oh, do you think so?" Beatrice said querulously.

"Why not?" Claire pushed her out the front door. The sun felt good on her face. A soft wind blew.

"How about down to the lake?" Claire suggested.

"That would be too hard."

Ignoring Beatrice's concern, Claire started down the slight hill. They were a block away from the road that ran along the lake. She carefully held on to the wheelchair as it gathered speed going down the hill.

When they reached the bottom, Claire parked the wheelchair next to a rock that offered a flat surface where she could sit. The water on the other side of the road danced with sun on its slight waves. She loved the way the low angle of the sun lit up the bluff line across the lake, showing the coulees as deep-green shadows cut into the hills.

"How about that?" Claire said.

"First time I've been out of prison."

"Prison, huh?"

"That's what it feels like."

"How's therapy going?"

"Look at me," Beatrice said. She held up her bad hand as if it were a dead bird. "I'm no good."

"It won't happen overnight. It's a slow process."

"I don't have much more time."

Claire asked, "Is there anything I can do?"

Beatrice acted as if she hadn't heard the question. Claire watched the old woman survey the scene in front of her.

Finally Beatrice said, "This is better. The fresh air is good."

"Beatrice, this isn't the end of your life. We won't let you rot away in there. How about coming to dinner at our house this weekend? Would you like that?"

Beatrice stared at Claire as if checking to see if the offer was a trick. "Can we eat something that isn't baby food?"

"Yes, I promise."

"That was a good barn," Carl Wahlund said as he whittled a spoon he was making from a piece of an old pear tree he had chopped down last spring.

Rich watched the five other men sitting in Ole Lindstrom's house all nod. They had formed a half circle around the fireplace: Edwin, Ole, Carl, Ted, and Pader. Carl was fairly new to the carving group.

All told, there were ten men who came to the group when they could. It was always at Ole's house. He had the biggest living room, and his wife made great black-walnut bars. She said she had to do something with all the walnuts that Ole brought home. The men each worked on their own project, sometimes sharing tools, less frequently giving a piece of advice. Minutes could go by without anyone talking.

Rich sat as far away from the fire as he could. The idea was nice, but he didn't think the weather called for it yet. They often had a fire going to get rid of the detritus of their work. He was carving a large bowl from the heartwood of a black-walnut tree he had cleared off his land. He was making it for Claire, his housewarming present for her.

"You talking about the Tilde barn? What happened there? I just saw it tonight as I drove by," Pader said. He came the farthest, all the way from Plum City, which was about a twenty-minute drive. If the weather was bad, he sometimes didn't make it.

"Nothing wrong with that barn," Edwin joined in. "I was the one who saw it start. I was driving by, and flames came out of the backside of the barn."

"Jeezus. That must have been something." Ole picked up the poker and stirred at the fire.

"You're not a-kiddin'. I got right on the horn and called the fire department. Listen, it was lucky they got there in time to stop it from jumpin' to the house."

"If Walter was alive, that fire woulda never started."

"You don't know, you don't know. These things happen."

"Walter was real careful. I think he rewired that barn not so long ago."

Rich sat and listened to the older men talk around him, the sound almost like waves lapping along a shore.

"Wasn't much of anything in that barn."

"Nope, there wasn't."

"Those dang soybeans are still rotting in that field. That woman beats all."

"What's the matter with her? She don't have the sense that God gave geese."

"You got that right."

Ole joined in. "My wife knows her sister, and the sister don't have much good to say about her."

Rich perked up when he heard that. Time to step in and get some information for Claire. "Sister? She has a sister around these parts?"

"Not that close. Over toward Madison. I think they're half sisters. Don't stay in touch."

"Do you know her name?"

"You know, it's her married name. Let me think on it. It'll come to me. I can almost hear my wife saying it. Give me a second."

The room went quiet except for the sound of knife blade against wood.

"You know, I think it's Parsons. First name of Debby. That's it. Debby Parsons. She and my wife keep in touch. They've been friends since way back."

"Claire might call your wife tomorrow to get the information."

At the mention of Claire's name, everybody looked up.

"What's up?"

"She's just checking on Patty Jo. The barn and the will that Walter left."

"Damn shame, I say, that his daughter didn't get that place," Edwin said. "What was he thinking, leaving the farm to that fool woman? Now look what has happened. The barn burned down."

"That was a good barn. Nothing wrong with that barn."

CHAPTER 13

The hand-painted sign on the old church door read FORT ST. ANTOINE INSURANCE ASSOCIATION in bright-yellow letters against a deep-blue background. Claire knocked on the door and then stepped in. The building smelled of old cigars and wet wool.

An older woman with a halo of white hair was sitting at a typewriter, punching away at a good clip, and an older gentleman was seated in an inner office, reading over some papers.

Claire stood in the doorway for a moment, looking in at the scene, the sun pouring in from the east, the two people bent over their work in separate rooms. It looked like an Edward Hopper painting.

"Can I help you?" the woman said, holding her hands above the keyboard as if she were going to levitate it.

When Claire had moved to Fort St. Antoine, her banker had told her that she could get her insurance from this small company. He explained that it was an association of farmers from the area, a private insurance company. She liked the sound of it, so she had bought her insurance from them. A representative had come out and helped her determine the worth of her house. He introduced himself and told her that he had known the family that had built her house. Once a year she got a mailing from the company, telling her how much money they had in the group and how much they'd had to pay out over the year. Twice a year she received a typed notice for a bill. She didn't want the woman to think she was there because of her insurance policy.

Claire looked down at her uniform. "I'm here on county business. I have some questions about how you investigate claims."

"You're Claire Watkins, aren't you? I remember when you started with us. I'm Lois Schreider. My husband could talk to you about that." She turned her head and yelled, "Stan, someone here." Then she turned back to Claire and waved her hand. "Go on in. He's hard of hearing, so speak up."

When Stan Schreider stood up, he reminded her of a crane. He moved his legs all of a piece. He was tall and lanky. She guessed he was a farmer because he had a lighter forehead where his feed cap sat while he cultivated his fields. His eyes were a soft blue, set into a pool of wrinkles. Claire thought he was in his late seventies. He came and shook her hand and pulled out a chair.

"You're a deputy," he said, and chuckled as he moved slowly back around the desk and sat down in his own chair.

"Yes, I work for the county."

"I've seen you around," he told her.

"Sometimes I stick out," she said.

"Like a sore thumb?" he asked.

"Sometimes," she admitted.

He held his palms together as if he were praying. His hands were crippled with arthritis and hard work. "What can I do for you?"

"I'm wondering how you go about investigating your claims."

"Well," he said slowly, and leaned back in his chair. "We might send someone out from the board to look things over. You gotta claim?"

"No. I was wondering if you do the investigating internally or if you hire someone."

"If we need to look something over, one of us does it."

"What if you suspect that it's a fraudulent claim?"

"I don't know why you're asking all these questions. We don't have many problems. We know all our customers pretty well."

"You've never had a suspicious claim?"

"One or two over the years, but it really hasn't been a problem. Do you have something in mind?"

"Well, I was wondering if anyone from your company had gone to look over the Tilde barn."

"We got a call on that. Walter's been with us for over fifty years. I think this is his first claim."

"Is that unusual to go so long without a claim?"

"Not particularly. Some years are bad. Those straight-line winds tore up part of the county three years ago. We paid for that, all right. Lots of claims that year. But Walter didn't catch the winds."

"Will someone go up and look at the barn?"

Stan Schreider looked at her over his hands and shook his head. "Might. That was an old barn. His wife said the fire chief thought it was caused by an electrical problem. He's probably right."

"What do you do if you suspect it might be arson?"

He looked at her, puzzled. "Why do you ask?"

"That does happen from time to time, doesn't it?"

"Not really. People don't need to create problems down here. They come on their own often enough. Walter was a good customer."

"Yes, but Walter's dead. It's his wife you're dealing with now. I was up at the fire. The fire chief didn't really take a careful look at the barn. There might be something you could discover if you went up there."

"Do you suspect something? We don't have many problems around here like that. Maybe you did in the city."

Claire decided she should explain why she was questioning him. "Walter died, as you know, very recently. His new wife has inherited everything. I'm just following up on the barn on the chance it might have been a case of arson."

"Yeah, I can see that. Well, if we find anything, we'll let you know."

Claire figured that was as much as she would get from him. "If I discover something about Patty Jo Tilde that might shed some light on the barn burning down, would you like to hear about it?"

He looked at her for a moment as if she were speaking a foreign language. Then he said, "Sure. That would be fine. We'll be taking care of the claim in the next week or two."

"Okay," Claire said as she got up to leave.

Lois Schreider stopped typing for a moment as Claire walked back into the room. Above Lois's head was a large stained-glass window left from when the building was a church. Jesus stood over the woman, blessing her with his open hands. Lois smiled at Claire. "You have a nice day now."

Patty Jo was spending her money. She had a piece of paper down in front of her, writing down all the money she would make from the sale of the farm. She had figured that Reiner would give her about $400,000 for the house and the 120 acres it sat on. She hadn't called him to tell him about the loss of the barn, but she was pretty sure he wouldn't care. One less building to take care of. As far as she knew, he was just going to pull it all down anyway.

She hoped to get about $20,000 from the contents of the house at auction. And then Walter had left her a nice nest egg of $180,000 in various stocks and bonds. The insurance for the barn would pay about $50,000. The pickup truck would bring in another $10,000. Well over a half a million dollars. She was collecting Walter's social security check now and could collect her own in another couple of years.

She was set for life. If she didn't go to the casino too often.

Nothing could stop her now. She'd shuck off this damn farm like it was an old skin and move into her new life. Any day now.

Patty Jo heard the sound of tires on the driveway and looked up to see a Pepin County squad car pull up in front of the house. She thought of pretending she wasn't home even though her car was sitting right out front. A friend could have picked her up for an event. She could have gone for a walk.

She watched behind the shadow of the curtains as the woman deputy, Watkins, got out of the car. But the deputy didn't head toward the house. Instead she walked over to the remains of the barn. This was not good. Patty Jo didn't need her messing around in there. The insurance company had assured her that they would process her claim lickety-split. They'd agreed to send the check in her name. Walter had put her name on the insurance policy at her request.

The deputy was standing in the doorway of the barn. Patty Jo couldn't have her snooping around, so she walked out the door and yelled, "Can I help you?"

The woman turned her head and waved as if they were friends, then came walking over.

"What a smell," said Watkins.

"Yes, the whole house stinks," Patty Jo agreed.

They stood on the porch. Patty Jo didn't intend to invite her in. She could state her business and be done with it.

"The sheriff said you called to let us know the barn burning down was accidental."

"That's right," Patty Jo said, wondering why the sheriff had sent someone out to talk to her about that. "You should know. You were here that day."

"Yes, I was. I wanted you to know that I'm the investigator for the county and offer my services. It's my job to look into such matters."

"Well, there's nothing to look into."

"No one you know who might have set the barn on fire?"

"No. Why would anyone do that?"

"Well, the reason I'm asking is it sounded like you thought the fire might have been electrical, but a friend told me that Walter had recently had the barn rewired."

Who had she been talking to? "I think he just did part of the barn. Not the whole thing. Anyhow, there still can be problems with it."

"Sure."

"You're a friend of Margaret's. Did she ask you to look into this?"

"I do like Margaret, but I've only met her recently." Watkins stared at Patty Jo, then went on to say, "I'm just doing my job."

Patty Jo didn't see how she could argue with that. "Well, I don't need your help."

"I was sorry to hear about your husband's death."

"Thank you."

"Did he have another stroke?"

Patty Jo wondered why she was asking about Walter. "The doctor wasn't really sure. He thought it could simply be failure to thrive."

"Mind if I take a look in the barn before I go?" Watkins asked.

"Oh, I couldn't let you do that. It's a liability. That structure could come down at any time. I'm having it bulldozed as soon as I can get some men up here to do it."

Claire nodded and turned to go.

Patty Jo stood and watched the deputy walk back to her car. She wasn't going to take her eyes off the woman. She was up to something, that was for sure.

When she was only a few feet from her squad car, the deputy turned and said, "Oh, a friend of mine knows your sister."

Patty Jo felt her heart drop into her feet. What had made the deputy mention that? Her sister was the last person on earth she wanted to know what she was up to now.

"You don't say. Small world," Patty Jo said.

In the late afternoon light, the land looked burnished, as if some large hand had rubbed at its surface until it glowed. The grasses were turning color, and while they didn't do it as dramatically as tree leaves, she loved their soft golden hues.

As Claire drove east from Durand, she had plenty of time to ask herself why she was pursuing this Patty Jo Tilde so hard. Or Patty Jo

Splinter, her name by her first husband. Or Patty Jo Johnson, her maiden name. She had checked her out on the computer and come up with nothing. The woman had no record.

Even today Patty Jo had acted like a woman with something to hide. She hadn't wanted Claire to get anywhere near the barn.

But Claire was sure her sense that something was terribly wrong wasn't just woman's intuition. She had worked in law enforcement long enough to know that men got this feeling too, and certainly as strongly as women. She had seen men become completely obsessed about catching a particular person.

One time a cop she worked with had sat outside a man's house for months, following him at night, convinced that the man was a serial killer. What he discovered was that the man was not a serial killer. He was seeing his wife's sister on the sly and so had not given straight answers when he was questioned.

Claire was taking some of her own personal time to drive toward Madison to talk to Patty Jo's sister. The drive took her through gently rolling hills with the occasional outcropping of rock or mound.

She had set up the meeting the night before and made it for late afternoon so that it wouldn't interfere with work. Rich would be home when Meg got there, and she told him she'd try to make it home in time to watch a rerun of *The West Wing.*

Rich had pointed out to her last night that she could simply talk to Patty Jo's sister on the phone. But Claire had learned that people were more open when you interviewed them in person. She wanted to see how this woman reacted physically to some of the questions she would ask about Patty Jo.

She felt pretty stuck, even if she did get something from the sister. She felt sure Patty Jo had torched her barn, but since the insurance company didn't seem to care, that might be a dead end. And she felt that Patty Jo might have been instrumental in Walter Tilde's stroke. But it would be impossible to prove that Patty Jo had withheld pills from him. What evidence could there be? Even if she found out that he hadn't been taking his pills, how could Claire prove it hadn't been his own decision?

As she turned into the small town of Whitewood, Claire decided she would stop trying to collect evidence against Patty Jo if the conversation with the sister produced nothing. She would give it up and get on with the rest of her work.

The town was three blocks long, and Debby Parsons lived next to the library on the far edge of town. A brick bungalow, she had said, with a white picket fence around it. "My roses are still in bloom—you'll get to see them," the woman had promised. When Claire said she was coming to ask some questions about Patty Jo, Debby hadn't seemed surprised.

The roses were indeed in bloom, sprawling over the fence like a red-and-green quilt hung out to air. Claire admired them for a moment or two, then walked up the sidewalk to the front door. She didn't even have a chance to knock on the door before a small blond woman appeared and introduced herself as Debby. She had her hair pulled back at the nape of her neck and wore a white shirt with blue jeans. Claire guessed her to be in her early fifties.

"Look at you in your uniform. Does a heart good to know there are women deputies out there. Come on in. I've put us in the porch. This time of day, it's so pleasant."

Claire stepped into the porch and saw that a table was set with china and linen. A white wooden swing hung on the far end of the porch and was covered with flowered pillows. Debby offered her a chair.

"This wasn't necessary," Claire began.

"No, but it's nice to have an excuse. My husband died about two years ago and I'm quite comfortable, but I don't have people over the way I used to. I thought this would be nice. What news have you of my sister? I haven't heard from her in almost ten years. Coffee?" Debby asked.

"Yes, please."

While Debby poured the coffee and offered a lemon scone, Claire told her what had been going on in Patty Jo's life. She mentioned Walter's death and the new will and the barn burning down, but she didn't place the blame on Patty Jo.

"Never even met this guy, Walter. But then Patty Jo and I were never close. You see, she was the adopted daughter."

"And you weren't?"

"Just one of those deals. Mom and Dad adopted Patty Jo when she was already five and they were going into their forties. They figured they were not going to have their own children. Then I came along two years later. Patty Jo did not take to me."

"She didn't like being a big sister?"

"I guess not. She left home at seventeen, when I was only ten. She got married soon after. She lived in the next town, so we saw each other once in a while. Then her husband died and she moved away."

"When was that?"

"Ten years ago."

Claire finished her scone and wiped her hands on her napkin. "That was delicious."

"Would you like the recipe?"

For a moment, Claire envisioned herself getting up on a Sunday morning and making scones. Rich had taken over most of the cooking, but she didn't have to relinquish all of it. "Yes, I would."

Debby offered her more coffee. Claire took half a cup.

"I'm going to ask you some awkward questions. I hope you don't mind."

"I was expecting them. When you called, my first thought was, *I wonder what Patty Jo's done now.*"

"Really?"

Debby nodded her head. "She was terrible when we were kids, always getting into trouble."

"Like what?" Claire prompted.

"I remember her finding my Easter basket and then eating all my candy before Mom could get it away from her. She was often caught taking things from people's houses. She was very jealous of anyone who had anything she didn't have. She got caught shoplifting as a teenager several times, but Dad always managed to have the charges dropped. Not sure that was a good idea. I think Patty Jo always thought she could get away with anything."

"What about fires? Was she ever involved in any incidents as a kid?"

"When she was pretty little, the slough behind my parents' farm started on fire. Turned out Patty and a friend had been playing with matches. Then, right before she left home for good, the shed behind our parents' house burned down. My father claimed it was because he had left some rags out, but I think my mother always suspected Patty Jo of setting the fire."

"There is a pattern here. I'm trying to understand her recent behavior. She seems like she's up to something."

"Doesn't surprise me a bit," Debby said.

"Any other examples of bad behavior you can think of?"

Debby stirred her coffee for a moment. Then she sighed and said, "Well, the worst thing she ever did, as far as I'm concerned, was kill her first husband."

CHAPTER 14

Claire allowed herself a second doughnut at the kaffeeklatsch. She usually tried to limit herself to one, but today she felt the need to bribe herself to keep quiet about Patty Jo. She couldn't spread gossip around, but she would have loved to discuss Debby's information with the crew gathered at Le Pain Perdu.

As she passed the plate around to see if anyone else needed another doughnut, Edwin Sandstrom stood up.

"I've got good news that I'd like to share with everyone. I wanted you all to be the first to know. We're going to get married," Edwin announced, holding up the hand of his bride-to-be, Ella Gunderson, to show off the ring she was wearing on her finger.

The kaffeeklatsch erupted: forks clanging glasses, hoots and hollers from the group gathered around the table. Stuart, the owner of the bakery, came running from the kitchen to see what was going on.

Claire had thought the two of them were up to something when they walked in the door that morning. They both looked like the cat that swallowed the canary, as her mom used to say. It had never occurred to her they might be engaged. Funny how events went in cycles or circles. She still wasn't used to the idea of Bridget and Chuck splitting up, and now a nuptial was being announced.

At the commotion, Meg looked up from her book. She had insisted on coming along this morning. Said she didn't feel like being home alone, but brought a book along in case it got boring. She was at the age, Claire had noticed, where she got bored when she didn't get her way.

Claire asked, "Is this like the reading of the banns?"

Ruth held up her coffee mug and proposed a toast. "To the nicest couple around. May you both live long and celebrate many anniversaries."

"For the time being, we'll each keep our own place," Ella said with a nudge to Edwin. "Just in case it doesn't work out."

Ruth offered her barn as a place they could hold the ceremony, since Ella wasn't particularly churchgoing.

Ella turned to Claire and asked her if she would be her best woman. "I don't have any nieces, and I like the idea of a strong law-enforcing woman to be there by my side."

Her request thrilled Claire. "I'd love to." She immediately wondered what she would wear. As Ella was having only one matron of honor, at least she wouldn't have to match someone else's dress.

"When's the wedding?" Stewart asked.

"Can't wait too much longer," Edwin quipped. "We've got our health, better act fast. We're thinking early November."

Ella turned to Rich. "How's your mom doing in the nursing home?"

"She hates it. She came to our house for dinner and didn't want to go back."

"I don't blame her," Ella said. "If she's up to it, ask her to come to the wedding. Who knows, maybe she'll meet some nice guy."

How wonderful to have something to celebrate, Claire thought. She was having a hard time pulling her mind away from the news from Debby. What was the most frustrating was that she still had no proof Patty Jo had done anything wrong in her whole life.

As if he had read her mind, Edwin nudged her shoulder to get her attention. "I've been meaning to tell you. I heard through the grapevine that Reiner has canned the idea of buying the Tilde farm."

"Really? I wonder why?"

"Well, what I hear is that he didn't want to get embroiled in a title problem because of probate, and he wasn't too happy about the barn burning down. He had planned to use it to store his plane." Edwin leaned back in his chair and laughed. "I bet that's got Patty Jo pretty rankled."

Claire thought about a rankled Patty Jo—not a good situation. She went back over what Debby had told her of Patty Jo's first husband's death. Dell Splinter was his name. They had been married thirty years. Then he had had a bad accident on the farm: a bale of hay had fallen on his head, causing brain damage. A week after he left the hospital for home, he had died, and there had been no autopsy; Patty Jo had him cremated. Debby said she was sure that Patty Jo had had something to do with it. When Claire pressed her to say why she was so sure, Debby said that Patty Jo had let something slip, just a casual comment.

"What?" Claire asked.

"She said that she couldn't stand to see Dell unable to do anything. That she had taken things into her own hands."

Claire had asked her if she had told anyone her suspicions.

"What could I do? Who would I have told?" Debby said. "I knew they couldn't prove anything. There was no body anymore. If she had killed him, I didn't know how she had done it. So I didn't say anything."

"Then why tell me?" Claire asked.

"Because you're the first person who's ever come sniffing around about Patty Jo. Not everyone sees who she really is. She can be charming when she wants. If she's killed her second husband, maybe you can prove it and put her away. I'd feel good about that. Stop her before she gets a third one."

* * *

Meg pumped her bike up the small hill that rose from Highway 35. She was on her way to Ted's house. Her mom had agreed that she could ride over and see Harvey. Ted lived right on the way. Meg had told him at school that she might go see the elk at Reiner's.

He seemed very impressed. "If you do, can I go with you?"

"I guess."

"Cool."

Her mom had made her call the caretaker and ask if it was all right to visit Harvey. The guy sounded surprised by the request but said sure, it was fine with him. He said Harvey's wound had healed up, and he didn't think Reiner would mind. That's what he called the owner, Reiner. She liked the sound of saying just the man's last name, like in a detective story.

Then she gathered all her courage and called Ted's house. Wouldn't you know, his mom answered the phone.

Meg had been very polite. "Hello, may I speak to Ted?"

"May I ask who's calling?"

"Yes, this is Meg Watkins."

"Oh," was all his mother had said, then Meg could hear her shouting, "Ted, phone."

When he said hello, Meg was surprised by how old he sounded on the phone. Like he was a teenager or something. "I'm going to see the elk," she told him.

"Count me in."

"I'll come and get you. My mom's letting me ride my bike."

"I'll be waiting by the driveway. When are you leaving?"

She told him it'd be immediately, then ran out the door, hopped on her bike, and headed toward his house. Meg wondered if she would have ever dared call him if it hadn't been for the elk. Funny how things worked out.

When she pedaled up to his house, she could see him leaning on the handlebars of his bike, watching her.

"You ride a bike like a girl."

Meg was fascinated by the way kids her age decided how a girl behaved and how a boy behaved. There was a whole list of such actions:

how you looked at your nails, how you looked at the bottom of your shoes, how you combed your hair.

"What do you mean?" she asked.

"You wobble."

Meg could feel herself getting mad. "Let's go. I told the guy I'd be there."

She started biking, pumping her legs as hard as she could. Wobble? She'd show him. She could hear Ted riding behind her, trying to keep up.

"Hey, wait up."

She slowed slightly, and he went tearing past her. She let him pedal down the next hill. Then he slowed and waited for her.

After that they biked next to each other, talking about school and their friends, until they got to the Reiner place.

"Man, this guy must be stinking rich."

"I guess so."

"Two houses and everything. My dad says he could buy the whole county if he wanted to." They both jumped off their bikes and started walking to the barn.

Meg nodded. "My mom says he thinks he's like the emperor around here."

Ted slowed down as they walked up to the fence. "I knew they had elk here, but I've never been up here."

Meg put down the kickstand, parked her bike, and reached into her fanny pack. She had cut up an apple before she had left home and put it into a Ziploc bag.

Harvey was standing in the fenced area, over by a big pine tree. She called his name.

"That's him?" Ted asked. "The Indians called them *wapiti.*"

"You want to feed him some apple?"

Ted looked at the apple, then over at the elk, which had started lumbering in their direction.

"No," he said, shaking his head and stepping back. "I'll just watch you do it."

Meg's heart opened up as she watched the elk approach. She was so glad to see Harvey. She was glad she had come to see him in his real home. It was good that he was back here, she realized, among the other elk, where he belonged. The fact that she could come over and see him whenever she wanted to made it easier for her to accept that this was where he would stay.

"Harvey," she called. He stopped and sniffed the air. She knew he recognized her smell.

He lowered his head as if he were fixing his eyes on her and then started to walk toward her again. She held a piece of the apple over the fence, and he walked right up to her and took it gently out of her hand. After he ate it, he presented his face to her, and she scratched his fuzzy chin. She had almost forgotten about Ted. He didn't seem as important as the big animal she was petting.

When she had one piece of apple left, she turned and looked at Ted. "Are you sure you don't want to try feeding him?"

Ted looked down at the ground. "It's good from here. I can see him really good."

Meg knew what it felt like to be afraid. She could see the fear in Ted's eyes and hear it in his voice. She wouldn't push him. "You don't have to be scared of this elk. He was bottle-fed, and that makes him really tame."

They didn't stay long. Ted wanted to get going. On the ride back to his house, he was playing the show-off again. Riding circles around her, trying to ride on his back tire. She pedaled her steady rhythm. She still had a long ride home.

At the end of his driveway, she stopped and straddled her bike. She thought he might invite her in, but he didn't. He just kept going and yelled back over his shoulder, "See you at school."

Riding back down his road, Meg was disappointed. She had hoped seeing the elk might be a good thing to do together. Somehow it hadn't worked, and she wasn't sure why. She didn't get boys.

As she was getting close to the turn on Highway 35, she saw a woman stopped in her car in the middle of the road. Meg noticed because there was no stop sign or driveway. She couldn't understand why the woman had stopped.

As she got closer, she could see the woman was looking around. Then Meg recognized her. It was Patty Jo Tilde, the woman whose barn had burned down. She had to be in her seventies. Her blond-gray hair looked like a helmet, like if you pushed your fingers into it, it might leave a dent.

"Hey, you, girl. Do you know the way to the elk farm?"

When Meg didn't say anything right away, Mrs. Tilde spoke again. "What's the matter with you? Aren't you from around here? I suppose your parents told you not to talk to strangers. I'm a neighbor, not a stranger. Do you know where the elks are?"

Meg didn't feel like talking to her. She didn't like this old woman, so she just pointed back down the road she had come from and watched the woman look back that way. Then the woman slammed her hand on the steering wheel and swore. Meg was surprised; old people didn't tend to swear. At least, not in public.

Mrs. Tilde drove right around in a circle in the middle of the road. When she got her car facing the right way, she stomped on the accelerator and roared away.

Meg closed her eyes and tried not to breathe the dust stirred up in the car's wake.

Jim Bartlett was not sure what woke him. A flickering movement. He had fallen asleep after drinking a six-pack of beer and watching the football game. All he knew when he pulled himself up in the big Naugahyde-covered recliner was that something was not right. He turned the TV off. It was midnight. There was a strange light coming from outside. He rubbed his eyes and went and looked out the window.

He couldn't believe his eyes. A fire was eating away at the elk barn. He rubbed them again. Then he felt a jolt go through his whole body. He didn't know what to do first. He had to get out there, but he had to let someone know. Help—he needed help fast.

He grabbed his boots and started pulling one of them on. When he had stuffed his foot in one boot, he realized he needed to make the phone call before he did anything else. He hobbled to the phone and dialed the fire department.

"Fire, Reiner place. The barn. Down Double E . . . That's right. Right by the road." He gave the woman his fire number.

He had dragged the boot with him and was trying to put it on with the phone stuck under his chin. The woman at the other end of the line said she would send a fire crew out as soon as they assembled. Who knew how long that would take? When he hung up, he knew he had to do something.

Then he remembered he had separated Harvey from the rest of the herd and put him in the barn. Jim swore and ran out the door.

It was cold, but he he could feel waves of heat coming from the fire. The fire was up high on the roof, so maybe Harvey was still okay—if the smoke hadn't filled the barn. If he could get to the door and open it, he hoped the animal would find its way out.

Jim ran to the fenced-in area around the barn and tried to open the gate. His hands were shaking, and he didn't seem to be able to work the latch. Goddamn it, he had planned to change that thing for the last month. Just hadn't gotten around to it. He yanked it off and ran into the pen. The barn door was shut. He grabbed it and pulled it open along its track. Nothing came out of the barn. He stuck his head in and saw the elk.

The big animal was at the back of the barn. The fire had broken through the roof, and a burning beam had fallen into the middle of the barn. The elk was afraid to run around it. Harvey was slashing his front feet at the blaze and kicking at the side of the barn, trying to get away. For a moment, it looked as if the elk would try to bolt by the blazing beam, but at the last second, he changed his mind and ran back to the false protection at the far end of the barn.

Jim had to do something or the animal would die. If he could put out the fire on the beam before the roof came down, he could get the elk out.

Jim knew there was a hose by the water trough. He ran and pulled it to the door. The smoke was starting to pour out of the barn, and he worried that the elk would be overcome by smoke.

He turned the faucet on high and aimed the stream of water at the blaze. It fell short. He covered part of the nozzle with his hand and forced the pressure up. He aimed the water higher and it started hitting the beam.

The elk was going crazy, charging and pawing at the back of the barn. Jim thought Harvey would hurt himself trying to tear a hole in the barn. Jim kept dousing the beam. The roar of the fire was getting louder. He was afraid more of the roof would cave in.

The fire on the beam subsided. Jim dropped the hose. He covered the bottom half of his face with his arm and ran into the barn. He got to the other side of the beam, and the elk came running up to him. He ducked behind the animal, and Harvey jumped away from him and bolted out of the barn.

Jim followed, but he tripped on the beam and went sprawling. As he fell, he tried to roll, but his boot was stuck. His leg twisted under him. He screamed in pain. Flat on the straw, he knew he had to get out of the barn. It wasn't going to hold together much longer. He started to crawl.

The fire sounded like a tornado. The suck of the flames pulled the air out of his lungs and into the towering blaze above. The heat pushed him down. The pain from his leg made movement almost impossible. He was afraid he wouldn't get out. He couldn't breathe. He was almost to the door when he heard the barn coming down behind him.

CHAPTER 15

Rain fell in the very early morning. Claire heard it tapping at the window before she crawled out of bed, thinking it would make everything a little harder to do today. But they needed the rain. It had been a dry late summer, and some good rains before the ground froze would help all the plants survive the winter.

Funny how she thought of those things now. When she'd been living in the city, it had never occurred to her to worry about the plants.

The drive to work was long, with waves of rain slapping the car as she made her way up to Durand and the Pepin County sheriff's department. Checking the level of the sloughs along the road, she figured a couple inches of rain had fallen. She planned on having an office day, catching up on her paperwork.

As soon as she entered the department, however, the sheriff called her into his office and told her she would be working on something else that day.

"I just got off the phone with Reiner. He's fuming."

"What now?" she asked. She sat down. She could tell the conversation would not be quick.

He said sarcastically, "Your lines of communication are down?

Usually I assume you know all that's gone on in the county before you walk in the door."

She ignored his tone. "What happened?"

"Reiner's barn burned down last night."

This announcement took Claire by surprise. She'd been uneasy about what Patty Jo Tilde might do next, but she hadn't thought it would be so dramatic or so quick. "You're kidding. Anyone hurt?"

"His caretaker just about got asphyxiated. Ended up in the hospital with a concussion, a broken leg, and messed-up lungs. I want you to go talk to him. Then run out to take a look at that barn. What's left of it."

"Do they know what happened?"

"Arson suspected."

"Is Reiner there?"

"He will be." The sheriff looked down and shuffled some papers around. "He says he's calling in help."

Claire didn't mind help. Especially with an arson. But she knew it made the sheriff uneasy. "Fine by me."

"A Dr. Wegman."

"Barney? Great."

"You know this guy?"

"He's the arson expert. Has his own business. I worked with him quite a bit in the Cities. He's a character. He travels around the country in a Citroën."

"A what?"

"French car. Low-slung body, big headlights. Looks like a bug. One cool feature is that you can lower the car onto its wheels, making it virtually impossible to steal. The thing is forever breaking down, but he keeps it running."

"Never heard of such a car."

"Don't think I've seen one in Pepin County since I moved here."

"You foreigners bring in the darnedest things."

Claire sat still for a moment, thinking. "That Tilde woman. The widow."

The sheriff nodded. "Two fires in one week is too much of a coincidence for me."

Jim Bartlett's head was tilted back on a crisp white pillow and his hand rested on his forehead. His leg, looking like a white sausage, lay on the hospital bed. Gauze frosted his cheek. He was puffing air through his cheeks the way people do when they're doped up on painkillers. Claire hated to wake him. He looked like he had had a rough time.

She sat in the chair in his room and closed her eyes for a moment, tired of this rainy day and what lay ahead of her. When she opened them, he was staring at her.

"What're you doing here?" he asked, surprised.

"Checking on you," she said.

He had raised his head to talk to her and now lowered it back to the pillow, wincing as he did. He closed his eyes, then popped them open as he said, "I hope you don't think I was responsible for that fire."

"Not particularly." Claire waited a moment, then asked, "Should I?"

"Can't a guy say anything to a cop without incriminating himself?"

Claire ignored his whine and asked, "Who do you think set the fire? And why are you so sure it was set?"

"I know that barn inside and out." He took a long breath and shook himself, as if he were still seeing something frightening. Then he continued, "It was built a year ago. The wiring is perfect. There's nothing left lying around that could catch on fire. I don't smoke when I'm around the barn. At least I try not to. It happened in the middle of the night. I didn't hear anything, but I can sleep pretty heavy."

"All right."

"Reiner is going to be really pissed about this, probably blame me. I want to keep my job."

"I don't blame you. Anyone come by the barn in the last few days?"

"Your daughter."

"I think we can safely count her out."

"She's a smart kid."

"Thanks."

"She brought some boy with her to see the elk."

"She did?" Claire was annoyed at herself for letting those words pop out of her mouth. How would she look as a cop when she didn't even know what her daughter was up to?

"Maybe he came back to the barn after she left," Jim suggested. "Boys like to play with fire."

"Thanks for letting me know. I'll ask her about him. Find out who he was. Anything else you can think of?"

"I don't know if you can tell this, but whoever started it did it on the side toward the road. When I came out of the house, the fire was only on the outside. The elk was in the barn."

"He was in the barn?"

"He got out. I got him out."

"Thank God."

"Almost got killed doing it."

"I'll find out who set this fire. You can tell them how you feel."

"That'd be good." His hand rose to his forehead again. His eyes closed. "Morphine and I don't get along. I think I'm going to be sick."

Claire stood. This was her cue to leave. "I'll get the nurse," she said.

Standing in the shelter of the overhang outside her school, Meg watched her classmates climb into school buses for the ride home. She felt a sense of relief. About once a week either her mom or Rich picked her up after school, and she loved it. Her bus ride home took nearly an hour. She was the last kid on the route, and while she had learned to entertain herself, by the end it was just pure boring.

Ted walked by and then turned back and gave her a weird stare. "What're you doing?"

Ever since the elk, he had been mean to her. She didn't quite understand it, but she figured he was mad because she had seen him be a chicken. For girls it wasn't such a big deal. Obviously it was for Ted.

"Waiting for my mom."

"I heard your elk might have got cooked last night."

Meg felt a sinking in her stomach. "What?"

"Didn't you know? That barn burned down last night. The one the elk was in."

"No way."

"I'm telling you, it did. My dad told me this morning. He went up and looked at the place. He said it was totally gone. To the ground."

"But Harvey?" Meg could feel herself on the edge of tears.

"Far as I know, he's okay. But maybe he went down with the barn." Ted shrugged. "They had a whole herd of elk. One wouldn't matter much."

Meg bristled. "You don't know anything. Just because you were scared of him. He's worth about a million dollars. They told me. There will never be another elk like him. The best elk in the world."

Ted laughed. "You sound like that elk is your best friend."

"Maybe he is." Meg saw the squad car pull up with her mother driving. "I'll find out right now."

She ran through the rain to where her mother had parked, and slipped into the car. "Mom, what happened to Harvey?"

"I should have known you would hear. He's fine. Completely fine. The caretaker got him out of the barn in time."

Meg burst into tears. She tried to hold them back, but it did no good. They pushed too hard. "I can't stand it. Why Harvey? Why would anyone want to hurt Harvey? You said he would be safe. You promised. But he's not."

Her mom reached over to hug Meg, but Meg shrugged her off. She was mad at the whole world.

"Meg, settle down. He's fine. I'm going to find out who did this." Her mom paused, then asked, "Meg, who did you take to see Harvey?"

How had she found out about that? Not that she had done anything wrong; she just didn't want to talk about Ted with her mother. "Oh, just this kid from school. He lives right by the farm, so I told him about Harvey and he wanted to come."

"What's his name?"

"Ted."

"He's a nice kid?"

"Of course, Mom. What d'you think? I hang out with losers?"

Meg slouched in the corner of the squad car and didn't bother to put her seat belt on. They were only going six blocks. Over to see Beatrice. She had seen her once since her stroke, and the change in the older woman had shaken her. What Meg had always liked about Beatrice was that she said what she thought. But she seemed to have gotten buried under a pile of vagueness. She wasn't quick anymore. She was slow and tired. Meg felt sorry for her but wasn't anxious to spend much time with her.

Her mom kept talking, telling her what she knew about the fire. Meg didn't really listen to her. She let the words roll over her like a wave. She felt like everything good was going away: Beatrice's spark, her friendship with Ted. And now Harvey was being threatened again.

"How was school?" her mother asked.

Meg heard this question every day. She usually tried her best to give Rich or her mom some kind of answer to it, but there really wasn't much difference day to day. This time Meg decided she'd try a new tack—tell the truth. "Kinda crappy."

"I'm sorry to hear that."

"Boring. Everybody is so slow. I finished the whole book we're working on, and we have to keep going back."

"You'll learn it even better that way."

Meg gave her mom a disgusted look. "You don't need to do that. Always looking at the bright side of things. Sometimes things are just crap."

Her mother pulled the car over to the side of the road. They weren't even to the nursing home yet. She turned and looked at Meg. "I'm sorry you had a bad day. Mine's been kind of crappy too. Days like that do happen. I hate to think of them happening to you, and so maybe I try to pretend they don't."

"Oh, it wasn't so bad."

"Maybe it will get better. Let's go see Beatrice. See if we can cheer her up."

When they got to the home, they found Beatrice sitting in a chair near the window, working on a crossword puzzle. She looked up at them as if they were strangers. Then, when she recognized them, a half smile snuck onto her face.

"How are you?" she asked, looking at Meg.

Meg decided to stick to the truth. "Crappy."

Beatrice looked up at Claire to see what she had to say.

"Crappy," her mom said. "How about you?"

"Really crappy," Beatrice croaked. Meg thought a glimpse of the old Beatrice seemed to come through at that moment.

They pulled up chairs and helped Beatrice work the crossword puzzle. She still was smarter than almost anyone Meg knew when it came to words. They didn't stay too long. Her mother said she had more work to do before the day was over. When they were leaving, Meg asked Beatrice if she liked jigsaw puzzles.

"I don't know. Haven't done one in years."

"How about I bring one over next week?"

"We could try."

Meg knew which one she would bring. Rich had given her one for her birthday that was all historical American figures, such as George Washington and Martin Luther King, Jr. When you put it all together, it made a picture of the American flag. As they were turning to go out of Beatrice's room, the woman whose barn had burned down walked by. Meg wondered what she was doing here. She marched by as if she were on a mission, her fake blond hair as stiff as a helmet.

"Mom, did you see her?"

"Yeah," her mother said, and when they reached the desk, they stopped and her mom asked the nurse about the woman. "Patty Jo Tilde? Why is she here?"

"Oh, she's been coming in ever since Walter's wife was here. Even though Walter died, she still comes to play bingo with everyone."

Her mom nodded, and they walked out the door. When they got into the car, Meg told her mom what had happened after she had gone to see Harvey. "I forgot to mention it, but I saw that woman driving around in her car. She asked me where the elk farm was."

Claire wanted to walk back in and spin Patty Jo around, demanding what she was up to. But she didn't want to make a scene at Beatrice's new place of residence. When she had the evidence she needed, she would take on Patty Jo.

CHAPTER 16

What Claire saw first as she drove up to Reiner's place was the Citroën parked in the shade with the trunk wide open. The car was a 1970 model painted a silver blue that enhanced its buglike qualities. The license plate read BURNOUT.

The rubble from the burned-down barn was black and still smoldering. Claire saw Barney Wegman standing knee-deep in the charred remains. He was wearing his usual uniform: blue jeans, knee-high rubber boots, a turtleneck shirt, and a fisherman's vest covered with pockets. He would have equipment stuffed in every pocket.

When Claire drove up he turned and saluted her. She was glad to see him, a solid, organized man in the midst of chaos.

"Hey, Doc. It's been a long time," Claire said as she approached the edge of the scorched earth. Luckily they had had that rain in the early morning. Even more luckily, it had stopped about an hour ago.

He strode up to her and then, surprising her, swooped her into a hug. "Claire, living in the country suits you. Course, the last time I saw you was a bad time for you."

Claire was a little flustered from the hug. She remembered the last time he had seen her. He had come to her husband's funeral, an act of kindness from a man who didn't give them out easily.

"That was a rough period. But I've worked through it and I like my life down here."

"Don't think I've ever seen you in uniform."

"Comes with working for the sheriff. I don't mind it. Don't have to decide what to wear in the morning." She looked back at his car. "You got here quick. That old crate didn't break down on you?"

"Hey, I found a new mechanic. Does this guy know his stuff! He swears he's going to keep that car running another twenty years."

Claire looked around. She had wondered if Reiner would be at the scene. "How'd Reiner get you out here so quick?"

Wegman looked back at Reiner's house. "He caught me at a good time. Plus, I know he's good for it."

Claire laughed. "You got that right."

"He drove down late last night and left this morning. He was plenty mad when he talked to me."

Claire looked around at the remains of the barn. "Find anything yet?"

"Give me a few minutes. What do you know? Have you talked to the caretaker about how it started? He was the first witness, wasn't he?"

"Yes, I've been to the hospital. According to him, it started on the side toward the road. He suspects arson."

"What about him?"

"I don't think so. That's my take. He's got a lot to lose. He likes his job, and the house comes with it. He made it pretty clear to me that he'd like us to find out who did it. If it was him, I'd expect him to be pushing the idea that it was an accident of some sort."

Claire offered to help, but Dr. Wegman told her to stay out of the mess, insisting that she shouldn't get her uniform dirty. "I'd rather not deal with any more feet in here than I have to."

Claire leaned on the squad car and watched Dr. Wegman work. He used a small brush to gently clean off pieces of metal sticking out of the ashes. He poked around in the burned shards and sifted through the charred wood. Occasionally he'd stick something in a small bag and bring it over by her for safekeeping.

At first she wasn't sure what he was using to dig through the rubble. Then she saw it was a plastic spatula. "You look like a cook."

He stood up and grinned. "With my fearless spatula? This thing is my favorite tool. With its soft edge, it doesn't abrade anything."

Bringing over one final bag, Doc stood next to her and surveyed the pile of samples. "That'll get me going. See what I find in this first round of samples." He looked up at the sky. "Doesn't look like it will rain tonight. Have you heard the forecast?"

"Not supposed to."

He turned to her and looked her over with much the same eye he had used to survey the scene. "What do you know?"

"About what?"

"Life in general. This fire in particular."

"In general life is quite good, but I'd like to know what's going on here. I think we might have an arsonist at work. This is the second fire we've had in this area in the past couple of days."

He raised his eyebrows and waited for her to go on.

"The first one was at a barn about three miles from here." Claire told him what happened at the Tilde farm. Then she told him about Patty Jo Tilde and how she had acted after the fire.

"So you think this little old lady did it?"

"I would not call her that, especially not to her face. She's got the tenacity of a rat terrier. When she gets her teeth into something, she doesn't let go. I think she's pissed at Reiner because he backed out of a deal with her."

"Could I take a look at the other barn?"

"This gets kinda tricky. Patty Jo and I don't get along, but I'll ask her. I suppose I could try to get a court order, but I don't know on what grounds. The insurance company has determined the fire was an accident."

* * *

Claire wanted to go home. Her workday was done. It was past five o'clock. Rich would be making dinner, Meg doing her homework. She had already gone home once today, to drop Meg off on her way to the Reiner estate. But she decided to tackle Patty Jo now. Dr. Wegman had said he'd be back to take another look at the Reiner barn tomorrow. If she could get permission to take him over to look at the remnants of Patty Jo's barn, it would be a more efficient use of his time.

Much as she didn't want to, she turned her squad car up the bluff instead of heading straight home. The road wound up through the trees and came out on top surrounded by a cow pasture. Off across the field, she could see the cows were heading home. They knew what time it was.

When Claire drove up to Patty Jo's house, she saw her car was sitting out front. So she assumed Patty Jo was at home.

Claire knocked on the door and waited. Nothing.

She stepped back from the house and surveyed its front. No sign of any movement. No curtain pulled back. No lights on. No sound at all coming from the house. Where was Patty Jo? Claire didn't see her as the kind of woman that went for a stroll in the late afternoon.

She might be hanging up clothes in the backyard. Claire decided to look. She walked around the house and thought she had come up empty until she turned and noticed Patty Jo sitting on the back steps, smoking.

Patty Jo hadn't seen her yet, didn't seem to know Claire was there. She was wearing jeans and a plaid shirt and looked younger than she usually did when she was dressed up. She was smoking the way Claire remembered people smoking before the habit had gotten such a bad name. Patty Jo would inhale, sit for a moment or two, then slowly let the smoke out in a lovely white stream that the wind blew away.

"I didn't know you smoked," Claire remarked.

Patty Jo didn't jump. She didn't even turn her head to look at Claire. Maybe she had known she was there after all.

She said, "I don't anymore. I gave it up. Walter didn't like it. Now, I come outside once a month to smoke one cigarette. It was the only way I could quit." She stubbed out her cigarette, rubbing it against the cement of the back steps. Then she turned and looked at Claire. "What're you doing back here?"

No niceties from this woman. Claire decided to get right to the point. "I don't know if you heard, but there was another barn burned down last night. The Reiners'. The fire investigator who's looking at the scene would like to come over and examine your barn. It might be the work of the same person."

Patty Jo looked as though she had taken a big bite of a lemon. "I don't think so. This fire was an accident."

Claire noticed what Patty Jo hadn't said: no questions about how the Reiners' barn had burned down, no guesses as to who might have done it, no possibility that this might be a way to get to the bottom of who had destroyed her barn. What was so frustrating was that Patty Jo was doing everything to look guilty, but Claire still couldn't get anything on her.

"This would be an enormous service to the county if you would allow us to do this. If a firebug is running around, we'd like to catch him."

"What do I owe the county? A big nothing. All the county is doing is trying to take my farm from me."

"That's not true."

Patty Jo stood up as if she was going to walk back inside the house, then apparently changed her mind. "You're behind this. I don't know what your interest is in all this or what Margaret has told you, but I don't want to see you on my property again. I will call the sheriff myself and ask him to keep you away from me. Get a restraining order if I need it."

Claire could feel her anger building. Her fingers got twitchy and her ears got warm. "It's my job as a deputy sheriff to try to prevent crimes from happening in this county and to try to solve them when they do. That includes your barn burning down."

"It wasn't a crime, it was an accident. Why don't you focus on what's happening to me? What about Margaret persecuting me? Trying to take away the farm. Have you done anything to prevent that?" Patty Jo spit the words at her. "And I saw you at the Lakeside senior home today. Are you following me? I want you to leave me alone."

Claire held herself back. No good would come of telling Patty Jo off. "I was visiting a friend. I'm sorry if you think I have something against you. I thought you might like to know what happened to your barn."

Patty Jo stood on the steps, looking down at Claire, and said quietly, "I don't care about the barn. I just want to be left alone. So please get off my property right now."

The house felt cold, so Margaret went and fetched the afghan that her mother had crocheted. She had persuaded her mother to use only green tones, so it hadn't ended up a hodgepodge of color. She found the afghan soothing and the fact that her mother had made it comforting. She wrapped herself in it and sat on the couch.

It was past midnight. She had slept for two hours, then woken up. This was an all-too-familiar pattern for her. In the last two years, she had gone from easily sleeping ten hours straight a night to being lucky if she could catnap for two to three hours at a time. Between having to pee and just feeling anxious, she couldn't stay asleep for long.

Margaret tried not to let it bother her. If she got up and read for an hour or so, she could often fall back asleep for another few hours.

She picked up the book she had left next to the couch, but it looked no more interesting to her now than it had last night. What she wouldn't give for a good book. They seemed harder and harder to find. Maybe she was just getting to be more difficult to please. Mark thought so. She opened the pages, then snapped it shut. She was tired of reading about women whose lives were falling apart. Women in jeopardy—these were women in apoplexy. Who wanted to read about her own life? Didn't people read to escape?

She stood up and didn't know what to do with herself. Her mind churned at this time of night. Maybe she should try to write a book about a woman who is afraid of nothing and conquers all.

Margaret looked around her house. She had a good life. Couldn't she get that through her head? She had a husband who loved her. Sure, he tracked in mud and didn't put the dishes away, but he brought her wildflowers when they were in bloom and did more than his fair share of the milking, claiming he liked it.

Maybe once she got through this transition phase of her life she would hit a good patch and try some new things. Get excited about life again.

If only they would get the farm. It would make all the difference in the world. She tried not to think about it, but it was hard not to fantasize.

After she'd heard about the will, she and Mark had decided to try to get the farm away from Patty Jo. They thought they might have a chance of proving that Patty Jo had unduly influenced Walter in the grief that had followed his first wife's death. They had filed for another injunction in probate court.

She had talked to the lawyer today, and he'd come right out and said not to count on it. He'd said their case was very difficult and there wasn't much to argue against in her father's new will.

"But the timing . . ."

"The woman was his wife," the lawyer reminded her.

"But they had only been married a few months."

"I'm aware of that. I don't know that it can matter in this case. The will was signed and witnessed."

"She never loved him," Margaret blurted out, and then regretted it. Why did she always have to make everything so personal?

Margaret walked to the front window. The moon was a small gleaming boat in the dark sky. The leaves hung still on the maple tree. She decided to walk out and check on the goats. Maybe counting goats instead of sheep would make her sleepy.

She folded the afghan and placed it on the couch, then grabbed her barn jacket, which hung by the back door, and slipped her feet into her rubber boots. Pulling the jacket over her flannel nightgown, she was sure she would be warm enough. The nights hadn't started to cool off much yet. The thermometer outside the kitchen window said it was still fifty degrees out. Not bad.

She opened the door and smelled the air. The sweet smell of decay. The leaves were starting to fall. One good wind and most of them would drop. Sometimes it happened in a weekend. It would be nice to get a few days of color before they fell.

She walked around the side of the house and stared at the barn. At first she couldn't believe what she was seeing.

A candle was burning in the window of the goat barn. She stood still and wondered if Mark had taken one of the automatic candles she put in the windows for Christmas and set it up in there. As a night-light for the goats? Not likely. But what other explanation was there?

She started walking quickly toward the barn. The candle was very short. What might happen if it burned all the way down? There was a lot of hay in the barn.

The candle exploded in front of her eyes, and the whole window of the barn filled with light. Margaret wasn't sure what had caught on fire, but she knew she had to stop it before it got out of control.

She yelled for Mark as loudly as she could but didn't stop moving toward the barn. She had to get the animals out.

She started to run and tripped over her nightgown. Sprawled in the dewy grass, she felt panic building inside her. She picked herself up, lifted her nightgown over her knees, and ran for the barn.

When she got inside, she didn't know what to do first. The fire had dropped to the floor and was lapping up the walls of the barn. The goats were restless in their stalls, and all of them stared at her with the fire reflected in their large eyes.

She had to get the goats out but decided to try to put the fire out first. There was no time to lose.

They always left a hose next to the water trough. She got it, turned it on full blast, and aimed at the barn wall above the fire. She started up high, then sprayed downward. She had to save the roof. If the roof went, they would lose the building. She soaked the wall and then worked on the fire. Freezing-cold water ran down her arms, but she couldn't stop.

Just when she thought she had control of it, the fire popped up again in the straw that covered the floor. She started spraying the floor. The smoke was getting pretty thick, and she knew that could do a person in—or a goat. She needed to get the goats out of the barn before it was too late.

She dropped the hose, which was still aimed in the direction of the fire, and hoped the stream would keep it under control. Then she ran from stall to stall and undid the latches. The goats started to push their way out, but they seemed stunned and sleepy. It was the middle of the night.

She sang to them the song she sang in the morning when she let them out to pasture: "You are my sunshine, my only sunshine." They butted her and poked one another, and she started to slap them on their backsides and push them out the door. Twelve goats. She counted their heads as they went out in the barnyard, then left them milling about.

Margaret took a deep breath and plunged back into the barn. The smoke was dense and made her cough. She grabbed a bucket, dipped it into the water trough, and threw a bucketful of water where the remains of the fire crackled in a pile of straw in the far corner of the barn. That did it. The fire was out. The barn fell into darkness. She caught her breath and stumbled outside.

Margaret walked into the milling herd of goats. They talked to her in their soft language and butted up against her thighs, nibbling on the edges of her jacket. She pushed her hands into their soft fur and tried to stop trembling.

CHAPTER 17

Daniel Reiner's black Lincoln Navigator sitting at the top of the driveway looked to Claire like a big block of coal. The chunky vehicle made the sleek silver-blue Citroën sitting next to it look even more foreign.

Reiner opened the front door and smiled at Claire. "Well, if it isn't my favorite deputy sheriff!" He stepped aside, but without giving her enough room to walk through the door without brushing by him. Claire decided to stay where she was.

"I need to talk to Dr. Wegman. His office said he was here."

"Come on in. He's here. We're having some coffee, and he's giving me the lowdown on this fire. He told me you stopped by yesterday. Not really necessary. I think we've got it under control."

"Mr. Reiner, when a crime is committed in this county, it is the sheriff's department's business. We need to be involved. You can't take over the investigation."

He smiled his big broad smile. Claire was sure he had had his teeth whitened, or maybe they were all caps. There was no way nature would allow a man of his age to have teeth that white.

"I guess I've been put in my place," he said in a manner that told Claire he didn't care what she had to say.

"Well, there's been another fire," Claire told him. "Probably set by the same person. I think it might answer some of Dr. Wegman's questions."

Dr. Wegman came up behind Reiner. "Claire, what happened?"

Reiner finally stepped back and gave her some space. Claire walked into the foyer and then followed the two men back to the living room.

When they all sat down, Claire told them what she knew. "I haven't been over there yet, but a fire was started last night at Margaret Underwood's place. She was the daughter of Walter Tilde, Patty Jo's husband. I think Patty Jo is on a rampage. We've got to stop her. We need some proof that she's behind this string of fires."

"Tilde," Reiner murmured. "But that's the woman I was going to buy the farm from."

"Exactly." Claire felt like giving him a gold star. "And you reneged on the deal and then your barn burned down."

"What do you know about this latest fire?" Wegman asked.

"Margaret was lucky to catch it before it got out of control. She managed to put it out. She told me it had been started with a candle."

Wegman rubbed his chin. "Makes sense. A woman would use a candle. Simple, effective, right at hand. Tough to detect once it's done its job. Let's get over there," Wegman said, standing up.

"I didn't hire you for this," Reiner said.

Wegman looked down at him. "Yes, you did. You told me to find out who had set your barn on fire. Have you changed your mind?"

Reiner settled back in the couch. "If you think it's what you need to do."

"We can take my car," Claire suggested.

Reiner stood by the door as they were leaving. Claire got the feeling he was hoping to be asked along. Not on her watch, she decided.

"You going to come back?" he shouted at Wegman.

"I'll come to get my car," Wegman called back as he climbed in the squad car.

After Claire turned out of the driveway, Wegman asked, "Who made him president?"

"Not much competition around here. He's got the money to ride roughshod over everyone."

Margaret came walking out of the house as soon as they pulled into the driveway. She looked as though she'd had a rough night. Her hair was pulled back in a loose ponytail and her eyes were pouched with dark shadows. Dr. Wegman asked her a few questions about the fire. Margaret offered them coffee, but he wanted to go right out to the barn to begin his work.

Claire took Margaret up on her offer and returned to the house with her. Margaret poured two big mugs of coffee and didn't even ask if she wanted cream and sugar. She pushed a plate of oatmeal cookies toward Claire. Claire took one. Lunch might be a while.

"Do you think it's Patty Jo?" Margaret asked.

"Do you?"

Margaret looked down at the table and smoothed the tablecloth with her hand. "I have no doubt."

"I suspect you're right. Now we have to prove it. Did you see anything before the fire started? Hear anything?"

"Not that I'm aware of. I wake up awfully easy these days. Almost any noise will get me out of bed. I might have heard something, but I don't remember anything in particular."

"Have you had any contact with her?" Claire asked.

"No. I haven't even seen her since the funeral. I've been glad. I'm almost afraid to go to town. I worry that I might run into her, and I'm afraid of what she'll say."

"She's got a mouth on her."

Margaret looked nervously around the room, stood up and walked to the window and flicked back the curtain, then came back and sat in her chair.

"I don't know where Mark is," Margaret told her.

"What do you mean?"

"He was so mad about the fire. He took off early this morning. I'm afraid of what he might do."

Claire hated to hear this. If Mark did something rash, it could make everything worse. "You have to talk sense to him. If we can pin this on Patty Jo, we'll be headed in the right direction. He needs to leave her alone."

"I know. I'll try to talk to him." Margaret looked at Claire. "Do you think she'll try again?"

"I can't say, but I doubt it. She knows you'll be watching for her now. I think you'll be safe, but you might want to rig up some kind of alarm to let you know if anyone comes near the house or barn."

"Maybe that's where Mark went. He would think of that." Margaret's voice said otherwise.

Rich picked up the clothes Claire had left in a pile on the floor last night. He threw them in the hamper in her closet. She wasn't the neatest person he had ever met.

Claire and Meg had certainly stirred up his life. Not that he'd thought living with them would be all romantic and fun, but he realized what a staid life he had been leading before. Claire didn't seem to ever let up on herself. Even when she did the dishes, she was thinking, usually about her job. Talk about taking work home—she carried it around with her in a backpack.

It was odd to be living with a deputy sheriff and learn about all the crimes that were being committed in this small county. He wasn't sure if the county was getting more dangerous, but since Claire had moved down from the Cities there certainly seemed to be an increase in crime.

But then she wasn't the only person who had moved down from the Cities. First the area had been discovered by the artists in the late seventies and early eighties. Then the tourists had followed. Once the artists had fixed up their houses and set up shops and restaurants, the rich folks had followed. He wouldn't be able to afford his farm and land if he had to buy it at the going rate now. Thank goodness it was paid for and he could keep up on his taxes.

The mayor of Fort St. Antoine had told him that in 1990 there'd been fifty people commuting from Pepin County to the Twin Cities. Now over five hundred people commuted. It wouldn't be long before the county would change from a farming community to a suburb of the greater metropolitan area.

Living with Claire on a daily basis, he found her more intense than he would have guessed, and also more crotchety. He liked it. If she didn't care for something, she said so. He didn't have to try to guess what she was feeling. It was right out in the open. But the downside was that he then had to deal with how she was feeling and do something about whatever it was.

When she came home from work that evening, later than usual, Meg and he had already eaten dinner and Meg had gone upstairs to work on some homework. Claire stomped in and slammed the door shut behind her. Her dark eyes were flashing.

He dished up a plate of mashed potatoes and meat loaf and sat down with her to watch her eat it.

"This looks great," she said, and slammed a kiss into his cheek. He could tell she was seething about something. He decided not to ask, and wondered how long it would take her to burst out with it.

She asked how his day had been. She praised his mashed potatoes. He had learned, early on, that she loved mashed potatoes. She ate everything on her plate with great energy. And then she exploded.

"I'm furious." Claire set her fork down on her plate.

"How unusual," Rich said.

"What is that supposed to mean?"

He wondered if he should try to explain. Sometimes he just dug a deeper hole for himself. "I'm learning that you often come home upset about something that happened at work."

"I'm a cop. Yes, I do bring my work home. I thought you might be interested."

"I am."

Meg came galloping down the stairs. "Hi, Mom."

Rich wanted a few moments alone with Claire, and he didn't think Meg should have to hear about all the gory details of her mother's job. "Meg, why don't you give us some time alone?"

Meg didn't pay any attention to his request. She sat down at the table with them. "What's up? Mom, you have a hard day?"

Meg got a smile out of Claire. "Yes, Meg. Thanks for asking. I'm a little pissed off."

"Don't worry about me, Rich." Meg turned back to her mother. "What're you mad about, Mom?"

"I'm just getting frustrated. I was over at Margaret's. It was their turn for a fire last night. . . ."

Rich had heard about it at the bank. "Stanley told me about that."

Meg nodded. "Mariah told me at school."

"So I was over there nearly the whole day, combing through her yard for any evidence. That arson investigator took back bagfuls. I'm mad because I think we know who's doing this and she keeps getting away with it. I'm hoping he can find something that links this fire with Patty Jo Tilde."

"See, Rich," Meg said, "I told you about her. That's the woman Mom and I saw at the nursing home. She looks like she could have been a school principal."

Claire started laughing. "Oh, Meggy. I think you're right. She does a little. Why does that make me feel better?"

Rich tried again. "Meg, have you finished your homework?"

She shook her head.

"Go on up and finish it. You can talk to your mom later."

Meg wrinkled up her face as if she had eaten something rude. "What's with you tonight?"

Claire nodded at Meg. "I'll be up in a little while."

Meg snorted and ran up the stairs.

Claire pushed away her plate. She hadn't quite finished her meatloaf. "I like to see Meg when I get home from work."

Rich felt he needed to stand his ground on this one. "I don't think you should talk to her about your work as much as you do."

Claire took her dishes into the kitchen. She came back out with a glass of water and stood looking at Rich. "I know how to raise my daughter."

Rich didn't say anything right away. This was dangerous territory. He needed to weigh his words. "Yes, but sometimes all she has is me."

The Grand Casino was located a few miles outside of Red Wing, Minnesota—about a thirty-five-minute drive for Patty Jo. First the Prairie Island nuclear power plant came into view, then right across the street the bright lights of the casino appeared. The one time she had taken Walter to the casino, he had laughed when he saw the two huge buildings were right next to each other on the banks of the Mississippi. "If the power plant blows, what'll go first is a bunch of gamblers."

Walter didn't approve of gambling and they'd stayed only a little while, long enough for him to lose $10 in the quarter slot machines. Patty Jo hadn't let him know how often she went. After he had his stroke, she had become a regular. One night she had won $2,000 in the dollar slots, her biggest haul. She didn't want to think about how much money she had lost since then.

Sitting in the casino's parking lot, she worried about selling the farm. A real-estate agent was coming out to meet with her early next week. She had to have that money. She had seriously racked up her credit cards, but maybe that would all change. Tonight she felt lucky.

When she walked in the front door of the casino, the first thing she saw was the new car they were giving away—a silver Mercedes. Patty Jo could see herself behind the wheel of such a vehicle. She would stay only three hours, she promised herself. Long enough to be there for the drawing for the car. Long enough to take advantage of her lucky feeling. All it took was being at the one right machine at the one right moment.

Patty Jo started out at a row of slots in the back room, the *Bewitched* row. She had once won a thousand dollars on a *Bewitched* slot machine. She remembered every machine she had ever been lucky at. She didn't like to stay at any one machine too long. Moving around gave her a sense that she was in control. The right place at the right time was her mantra.

At the end of two hours, Patty Jo was down over $1,000. She had to get back to even. When she did that she would leave. She needed to take out a little more money on her credit card. One thousand would get her back in the clear. She went to the cashier and got the necessary money.

Just as she watched her last twenty credits disappear from the screen of the slot machine, she heard them calling the numbers for the drawing. She sat stunned. She had lost over $2,000. Her worst night ever.

Patty Jo held the entries for the car in her hand. Every time she had come into the casino in the last week she had been given an entry. But the numbers called were never hers. She knew she shouldn't keep sitting at a slot machine when she wasn't playing. That was considered bad manners at the casino. But she didn't want to leave. She felt so empty, as if she had been gutted.

She walked out the door of the casino and was surprised by how dark it was outside. She hated the idea of going back to that cold and empty farmhouse. She hated that place. If it wasn't for Margaret and her friend the cop, she would have already sold the farm. Why was that deputy Claire Watkins sticking her nose in? She was ruining everything.

As she drove, she remembered the address she had written down before she went to the casino, Claire Watkins's address in Fort St. Antoine: 159 High Street. She had come across it when she was looking for someone else's number. Maybe she should swing through Fort St. Antoine to see what the deputy sheriff's house looked like. See if she had any outbuildings.

CHAPTER 18

Bridget sat and stared out at the driveway, watching for Chuck's truck. It was nine o'clock at night. Chuck had said he would be there at nine. Bridget could hardly wait to see Rachel.

This was the first time Bridget had been home alone without Rachel. She had thought she would get many things done without her young daughter hanging on her. Instead, she had been stunned by how physically debilitating Rachel's absence was. She felt as if a limb had been cut off her body. She kept glimpsing a small child ducking behind the dining room chairs, crawling on the rug in the living room.

Bridget had been surprised when Chuck asked if he could take Rachel one night a week. She had agreed. Bridget was pretty sure he would just take Rachel over to his mother's house and have dinner there, letting his mother tend to the baby. However, it was better than nothing. She did not want Rachel to grow up without knowing her father and his family.

When Chuck picked Rachel up at five o'clock, they said very little to each other. Rachel began to fuss as Chuck carried her out to the car. Bridget was afraid the baby might start crying, but she went into her car seat with wide eyes and no breakdown.

"I'll see you about nine," he said, and drove away with Rachel staring straight ahead in the backseat, not seeing her mother waving goodbye.

Bridget went into the house, sat on the couch, pulled a pillow into her lap, and cried. She had managed to make a grilled cheese sandwich and had cleaned the kitchen, but the laundry still waited in piles upstairs in her bedroom. Maybe the babysitter would do a few loads for her tomorrow.

Ten minutes after nine, headlights turned up the driveway. Chuck's truck parked, and he popped out but left the vehicle running. Obviously he had no intention of staying. He opened the door of the truck and leaned through to the back of the crew cab to get Rachel. Bridget ran out the door, eager to get her hands on her daughter.

"How'd she do?" Bridget asked as he deposited the sleeping child in her waiting arms.

"I think okay." Chuck reached out and adjusted the blanket Rachel was wrapped in. "Mom had to go and feed her some cake. I hope you don't mind."

"No, that's fine. A little cake won't hurt her."

Chuck took a step backward and looked like he wanted to jump back in the truck to get away from Bridget.

Bridget quickly asked, "So you are going to do this again?"

He stopped and said, "I'd like to. Is it okay?"

"I think it's a good idea."

Chuck looked down at Rachel. "She only cried once, and when I picked her up, she stopped. She's starting to talk."

"I know. What did she say?"

"Well, Mom was trying to get her to say 'daddy.' "

"Did she say it?"

Chuck gave a bashful smile. "I think so. It sounded like she did."

Bridget could hardly stand the thought that Chuck's mother was teaching Rachel to talk to her father. Why hadn't Bridget been able to do that? What was wrong with her? What had gone wrong with their relationship?

He climbed into his truck and drove away. As Bridget carried her into the house, Rachel opened her eyes.

"Oh," she said in her thin, high voice, then, "Momma, Momma," pointing her little finger at Bridget's nose.

"Hi, my sweet girl," Bridget said, and carted her off to bed.

Rachel was already falling asleep again. Bridget tucked her into her crib and snuggled her favorite blanket close around her face. She saw a smear of chocolate near her ear but decided to leave it until morning. Other than that, her daughter was perfect.

Bridget curled into the rocking chair in Rachel's room, trying to sort out all she was feeling. Maybe she had never given Chuck enough room to be a father. Maybe it was all her fault.

The phone rang. Bridget hurried to get it, not wanting Rachel to wake up.

When Bridget picked it up, a woman's voice said, "I know where you live," and hung up.

Claire watched the wrinkles disappear from her uniform as she ironed. Rich was watching the football game, but with the sound low so that they could talk. Ironing clothes was meditative for her, even therapeutic, but tonight she felt antsy, unable to sink down into the cotton landscape of crisp fabric folds.

In their division of labor, Claire had taken on the task of keeping all their clothes clean. She hoped it balanced out. Often she felt like he was doing more. Maybe she should take on a house project.

"What would you think of me painting the living room?" Claire suggested. "I think it looks dingy."

Rich grunted. "Dingy? I painted that two years ago."

"Maybe it's the color."

He turned and looked at her. "That might be nice, but you'd have to do it soon before the weather turns bad, while you can still have all the windows open. It would take a week or so. How would you have the time?"

"Well, let's at least pick out a color. I feel like I should be doing more around here."

"You're doing your share."

Claire set down the iron and came and stood in front of Rich so he couldn't see the TV. "So what do you think? Is this living together working for you?"

He looked up at her with a questioning look. "Are you having second thoughts?"

"Not at all. I just thought it's been a couple of months and maybe we should talk about it."

"I think the Vikings are about to get their asses kicked," he teased her. He craned his neck so he could see the TV, but she moved to block his view.

"Don't you want to talk?" she said.

"Come here," he said.

She plopped herself down in his lap.

He kissed her on the nose. "How do you feel?" he asked. "You're the one who brought this up."

"How do people stay together? Why are Bridget and Chuck separating? I'm just thinking about all this. I don't know if I'm holding up my end of the bargain with you."

"What bargain is that?"

"You know, doing enough around here. Making this a home. Being a real partner."

Rich pulled back and looked at her. "I'm not complaining. You always want to know how I'm feeling, but it's harder for you to talk about how you're feeling."

Claire scrunched up her face. "I don't know."

"Try." He poked her gently in the ribs.

"Hey, no poking." She leaned back against him and didn't say anything right away. "I think I'm feeling jealous of the time you get to spend with Meg, and I'm also feeling weird because you're taking on the role of father for her. I know that sometimes when I'm working hard on a case I can get pretty absorbed, and I don't know if it's fair."

"Well, the Meg stuff we are going to have to work out. I don't want to take over from you, but I should get to tell her what to do once in a while."

"I know. Sorry about the other night. I think I felt guilty about you doing it all and wanted to take a stand. To be her mom."

"You know, you don't need to be working. This house is paid for. I make enough money for both of us. I've got quite a bit put away."

Claire thought of what it would feel like to not go into work to-morrow, to get up and make breakfast for Rich and Meg instead. Meg would go off to school, Rich would leave to drive a load of pheasants up to the Cities, and she would have the day to herself. The thought of all that time alone scared her. "Oh, I couldn't stop working. What would I do? Who would I be?"

"I'm not saying you should."

"Do you want me to?"

"We've been there before, Claire. Not if you want to keep working. That decision is totally yours. Now that we're living together, I don't mind you working so much. As long as I get all the rest of your time."

"That's enough?"

"For right now it is," he said. Lowering his voice, although Meg had gone to sleep an hour ago, he added, "And I get to take advantage of you whenever I want."

"Which is not often enough," she teased.

He undid the buttons on her shirt, leaned down, and kissed her neck. It felt like raindrops. She melted a little.

The phone rang. Claire thought of letting it go. She was more inter-ested in how Rich was making her feel. But it was almost eleven o'clock, and no one made a casual phone call at that time of night. She knew she had to answer. Reluctantly, she pulled herself out of Rich's arms.

Patty Jo sat in her car down the road from the deputy's house. She had driven by the house for the last few nights, wondering if she should start a fire. Just a small fire.

There was only one light on in the living room, one light on upstairs. She had seen someone walk past a window, but that was a while ago. Maybe the woman was reading in bed.

Patty Jo had tried to go home tonight, but her anger would not let her sleep. Once she got the idea in her head, she could think of little else. Although she knew it might not be smart to take on the deputy, Patty Jo felt untouchable. Who was going to believe that an older woman would do such a thing? She had never been caught before. But she was sure the deputy would know who had done it. This was what she wanted—to make the deputy know who was in control.

Patty Jo had called the sheriff and asked him to keep Claire Watkins away from her. She listed all her complaints against the deputy and then tacked on a few for good measure. He listened to her politely and assured her that he would take care of the matter, but he also said that Deputy Watkins was doing her job. Patty Jo had hung up the phone feeling even angrier.

The light in the upstairs room went out. The house sat quiet. The downstairs light was so faint, she decided it must be some sort of night-light.

Patty Jo savored the feeling of power that expanded throughout her body. What a surprise this woman would wake to. What a shock, what a horror. She would look out the window and see her garage on fire. All she would be able to think of was the fire. It would fill her mind.

Patty Jo decided to wait fifteen minutes more and then proceed. Give Watkins enough time to fall asleep. There was a half-moon, which would offer her just enough light to see her way.

The back of the detached garage was where she would start the fire—where no one passing on the road could see it. That way the fire would get a good start before the deputy would even be able to notice it from the house.

Waiting made Patty Jo want a cigarette. That feeling lasted a few days after she had her monthly smoke. The price to pay for a little pleasure.

She leaned back in the car seat and thought of learning to light fires. Her father had let her start the fires in the old burn barrel in the backyard. He'd told her that she was to light matches only when he was with her. He would hand her the big red-and-blue box of matches. As she struck the match against the side of the box, the small red tip would burst into flame, giving off a faint smell of sulfur. Excited, she would fling the match into the pile of papers, and it would explode in color and light.

She gathered up her equipment. Keep it simple—that was her motto. A candle, some matches, and a pile of soaked rags. Didn't take much to get these old wooden structures burning. They were kindling. They went up in a flash. Too bad she couldn't stick around to watch. She loved everything about a fire: the dancing flames, the burning roar, the sweet smell of smoke.

As if to urge her on, an owl called from the bottom of the bluff, a quavering shriek. Patty Jo took it as a sign. She patted her pocket and found the matches. No one had driven by, no one could see her. Everything was working out perfectly. Once she made up her mind to start a fire, she felt like she went into automatic pilot; the act took her over.

She turned off the overhead light in her car before quietly opening the door. She loved this part of it. Blood fizzed through her veins with excitement. She left the car door slightly ajar to avoid the noise of shutting it and ran to a tree in the yard. All was quiet. The owl was silent. She stepped out from the shadow of the tree and walked quickly to the side of the garage. Then she slipped behind the garage and was hidden from the street and the house.

Patty Jo checked out the back of the garage. The propane tank was tucked right between the garage and the house. If the fire burned hot enough, the tank might explode. That would be exciting.

Crouched on her knees, she made a nest of the rags and set the candle in the midst of them. Once she got the candle to stand up by itself, she lit a match. She held it to the wick of the candle and it caught immediately. Such a calm night—no wind to blow it out. The flame pulsed in the night air, greedy.

She crawled backward and then stood up and dusted herself off. The candle hardly even showed, sheltered as it was by the rags. It might be an hour or two before it reached the rags. She would be home, having a drink and then climbing into bed. As she fell asleep, she would think of the building burning down.

Just as she was turning to leave the yard, an outdoor light came on overhead. It startled her so much, she froze for a second. Then, dropping the matches, she started to run.

The first sound Claire heard when they parked the car in front of her old house was an owl under the bluff hooting its thin, haunting song. The second sound she heard was that of someone running along the side of the road.

Then she heard her sister screaming from the front door of the house. "Hurry. I see fire by the garage."

Rich asked, "What do you want me to do?"

"Help Bridget," Claire said as she started to run after whoever was getting away.

The arsonist was already more than half a block down the road, although not running very fast. Claire could see an outline of a person and guessed from the size that it was Patty Jo. Who else could it be? She was not going to let that woman get away. Claire put on a burst of speed and had almost caught up to her when she reached a car parked alongside the road.

The runner pulled open the car door, jumped in, and started the engine with a roar. Claire ran straight toward the car, determined to stop the vehicle. She couldn't see clearly enough to determine if it was Patty Jo's car. It came straight at her, but she didn't waver. It slowed as if waiting for her to leap to one side. She thought she caught a glimpse of Patty Jo inside, screaming at her to get out of the way. Then the car lights came on and blinded her.

When the car was almost on top of her, she leaped forward and clambered onto the hood. Grabbing the windshield wipers with one hand, Claire slammed her other hand onto the glass. Now she had a good view of Patty Jo, who was glaring at her.

The car came to a sudden stop and Claire slid down on the hood, her hands holding tight to the wipers. She didn't know how long she could hang on.

Then the car backed up. Sliding around, Claire finally lost her hold on the wipers and fell off the car, landing on her side. She jumped up and watched as Patty Jo swerved the car off the road and into a ditch. When Patty Jo tried to go forward again, the car wheels spun and whined beneath her.

Claire jumped into the ditch and pulled open the driver's door. Patty Jo came tumbling out of the car. She sprawled on the dead leaves in the ditch and swore at Claire.

"Don't waste your breath, Patty Jo. I've heard it all." Claire reached down, grabbed the older woman's arm, and pulled her up.

"Get your hands off me!"

"This time you're not getting away with it."

"I don't know what you're talking about." Patty Jo seemed to shrink before Claire's eyes as if she were afraid. *What an act,* Claire thought. *This woman isn't scared of me. She knows exactly what she's doing.*

"This is your last fire."

CHAPTER 19

In the movies the villains gave it up easily. Shine a bright light on them, keep them up all night, and they broke, told you everything.

Claire glanced at the sheriff as they drank coffee in his office. She had never seen him look so tired. Nor had she seen him with this much beard stubble before. She hadn't realized that he was one of those men who had to shave twice a day to keep a clean chin.

It was three-fifteen in the morning. Patty Jo Tilde was sitting in the back room waiting for her lawyer.

Patty Jo had talked to them for three hours, claiming it was just by chance that she had been down the street from Claire's old house when a candle was lit by the back of the garage, propped up on kerosene-doused rags. She wouldn't change her story even though they didn't believe it. No one would believe it. Patty Jo stuck to her claim with the ferocity of a small terrier holding on to a leg bone.

They had tried everything. Claire had been bad cop, the sheriff good cop. Then they had switched as the sheriff got belligerent and Claire tried to calm him down. At the moment they were both drinking coffee simply to stay awake. By constrast, Patty Jo seemed wide awake and had finally insisted on seeing her lawyer about half an hour ago.

The lawyer arrived, clean-shaven and ready for the day. He was dressed in a business suit and carrying a briefcase. He and the sheriff shook hands, obviously old acquaintances. Then the sheriff introduced Claire.

The lawyer introduced himself. "Joe Pelke."

They shook hands. Claire wished she were in uniform. She had been wearing an old flannel shirt of Rich's and jeans when Bridget had called.

"How'd this happen?" the lawyer asked.

"Claire can fill you in." The sheriff turned to Claire.

"My sister is living in my old house. I've moved. She got a strange phone call, a woman saying she knew where she lived. Then last night, as she was putting her baby to bed, she noticed a car parked down the street. Well, you know Fort St. Antoine. There are no strange cars. She called us because it was making her nervous." Claire looked down at her clothes again. "I told her I'd come by and check it out. When Rich and I got there, a fire had been set back by the garage and Patty Jo Tilde was running away from the scene."

The sheriff jumped in. "Claire got to the scene just as Patty Jo was leaving. They caught her red-handed. And she still insists it was just a coincidence that she was there. It was nearly midnight. No way it was a coincidence." The sheriff was getting angry talking about it.

"Why would she do this? Why would she set the fire?" the lawyer asked.

Claire stepped in. "We believe Patty Jo thought she was torching my property. She didn't know I didn't live there anymore. My sister moved in last month."

"Why would she want to burn down your garage?" the lawyer continued.

"We think this isn't the first fire she has started in the last few weeks. She's been our main suspect in a series of arson fires. She has taken a dislike to me because I'm the investigator on the cases."

The lawyer looked Claire over and didn't say anything. He nodded. "I need to talk to my client."

The sheriff said, "Talk sense to her, Joe. We've got her over a barrel here. Help her see that. It's a first offense for her. No sense in this going to trial."

"I'll talk to her," the lawyer said.

They let the lawyer into the room where Patty Jo was sequestered. Then the sheriff tipped his head back toward his office, and he and Claire left Joe with his client.

At first Claire and the sheriff didn't even bother to talk. Then he looked at Claire and shook his head.

"What?" she asked.

"I wish you hadn't gone to see Patty Jo the other day. Now I've got it on record that she filed a complaint about you."

Claire felt ready to explode. She took a sip of coffee, which tasted as tired as she was, and said, "I had to go see her. Fire investigation, remember? Plus, I think it will work to our advantage. It goes to motive."

"Damn, I hope you're right." The sheriff rolled his shoulders, stretching. "But you didn't actually see her with the stuff. You didn't see her light the candle, and she didn't have anything on her when you caught her."

"Yes, but we caught her on the scene as the fire started. What do we need, photos? She was the only person in the vicinity. The fire was lit. Rich was there too, and my sister. There is no way she's getting out of this."

"Couldn't even pull a print off that candle. That's bad luck. What next?"

"Don't let her age or demeanor throw you. We follow procedure. She talks to her lawyer. I hope he straightens her out and convinces her that she needs to plead, and she tells us what happened. But either way, she's arrested, she goes to jail. I go home. So do you. Tomorrow we get a search warrant for her house and barn. The good doctor goes in with me and we figure the whole thing out. We charge her with at least one count of arson, and maybe four."

The sheriff rubbed his scruffy chin. "You're right."

Claire shook her head. "She can wear a person down. Let's go pay another visit to her. See if her lawyer has made her see reason."

They walked down the hallway and then punched in the code for the jail cell. Although they had an interview room outside of the jail block, they had interviewed her inside. Often it made a bigger impression on someone if they were taken directly into the jail.

Pelke looked up as they entered the room and gave them a weary shake of the head. Patty Jo ignored them. Claire couldn't stand to think about what Patty Jo had tried to do. Her sister and her young niece might have been dead right now if the garage fire had jumped to the house.

The lawyer said, "Mrs. Tilde is adamant. She says she had nothing to do with the fire. She says she was driving by, noticed the fire, and stopped to see what was happening."

"Oh, this is a new twist," Claire said. "She's lying."

Patty Jo screamed at Claire, "It's all your fault. You've got it in for me."

Something snapped in Claire. She stood and shouted right in Patty Jo's face. "You're not getting away with this."

The sheriff grabbed Claire by the shoulder and pulled her back while the lawyer placed a restraining hand on Patty Jo's arm.

Claire slumped. The sheriff let go of her. She walked out of the room and leaned against the smooth walls of the jail hallway. As her anger washed through her, she started to shake.

The sheriff came and stood next to her, not looking at her. "You're tired. You need to go home."

"I'm sorry." Claire felt ashamed. "She's getting to me."

The sheriff nodded. "You've done what you can do." He turned and put an arm over her shoulder on the wall and leaned in close to Claire. She could see his tired eyes as he said, "She's not worth it. You saved your sister."

"What's she going to do next time?" Claire asked.

"We'll see to it that there's no next time."

The lawyer walked out and said, "I think my client needs to go home. We can do a signature bond."

The sheriff shook his head. "I don't believe that will be sufficient. She's going to jail, and we're going home to bed."

Pelke looked at both of them. "She's an old woman. Are you sure you want to book her?"

The sheriff spoke clearly in his rough voice. "She had no trouble wandering around my deputy's property at midnight—a time when most decent folk are in bed. I don't see that it should bother her to sleep on a cot in a jail cell. She needs to know that the one action leads to the other. I don't care how old she is."

Margaret slept for a few hours, then tried to stay in bed, hoping she would fall back asleep. But at four in the morning, she gave up and crawled out of bed. In the kitchen, she put on a pot of coffee. She looked out the window and saw that Mark's car was still gone.

He hadn't come home last night. She wasn't sure where he had gone. He hadn't even called. She hoped he had fallen asleep in the car outside some bar and would wander home when he woke up.

She felt as though a wild animal were living inside Mark and slowly taking over his soul. He was turning into someone she didn't know anymore. Sometimes despair did that to a person—turned them sub-human, made them cease to believe in anything. What was it worth to have a soul if there was no god?

She had tried to love him out of it, but what Mark couldn't stand was how unfair it was to her. If he had been the one attacked, defeated, he could have been comforted. But he thought he should be able to defend her from evil. When he couldn't, he gave in to total despair. She saw it in his shoulders, in the way he carried himself around the farm these days. He looked as if he were carrying a hundred-pound feed sack in his arms and couldn't find a place to put it down.

If only she were feeling better herself. If only this weren't happening when she felt as though she didn't know herself anymore. If she were in better shape, she could help him with his burden. Maybe she needed to try a little harder.

His car pulled into the driveway. The sun wasn't up yet. He sat in the car for a few moments, looking like he might fall asleep.

Mark got out of the car and slammed the car door so hard that it sounded like a gong. Margaret jumped. His tantrums scared her, but his anger had never been turned on her. More often he turned it on himself. Inanimate objects received his blows. Once he had broken his hand by smashing it into a wall.

He never hurt the goats. He treated them like children. But she worried about the damage he was doing to himself. All she knew was he was a good man and she loved him. She didn't think the drinking helped him at these times.

She went to the cupboard and pulled out some flour and a big mixing bowl. Then she grabbed a carton of eggs out of the refrigerator and stirred up some pancake batter.

When he walked into the house, the griddle was hot.

"You want some pancakes?" she asked.

He nodded, showing no surprise at seeing her up. He sank into the chair he always sat in, at the head of the table.

"I'm sorry," he said, not looking at her.

"Why?" she asked.

"For doing this to you."

"Well, stop."

He lifted his head. "I wish I could."

Margaret poured in three pancakes and watched the bubbles push up in the batter. "What?"

"I can't stand it, Margaret. I've let you down. I should have made sure about the will. I should have stopped all this from happening. Patty Jo has won, and there's nothing I can do."

"And there's nothing you could have done. We didn't know how bad she was."

Margaret flipped the pancakes. Mark seemed to shrink in front of her eyes. She worried she would lose him in some way.

Mark didn't say anything. He sat staring out the window. He looked like he had been beaten up, his shoulders slumped over, his face darkened from fatigue. His attitude wore her out as much as what Patty Jo was doing to them.

She took the spatula, scooped up one of the pancakes, and, without thinking, threw it at Mark. The pancake hit him right in the face. He jumped and stared at her.

She yelled, "Stop this, Mark. You've got to stop acting so defeated. If you keep on like this, then Patty Jo will really have won."

Meg hummed a nonsense tune as she fed the pheasants. If she sat really still, the pheasants forgot she was there and would walk all around her, eating their food. She would watch them, and after a while she would turn into a pheasant, her skin growing long, colorful feathers. *Metamorphosis.* She liked that word. Long and intricate.

Rich leaned in the barn door. "Want to go get apples?"

In a nanosecond, she changed back into a girl kneeling on the floor of the barn. "Great idea." She looked at the house. "What about Mom?"

"She needs to sleep. She got in real late last night. Run and get a jacket. Leave a note for your mom telling her we'll be back for lunch."

Meg did as she was asked, then jumped into the truck next to him and they drove to the top of the bluff.

Meg loved to do errands with Rich. He was easily coerced. For example, if they drove by a Dairy Queen, he always thought a dip cone sounded like a good idea. He had the good qualities of a dad and the easiness of an indulgent uncle. Plus, she could talk to him.

She asked him the question she had been saving for such a private moment. "Rich, when did you have your first girlfriend?"

"You mean your mom?"

Why did grown-ups do that? Act as if kids couldn't stand the thought of the adults having a life before the kid existed. "No, I know better than that. I know you were married before. Seriously."

"Oh, seriously. Why didn't you say that in the first place? I remember I liked Jane Goody in third grade."

"Your first date?"

"Oh, sometime in high school. Samantha Lundgren. I think I even took her to the prom one year."

"If you liked a girl, how did you let her know?"

"What are all these questions about?"

"Don't tell Mom."

"Can't promise that, but I probably won't."

"Well, I thought this one kid liked me, but now he's treating me mean."

Rich wondered what he would think of Meg if he were twelve—too cute and too smart, probably. "That's too bad."

"Is there anything I can do?"

"Do you like him?"

Meg thought for a moment. "I like him when he's nice to me."

"That makes sense. Well, if you want to try something, you might do one clear thing to let him know you like him, that you think he's special. If that doesn't work, forget about him."

"Like what?"

"I don't know. What do you think would get the message across?"

Meg paused again, then asked, "What if I gave him a copy of my favorite CD?"

Rich grimaced. "That would be like bribing him."

"What if I paid a lot of attention to him? Like really listened to him, asked him questions?"

"That might work."

When they got to the apple orchard, they were handed a basket and told to walk out to the farthest row behind the barn. Rich carried the basket. The trees in the orchard were pruned so that the branches were close to the ground, easy to pick from. The apples glistened in the sun, and Meg imagined she could smell them, a sweet, tangy fragrance that made her want to chomp into one.

As they went past a row, Meg saw Ted's family was there. She caught a glimpse of Ted throwing an apple at his sister.

"Hey, I'll catch up with you. I see some friends," Meg told Rich.

He nodded and kept going.

Meg knew Ted's sister, Amelia. She was one grade behind them. "Hey, Amelia," she hollered out.

Amelia stopped running away from Ted and ran toward Meg. She hid behind Meg, and Ted came running up with an apple in his hand. When he saw her, he stopped and smiled, then tossed the apple at Meg. She was pleased when she caught it.

"Hey," Ted said. He looked cute. His nose was peeling and his brown hair was falling in his eyes.

Ted's mother hollered at him. "Ted, go get another basket, would you?"

"Okay."

"I'll go with you," Meg suggested.

Amelia joined them. "Me too."

Meg was disappointed, but Ted said, "No, Mealybug. You go help Mom. I don't need you tagging along."

The two of them started walking back toward the big red barn. "What're you up to?" Meg asked.

"Oh, you know, not much."

"Yeah."

"I went out hunting this morning."

Meg didn't like that Ted hunted, but she knew it was an important part of his life. His dad took him deer hunting in the fall, and he talked about it a lot.

"What were you hunting?"

"Not much is in season. I got a squirrel."

"You shot a little squirrel?"

"Not so little. He weighed about a pound."

Meg tried to refrain from saying anything else negative, but it was a trial. She decided to ask him a question. "What's the biggest thing you ever shot?"

He turned and stared at her as though she were trying to trick him. "Why're you asking?"

"Just interested."

"You really want to know?"

She nodded her head and prepared herself. She already felt sorry for the poor deer.

"Well, I wasn't ever going to tell you, but you asked. It was an accident. I was scared." He pressed his lips together, then said, "I shot that elk."

Meg stopped in her tracks. Ted told her that the elk had come at him in the woods and he had been scared and shot at it, but she could hardly listen.

She thought of Harvey and knew she couldn't say anything to Ted that wouldn't be mean. She turned around and ran down the rows of apple trees.

CHAPTER 20

The quietness of the house struck Claire when she awoke. Ten o'clock. She hadn't slept that late in years. Five hours of sleep would have to do. She had a busy day ahead of her.

As she pulled on her uniform, she remembered what she had done, standing in front of Patty Jo Tilde and screaming at her. Good thing the sheriff had been there to stop her from doing anything more.

Claire sank down on the floor, the anger pumping through her all over again. She couldn't stand the thought of anyone hurting her family. She had to get this woman safely behind bars for a good long while. Four counts of arson might do it.

A distant train clattered along the track heading up to the Twin Cities. Other than that she could hear no noise. No one else was home. She rarely had the house to herself. Claire wished she could stay and enjoy it, but she needed to get moving, even if it was Saturday. She could take a day off next week. She wanted to search Patty Jo Tilde's house before the woman was released from jail.

Claire stumbled into the kitchen and found a note on the table from Meg that read: *Went to get apples. Be back shortly. Kisses, Meg.*

Claire smiled. Apples and her sweet daughter. She looked over at the coffeemaker and saw that Rich had left her a couple of cups of coffee. Better and better. Then she saw the sack sitting next to her favorite mug and knew that he had also left her some pastry from the bakery.

She poured coffee into her mug, grabbed the pastry and the cordless phone, and went out onto the front steps to call Dr. Wegman.

He answered it on the first ring. "I'm cruising at seventy miles an hour down the freeway. What can I do for you?" His cell phone crackled and cut in and out as they talked.

"We're going to try to get into Patty Jo's house today. Thought you might like to be part of the team. We caught her lighting candles around my old house last night. And it wasn't for a prayer meeting."

"What time?"

"I'm hoping by midafternoon. The sheriff's tracking down a judge. Anything I need to remember to put in the search warrant?"

"Be as broad and vague as you dare. Be sure to include phrases like 'ignition materials,' 'fire paraphernalia,' and—why not—'combustibles.' "

Claire wrote the phrases down on her notebook. "Got it. This warrant will be a work of art."

"I'm playing eighteen holes, but I'll keep my cell phone on. Where should I meet you?"

She told him the Tilde farm.

"Do you have her in custody?"

"Yes, but she's not talking. Or rather, she's claiming it was just a coincidence that she was at my house at midnight when a fire started."

"So she's a nut job. Arsonists usually are. With some luck she won't need to confess to anything. I'm expecting the whole story to be in her house. You just have to know how to read it."

Meg was not happy to see her mom dressed in her deputy sheriff's uniform. Working again today. Meg had been counting on spending some time with her mother that afternoon.

"Apples!" her mother said in a pleased voice.

"What's with you?" Meg asked. She wanted to prick her mother, jab her, make her feel the same disappointment Meg did.

"Maybe I'll make an apple pie," her mother suggested.

Rich handed her a bag of apples. "Be my guest."

"When?" Meg asked, not believing her for a moment. Oh, sure, she believed that her mom wanted to make a pie, but not that she would ever get around to doing it. "When are you going to have time to do that? You're going to work today, aren't you?"

"Yes, but it won't take long. I'll be back long before supper. You want to help me make the pie?"

Meg didn't want to count on her mother. No promises. "We'll see. My last pie was a disaster."

Meg recalled the pumpkin pie she had made for Thanksgiving. It had looked glorious. But she had inadvertently confused the sugar and salt, and it had tasted like crap—a bitter blow for a budding baker.

"Have we got enough butter?" her mother asked Rich.

Rich nodded. "We're good on butter."

"I'm off to work. Trying to get a search warrant for Patty Jo's. Looking forward to tearing her house apart."

"Do you have to clean up your mess?" Meg asked. She had a lot of curiosity about certain aspects of her mother's job.

"What do you mean?"

"When you search someone's house? Do you clean up?"

"No. We're usually careful. We don't make that big a mess. In Minneapolis, narcotics occasionally trashed a place—ripping open pillows and slashing couches looking for drugs. But we don't destroy anything. We just look through everything. Sometimes, if we're lucky, the people even tell us where to look."

"Hey, we got news for you." Rich grabbed Claire by the shoulders. "We might have figured out part of the mystery of Harvey. Tell her, Meg."

"Only if you promise that my friend won't get in trouble. He didn't mean to do it. He was afraid."

Her mother said, "Meg, I'll try to protect him, but I need to know what happened."

"When we were at the apple orchard today we ran into this kid from my class, Ted. He told me he shot Harvey. But it was an accident."

Her mother thought for a moment. "An accident? What happened?"

"Well, he was out hunting. He hunts squirrels. It's legal, Mom. He told me. Anyway, all of a sudden he saw this elk. But he didn't know what it was. He was scared, so I guess he shot it."

"Ted shot the elk. But he wasn't near the farm, right?"

"I don't think so."

"So who cut the fence?"

Rich said, "Maybe someone cut the fence to let the elk out and then Harvey got shot later. Maybe the two events aren't related."

"That's what it could have been," Meg chimed in.

"And with the info that Meg gave me, I don't think it could be Patty Jo." Her mom's voice darkened. "Much as I'd like to blame her for everything bad that ever happened."

Meg was glad she had done something to help, but she wasn't clear what it was exactly. "Why's that, Mom?"

"Well, you said Patty Jo asked you where the elk farm was. She wouldn't have needed to if she had already been there to cut the fence."

"So who cut the fence?" Rich asked.

Claire climbed into the squad car. "Good question."

Staring through the hole, Claire could see Patty Jo sitting in the corner of her cell on the edge of her cot. They had given her a private cell. The orange jumpsuit she was wearing hung on her. She had rolled up the sleeves and the legs. Orange was not one of her best colors. It made her skin look sallow.

Claire waved the signed search warrant in front of the window to get Patty Jo's attention. Then she spoke through the slit in the door. "Patty Jo. We're going to your house."

Patty Jo turned and looked at Claire. "What?"

"We're going to search your house. I'd like the key to your house. Is it in your purse?"

Patty Jo stood and walked up to the door, then peered through the peephole. "Do I have a choice?"

"Not really." Claire could see Patty Jo think about it. Most people would hand over the key, but Claire couldn't tell with this strange woman.

After a moment, Patty Jo told her the key chain was in her purse, being held by the bursar.

Claire brought her the keys, and Patty Jo showed her which one was the house key.

"Anything you want to say today?" Claire asked. "Before we go into your house? We are specifically looking for the materials you used to start the fire. If you tell me where they are, we won't have to dig up your whole house."

"I didn't do it."

"Do you believe yourself when you say that? Have you said it so many times now that you've persuaded yourself?" Claire knew she shouldn't bother talking to her anymore, but she was curious.

"You think you know me, but you don't," Patty Jo said.

"No, I don't think I know you at all. That's why I'm asking."

"You can prove nothing."

"That will change soon."

Patty Jo looked at her and snorted. "You won't find anything."

Claire felt her heart sink. The woman was as good as admitting she had done the deed, and also saying she knew enough not to leave a trace. Claire hoped to prove her wrong.

When Claire drove up to the Tilde farm, the Citroën was parked in the driveway. She was surprised that Dr. Wegman had beaten her to the scene. She wondered when Doc started charging the client: from when he left the golf course, from when he arrived at the scene, or from when he started working? Maybe she should think about retiring and going into private practice. Perhaps when Meg graduated from college in ten more years.

The Citroën was empty. She guessed Doc had gone into the barn. Burned-out buildings drew him like a moth to a flame. She was glad she had included the barn in the search warrant. A matter of similar crimes, she had explained to the judge.

The sheriff had asked if she wanted to take anyone else with her to search the house. Usually they would have four or five deputies do a search, but she knew that more hands would not make this task easier. For the most part, she was going to give Doc his head and just follow him, especially in the barn. He was the master at the art of arson investigation. She knew she would learn something.

Claire peeked into the remains of what was left of the barn. The charred beams were still holding up a few sections of the wall, but it did look like a good gust of wind would topple the whole fragile structure. Dr. Wegman was crouched in the far corner, stirring through the ashes.

Without turning his head, he said, "It started here."

Claire hesitantly took a couple steps into the open area of the barn. "How can you tell?"

"Work backward. The fire spread out from here. I can see the way it moved through the barn." He stood up and waved his arms to show her where to look. "Up and out. Whatever caused it to combust began at this point."

Claire covered her mouth and tried to breathe into her hand. The dust from the stirred-up ashes was getting to her. "Do you want to keep looking here, or would you like to start in the house?"

"Why don't you go to the house and open it up and do a walk-through? See if anything jumps out at you. You might see something I won't notice. This is a woman we're talking about."

"You sure you don't need me here?"

He turned and looked at her. "I know you don't want to be in this barn."

"I don't mind."

"Liar." He waved her away. "I'll join you in a few minutes."

Claire turned and left the barn thankfully. Even the smell got to her. Once, in Minneapolis, she had had to help sift through a house where three people died. Only their bones remained. She had had nightmares for months afterward. The smell in the barn brought that back vividly.

Claire went to the house and stood on the porch, looking around. Patty Jo Tilde had left this house last night not knowing she wouldn't be coming back. So Claire would walk into a house that was not prepared for her visit. Better and better. She would get much more of a sense of who this woman was. Claire put on her gloves.

She fitted the key into the lock and turned. The door opened easily, and she walked into a small entryway that led into the living room and then to the dining room.

The house had probably been built in the twenties or thirties. It had a bungalow feel to it, even though it was two stories tall. The house smelled stale, as if it had been shut up for a long time. There was a scrambled feeling to it. Boxes everywhere. As Claire looked around, she realized the furniture still was where they had put it when they moved things back into the house after the auction.

Patty Jo Tilde wasn't really living here anymore; she was perching, ready to take flight at any moment. She was on her way out the door. Claire was glad they had caught her before she ran.

The kitchen was the only room downstairs with any semblance of organization. Claire decided to take a look upstairs before she started to look for specific items on her warrant.

She climbed the stairs and found four bedrooms and one bathroom all off a central hallway. None of the bedrooms was large. One was filled with boxes from the auction. One had a bed but no bedclothes. The other small bedroom to the front of the house must be the one that Patty Jo was using. The sheets had been pulled up, but the bed wasn't dressed. A book was next to the bed, a Harlequin romance with a bear of a man on the cover hugging a blond woman. The room was neither tidy nor messy. It just looked lived-in but clean.

The larger bedroom with a double bed in it did not look as if it had been used recently, but the bed was made with a chenille bedspread. Claire guessed that had been Walter and Patty Jo's bedroom when he was still alive. What did it mean that she didn't sleep there anymore? Guilty conscience? Not really proof of anything. Women who had loved their husbands and mourned their passing often didn't sleep in their conjugal bedroom after the death of their spouse.

Claire walked to the window of the large bedroom and looked out over the land. From this vantage point, she could see the decomposing soybeans, left to rot in the field. No wonder Edwin was irked. More than the neglected bedroom, the rotted crop showed the contempt Patty Jo held for her husband. Still not evidence to bring to a jury.

Claire unlatched the window and opened it. A soft cool breeze filled the room, lifting the curtains. This whole place needed to be aired out. It was time to see what she could find.

The first place to look for candles, matches, and any accelerants was the kitchen. Claire walked down the stairs and scanned the kitchen. Pretty makeshift. Patty Jo had moved most everything out and hadn't really put much back into its proper place. She had not settled again. Claire opened cupboards and found most of them bare. A few canned goods on a shelf in the pantry, a bag of flour, canned tomatoes. In the sink, a coffee cup with a pool of the dark brew in the bottom and a plate with bread crumbs on it. A snack before Patty Jo went out to start her last fire?

Claire looked in all the logical places: under the sink, in the bottom of the pantry, in all the drawers. She found no matches, no candles. Then she went to the dining room. An oak built-in sideboard with glass-paned doors filled up one wall. Claire methodically went through the whole piece and found only one drawer of interest. Old Christmas candles, red and green, still stuck in Santa Claus candlesticks. She bagged them even though she knew they didn't match the candle they had found at the last arson scene. That candle had been white. There were no white candles to be found.

Doc walked in the front door. She held up the bagged candles. "This is it so far."

"Don't think they're a match."

"You know, if she bought white candles down at the Cenex and we found them here, wouldn't they be a match for most of the candles in the county?"

"Good point." He looked around the house. "Moving?"

"I told you about the auction."

"Oh, yeah. Why don't you keep at it in here? I'm going to go check out the garage. The usual spot to keep most accelerants."

Claire decided to scour the upstairs. She went through every bedroom. In the master bedroom side table she found an old tube of K-Y jelly. *Good for them,* she thought. At least the old guy got something out of her. She bagged a pack of matches she found wedged under a chest of drawers as a shim, but wondered if they were too old to even light anymore.

She finished off the living room, then decided it was time to go down in the basement. She had always hated basements—some primordial feeling left over from dungeons, she imagined. This was a particularly damp and creepy basement. After stumbling around in the dank rooms with a dirt floor, flailing at old crystalline spiderwebs, she found calcified bar bait, poison left out for mice. *Nothing that had been down in this damp basement longer than a day or two would ever burn,* she thought as she climbed back up the rickety stairs.

Wegman and she converged on the porch and both sat down to go over their loot.

"Nice porch," Doc said.

"I wish we had a beer," she said.

"Sounds good. We've got diddly here."

They both looked at the pile of bagged items: stubs of red and green candles, old matches, a can of kerosene from the garage, and various burned items from the barn. Not much to go on.

"I'ver never liked arson investigations," Claire confessed. "Too tedious."

Doc nodded. "That's what I like about them. You need to be tenacious. What I really love is finding these timers some arsonists use. Guys often create these elaborate timers to start fires. Then, when the fire is done, we can dig through the ashes and find them. They prove that the fire was deliberate and often give us a clue as to who started it. But a candle gives us nothing. They don't last through a fire. Even if they do, they don't prove it was deliberate, and they give us no clue as to who started it."

"I said I didn't like arson."

"The problem is that our perp is a lady. Women have more common sense than men. They keep it simple."

CHAPTER 21

"It doesn't matter how much of a feeling you have about this, Claire. You know that." The district attorney, Mary Ann Jacobs, was even more rumpled than usual. She was wearing a suit that looked as if it had spent the night on the floor of a damp closet. Claire wanted to reach out and dust it off. A few white threads clung to the shoulders, but she resisted.

"I can't believe we can pin only one of these fires on her."

"Let's hope we can even pin that one on her. Patty Jo Tilde has no record. She's sixty years old. Who's going to believe she started these fires? I don't have a good feeling about this." She motioned Claire to follow her. They started walking from the sheriff's department to the county courtroom, which was down the hall and up a floor.

"What judge do we have?" Claire asked.

"Leonards."

Claire felt her heart sink. "He wouldn't make a serial killer post bail."

"He believes in keeping people in the community. He thinks we are still the Pepin County of fifty years ago."

Claire lowered her voice. The hall was empty, but you never knew who might come out of a door. Wouldn't do her any good to get in bad with one of the judges. "Which was when he should have retired."

"Can't make him." Jacobs stopped and turned to Claire. "If only we had a witness to place her there. What about your sister?"

"Bridget didn't see anything. She called us because she saw a car parked down the street, but she stayed with her daughter. I told her not to go investigate. She was scared to death."

"I bet. And neither you nor Rich really saw anything."

"When we found Patty Jo, she didn't have anything in her hands, but we found the matches about fifteen feet from her. The candle had burned down fairly far and we found no fingerprints on it. Maybe she held it with the rags. She wasn't wearing gloves. How much more evidence do we need?"

"No fingerprints on the matches."

"Not anything they can distinguish."

"Patty Jo Tilde is sticking to her story. She was coming home from the casino, drove by your house, not even knowing it was yours, and saw the fire."

"Then why did she run away?"

"She said she saw you and got scared that you would blame it on her."

"What a bunch of marlarkey."

Jacobs laughed. "I haven't heard that word since my grandfather died."

They reached the courtroom door. Claire nodded to let the district attorney enter first.

"Do the best you can," Claire whispered.

Fifteen minutes later, Patty Jo Tilde was out on a signature bond. The judge saw her neither as a threat to the community nor as a flight risk. Claire had her say, but the judge bent his head and examined his robe as she was talking. Patty Jo had been quite personable on the stand and somehow made her unbelievable alibi sound almost plausible. An effective quaver in her voice was the topper.

After the judge's decision, Patty Jo walked out a relatively free woman. On her way, she paused to shoot a venomous look at Claire.

Claire stayed seated in the courtroom for a few moments after Patty Jo left. She did not want to run into Patty Jo again. She needed to stay calm and focused on finding more evidence against the woman. She also decided she'd better tell Rich to install motion detectors on the house, barn, and driveway. They had been talking for a while about putting them in. No better time than when an arsonist was on the loose. She did not trust Patty Jo Tilde, even if the judge thought she was harmless.

Bridget explained to the older woman why she couldn't fill the prescription her husband needed. "Your doctor didn't sign the prescription. It's against the law for me to fill it for you."

The older woman looked up over the top of glasses that were sliding down her nose. She was probably in her mid-eighties and totally befuddled. "He's in the car. I picked him up at the hospital and he needs this medication for tonight." The woman's hand shook as she reached for the incomplete prescription. "He had a bad heart attack, you know," the woman added.

Bridget wanted to walk around the counter and hug the woman, she looked so overwhelmed. She reached out and took the prescription back from the woman. "Why don't you take your husband home and get him settled? Call me in about an hour. I'll try to track your doctor down and get a verbal okay on the prescription. It should be fine," Bridget reassured the woman, trying not to look at the five other customers who were waiting in line. Tracking a doctor down after hours could be rough.

The woman looked up at Bridget. "I don't know what to do without him. We've been married fifty-three years."

"We'll get him his medications. Call me." Bridget handed her a card with the pharmacy's number on it.

"I'll call you," said the woman as she walked off.

Bridget looked down the line of customers and saw that the last one was her husband, Chuck. She was quite sure he didn't need a prescription filled. What if he was here to create a scene? What if he wanted to buy some condoms from her? She stepped away from the counter long enough to place a page in to the doctor and then took care of the next three customers.

The fourth customer was a teenage girl with a yeast infection. The girl was so embarassed that she was whispering her questions to Bridget. Bridget had to lean close to answer her, had to tell her that it might take a day or two for the itching to stop. The girl nodded.

Bridget added quietly, "Everyone gets yeast infections."

"Really?" the girl asked.

"Absolutely. Just part of being a woman."

That appeared to be what the girl needed to hear. She walked out, already looking better. Nice when reassuring someone could be so easy.

"Can I help you?" she asked Chuck. She was glad he was the only customer at the moment.

Chuck smiled at her. He had a way of making her feel that only she could cause him to smile like that. He looked better than when she had last seen him, better rested. "What're you doing for dinner?"

"Going home."

The doctor she had paged was on the phone. Bridget asked Chuck to give her a moment. She got the verbal okay on the prescription and went back to Chuck.

"Can we talk?" he asked softly.

Bridget looked back at the pharm tech who was working with her. She hadn't taken a break yet this afternoon; she could step outside for a few minutes. She'd rather not have a talk with Chuck in the store—who knew what might happen. He had never showed up like this before.

"Give me a minute." She told the tech that she was going to take a break, took her smock off, and grabbed her purse.

"How about a Coke at the dime store?"

"Sure." They walked down the street to the old dime store and sat at the fountain. A blond, ponytailed waitress came up with an order pad. Chuck asked for a Coke, and Bridget decided to swing out and have a root beer float. She hadn't had time for lunch.

"What's up?" She swiveled on her stool and looked at him.

Chuck leaned on the counter with both elbows and wouldn't meet her gaze. "I think we should give it another try."

"Give what another try?"

"You know," he said.

"No, I don't." If he wanted it, he could learn to say it.

"Us." He turned and looked at her. "All of us. Our family. I think we made a mistake."

"Which one?"

"What?"

"Which thing was a mistake? Getting married, having a baby, or splitting up?"

"You moving out."

"Don't you dare put the blame on me. You left the marriage long before I moved out. You were no father to Rachel."

The waitress put the Coke and the root beer float down in front of them. Bridget couldn't believe she had agreed to talk to Chuck. It was going nowhere. She took a sip of her float. Such a nice combination, the snappiness of the pop and the smoothness of the ice cream.

He didn't flare back at her. Instead he said quite calmly, "I'm not trying to blame anyone."

"What do you want to do?"

"I'd like to take you out. You and Rachel. Maybe go up to the Mall of America or the zoo or something that families do."

"I don't get it. What are you up to?"

Chuck stirred his Coke. "Nothing. I'm not smart enough for that. I just know what I want."

"That's the smartest thing in the world—to know what you want. Most people never figure that out."

He turned to her. "Do you know?"

She had pondered that question every night, alone in bed. "Not anymore."

* * *

Patty Jo had never thought she would be glad to be back at the Tilde farm, but she was. She left her car parked right in front of the house. All she wanted was a bath. Something to eat. Maybe a beer. Then she was going to bed. She hadn't slept at all last night. The jail cell was cold and the light down the hall never went out.

The house was cold. She hadn't set the furnace yet. She walked over and turned it on. The noise of it kicking on rose from the basement. It would take a while for the house to warm up. She walked upstairs and started her bath running.

All in all, she felt good about what had happened. When the deputy had caught her by her car, she'd thought it was all over for her. Luckily she had dropped the matches. That made it as if she hadn't done it. All she needed to do was stick to her guns. Tell her story again and again. Keep it simple. Just happened to be driving by. Stopped on impulse. The fire was already started.

Patty Jo made a peanut butter sandwich after finding an old jar left in the fridge. She fried the sandwich in butter and poured herself a glass of beer to have with it.

Patty Jo knew the court date for the will was coming right up. She didn't think there was any way they would take away what was rightfully hers. But it had happened to her before.

Patty Jo thought of that deputy going to talk to her sister, Debby. How had that happened? What had Debby told her?

When she had been an only child, her parents had given her everything. And then the new baby came. She was supplanted. After that she was never good enough, always second best to her little sister. She remembered her mother telling her, "You're special. We chose you to come and live with us." Then why did Debby get everything that Patty Jo had ever wanted—all their love?

Patty Jo left the sandwich crust on the plate and pushed it away but finished the beer.

When she was done, she went to her special drawer and pulled out her pack of cigarettes. After a meal had always been her favorite time to smoke. But she couldn't find any matches. She knew she had left some with her cigarettes. The cops must have taken them. Damn! How awful to think they had been all through the house. What else would she find missing?

Patty Jo turned on the gas burner on the stove and rolled the tip of her cigarette around in it until it glowed red. She wasn't going outside this time. She was sitting right at the table and smoking in the house. She had thought of taking up smoking again but decided that persuading her to quit was one of the good things Walter had done for her. She knew it was better for her, she'd live longer, and she was ready to enjoy her new life.

Margaret, Debby. They could have their stinky little lives. She was going to move on to bigger and better things. But there was one person she needed to take care of before she left.

CHAPTER 22

Clouds were stuffed into a dreary, lumpy sky. Margaret stared out the car window while Mark drove her to Durand. They weren't talking.

She looked down at her dress, a printed cotton shift. She had put on a sweater over it. That way, if she had a hot flash, she could pull the sweater off. Her purse sat in her lap with her hands folded over it. Her lips, she could tell, were drawn into a tight line. She was nervous and tired. She wanted to be at home milking the goats, anything rather than on her way to Durand.

She didn't understand why they couldn't just tell her the verdict over the phone, but her lawyer said she had to come down to the courthouse. He claimed she had to be there to sign some papers. She hadn't really wanted Mark to go with her, but she hated to go by herself. In the end, she had agreed to him coming along. She was worried that he would get so angry again. Who knew what he might do?

Mark had turned into someone she didn't know. Maybe menopause was catching. Maybe Mark was so deeply linked to her that he was going through it too. What scared her the most was that she found herself contemplating horrible things to do to Patty Jo if the older woman won the case. And if her mind was going in that direction, she hated to imagine what Mark was thinking of.

They drove into Durand and turned up the hill to go to the county government center. Although she had visited the Farm Bureau there, she had never gone to the courtrooms or sheriff's department.

Walking into the courtroom, she was reminded of a small chapel. All the seats were wooden benches like pews in a church. The desk the judge sat behind was like an altar and his chair like the throne of a priest. To continue the religious theme then, Patty Jo was the penitent. But, of course, she wasn't penitent. She looked bored, like she had no reason to be there.

The clerk of the court called their case. Margaret kept having visions of this as a religious ceremony; she saw the clerk as the acolyte announcing the readings. The judge looked up and said he had reviewed everything. With his flowing dark robes, he was like a pastor. She was afraid of his sermon.

He called Patty Jo and Margaret up to stand before him. Margaret had a bad feeling. He was an older judge.

"I'd like to ask you some questions," he said to Margaret, his eyes on her.

His stare convinced Margaret that things were not going to go her way. In his voice was a reprimand. He was going to teach her a lesson.

"You were told of the changes in your father's new will?"

"Yes, after he died. I didn't know he had changed it before then."

"Your father died of a stroke. Is that right?"

"Yes, your honor."

"At the time of this will, he was of sound mind?"

"The will is dated before his first stroke, so yes, he was."

"This will was legally drawn up?"

"I don't know. I assume it was."

"So I don't understand what we're doing here. Why have you questioned your father's will?"

Margaret thought of not answering his question. She didn't think he really wanted to know why. But then she decided to have her say. She had already lost, she knew, but maybe saying it out loud in a court of law would make her feel better.

"My father loved me. I know that for a fact. I am his only child. We were very close. He always told me I would get his farm. He told Mark, my husband, that we would get it. We had planned on it for years. Mark called it our social security, our IRA. My dad never told me he had changed his will. My relationship with my father was always good until Patty Jo came along."

Margaret tried to think how much she could say. Her suspicions might get her in trouble. "I think Patty Jo had some kind of hold over my father. She kept him away from me, not even letting him come and have dinner with us anymore. I wouldn't put anything past her. Don't get me wrong—I expected my father to leave Patty Jo something in his will. But I can't believe he didn't leave me the farm."

Margaret's voice started to crack. She was on the verge of tears, but she kept talking. "Don't you see? She doesn't even want the farm. She's left the crops to rot in the fields. My father would have hated that. She's just going to sell it. She's a horrible woman. She doesn't deserve to have the farm."

The judge sat with his head dropped, his chin doubling up underneath. Margaret wondered if he had dozed off. Then he lifted his head. After a moment of consideration, he said, "The law is not about determining who most deserves the farm. It's about determining who has inherited the farm. And I'm afraid that seems very clear in this case. If you could bring to the court any evidence that your father was coerced into changing his will, I would entertain this petition, but as it stands, I feel you have wasted all of our time."

He turned to Patty Jo. "I'm sorry that this has held you up. I do find the will valid, and you are assigned as executor and claimant of the estate of Walter Tilde."

Margaret couldn't help saying one last thing. "My father loved me."

Patty Jo turned to Margaret for the first time since entering the courtroom. She said, "He loved me more."

* * *

The dwarf Nigerian baby goat Claire was holding in her arms was about the size of a cat. She had stopped by the Underwoods' to pick up more of their feta cheese and to see how Margaret was doing after the court decision went against her. Claire ended up holding a three-day-old baby goat, a bundle of legs wrapped in coarse black and white fur.

The baby goat was an accident, Margaret explained. "They're not supposed to be born in the fall. The stud goat got out of its enclosure and impregnated the nanny out of season.

"This has never happened to us before. The mother goat isn't being very motherly, and I'm stuck bottle-feeding this little one. With winter coming on, I'll have to keep it in the house with us. The timing is bad."

Claire stroked the wiry hair of the small animal and felt herself falling in love. It snuggled into the crook of her arm, nosing its way in until its head was hidden. Then it fell asleep.

"I'm sorry about the will," Claire said, watching Margaret.

The woman never seemed to sit still. Whenever Claire was at her house, Margaret was working on something: dinner, dishes, darning. At the moment she was canning, putting up a few more quarts of spiced apples. It was one of the many activities Claire had sworn she would learn when she moved to Fort St. Antoine, but she never seemed to have the time.

Margaret leaned against the stove and pushed her hair out of her face with her forearm. "I'm glad it's over. I don't want to think about it anymore."

"We can't prove Patty Jo started your fire."

"I know. I've accepted that too. She'll sell the farm and leave. We'll be done with her. She's destroyed my family and I hate her for it, but she'll be gone and I'll still have my own good life."

Claire couldn't believe what she found herself saying next. "I hate her too. She's the most evil woman I've ever met."

Margaret closed her eyes and then, after a long moment, opened them with relief. "Oh, God, thank you for saying that. It helps to not feel so alone in all this. She *is* evil, isn't she? There's no other way to put it."

Margaret walked over to the table and sank down into a chair. "I think she had this all planned out from the moment she met my parents. She saw my mom was getting sick with Alzheimer's and figured she wouldn't be long in the picture, and then she married my dad, who she knew wasn't in good health either. She knew he was a wealthy farmer. She wanted it all for herself. And she got it."

"I'm so sorry."

"I don't know how you fight evil like that. All I can think is that you live your own life the best you can. Who would want Patty Jo's life? Who would want to be her? Isn't that it's own best punishment?"

"It might be, but since she doesn't have a conscience, she never feels guilty about what she's done."

"No, but she's mired in her own yuck."

"Who's mired?" Mark walked in.

Claire didn't think Mark looked good: bloodshot eyes, hair overgrown, dark look on his face.

"Patty Jo. We're talking about how evil she is," Margaret explained as Mark walked over to the stove and sniffed the bubbling apples.

He spoke so loudly he nearly growled. "Evil? I don't know about that. She thinks none of the laws we live by apply to her. She should be wiped off the face of the earth."

The baby goat lifted its head up at the sound of the raised voice. Claire stroked the coarse hair on its nose.

"Mark," Margaret said, disapproval in her voice.

Mark wiped his face. "I'm sorry. But she's a menace. Someone needs to do something about her."

When Claire walked into Lakeview Manor she found Beatrice sitting on a bench by the front door.

"Good to see you up and about," Claire said.

Beatrice turned her head slowly and looked up at Claire with a bit of disdain. "Don't do that to me, Claire. Don't talk to me like I'm a child."

Claire was amazed how much Beatrice's verbal abilities had improved since she'd come to the nursing home. The sharp tongue she was known for had returned.

She sat on the bench beside Beatrice. Might as well get on her level. "Sorry. I didn't mean to talk to you like a child. I *am* glad you are up and about."

"They make me."

"Don't you want to get up?"

"Not always. You know, when I lived on my own, sometimes I stayed in bed for part of the morning, just thinking and reading. I enjoyed it."

Claire had moments when she really liked the old woman. She wished those moments would last longer. "That does sound nice."

"Why are you here?"

"Well, I wanted to see if you had given the invitation to go to Edwin and Ella's wedding some thought."

"I don't know these people."

Claire bit her tongue for a moment. Beatrice had lived in Fort St. Antoine for over forty years before moving to Rochester ten years ago. "You do know them. You knew them from when you lived here."

"But not very well. Just to say hi."

"Meg would love it if you came. We would all love it."

Claire watched Beatrice think about it. Finally the older woman raised her head and said, "But I don't have anything to wear."

"Before the wedding you and I can drive over to your apartment and get you some more clothes."

Beatrice nodded. "I'd like that."

Claire spent half an hour with Beatrice, walking the halls, since it was cold outside, and then going back to her room and trying to fit a few more puzzle pieces together from the thousand-piece puzzle that Meg had brought her. It was a picture of horses, one of Meg's many favorite animals.

As they were sitting close together, working the puzzle, Patty Jo Tilde walked by. She stopped and said hello to Beatrice.

Beatrice said, "Hello, Patty Jo. Are you feeling lucky today?"

Patty Jo glanced at Claire, then said, "I'm on a roll," and walked away.

Claire stiffened. "How do you know her?"

"Oh, she plays bingo with us. A good woman. Her husband just died here recently. She took such good care of him. Visited him every day."

Claire didn't want to tell Beatrice all she knew of this "good woman," but she felt she should warn her. "I would watch her, Beatrice."

CHAPTER 23

The thermometer attached to the oak tree in the backyard read forty-five degrees. With no wind, leaves fell down like a soft golden rain in the bright sunlight. Rich suggested they walk to the bakery rather than drive. He thought some exercise would do Claire good. She hadn't slept well last night. Also, it would give them time to talk, just the two of them. They didn't get as much alone time now that they were all living together.

"I'm worried about you," he said when they were down the driveway and walking toward town.

"Is that an eagle?" Claire pointed at a large bird floating low over the road.

"No, it's a vulture," Rich said, then patiently pointed out the differences. "See the wings? They're held in a V shape, while a bald eagle's are usually out flat. The rumpled edges on the wings you see only on the vultures. And then there's the absence of a white head, although the immature eagles don't have white heads." He grabbed her hand. "I'm still worried about you."

"I'm worried about me. This woman has got me going. She's pushed all my buttons."

"Patty Jo won't try anything now. She knows you all are watching her."

"Rich, you don't know what people like her can do. Sociopaths. They are able to rationalize any behavior. Patty Jo's worse than you can imagine. Unfortunately, I've met more than my share like her. They don't believe the rules apply to them. They don't feel remorse or guilt. She would do something to your mother just to get back at me."

Rich had felt so good when they were able to get his mother into Lakeview Manor, to have her so close to him and not have to worry about her from a distance. Even after Claire told him what had happened yesterday, he didn't think there was anything to worry about. She was being watched by all the nursing staff. Probably the safest place for her to be.

"Not with everyone around."

"I suppose you're right. I just hated seeing Patty Jo talking in a friendly way with your mom. It's probably an overreaction. Plus, I don't think it would do your mother any good to have to get used to a new place. She obviously can't go home yet. I just have a bad feeling. With any luck Patty Jo will be found guilty of arson and put away for a while."

They turned up the main street and saw Edwin's old pickup truck already in front of the bakery. "Let's see how the about-to-be-weds are today."

Ella and Edwin were holding court at their usual table with most of the kaffeeklatsch gathered around. Rich was glad to see Claire's spirits rise as they joined the crowd. Ella talked about the arrangements for the wedding and the barn dance that would follow.

Claire announced, "Beatrice said she would come. She just wants to be sure she has the right outfit."

Lucas, the bookstore owner, straightened his shirt collar. "I've been spending a great deal of time thinking about what I'm going to wear too. I'm so relieved to hear black is now in style for weddings."

Ella laughed. "I expect all you men to be in full tuxedos. With cummerbunds."

Rich confessed, "I not only don't have a cummerbund, I don't know what they are."

Claire poked him. "Yes, you do. Those pleated, sashlike things that go around men's waists when they wear tuxedos."

"Oh, I thought those were corsets."

Edwin turned to Claire and said, "Hey, I hear Patty Jo tried to set your old house on fire. What's she up to?"

Rich watched as Claire set her lips. She didn't like to talk publicly about a pending case. He could tell she was struggling to find the appropriate comment. "Yes, she was caught near the scene of a crime. Another fire."

Edwin continued. "At your house? Where your sister is living? I hope you threw the book at her."

"We tried, but it didn't stick. She's a free woman at the moment. I saw her at the nursing home yesterday. It makes me nervous for Rich's mom."

"I don't like that woman," Edwin announced to the table. He asked Claire, "You think she might try something?"

"You never know."

Rich hated to see Edwin egg Claire on. She was already so worked up about Patty Jo. He decided to jump into the conversation. "But what could Patty Jo really do? How could she hurt my mother in the nursing home?"

Claire countered, "Well, women work differently than men. They tend to be more underhanded in how they kill people."

Ella leaned forward. "Like how?"

"Actually, there have been many instances of women as serial killers—nurses who euthanize their patients. They often go undetected."

"Yikes," Edwin said. "How do you know that if they're undetected?"

"Some finally trip up and their other victims are discovered. Also, women tend to use poison to kill people."

"Like Snow White and the witch with the apple."

Claire stood up as if she had just remembered something. She looked at Rich, and he could tell she was not going to be able to relax this morning and linger over coffee. "She visited Margaret's mom while she was in the nursing home too."

Rich stayed sitting. "So?"

"I think we need to go. I want to check on some things."

There would be no persuading her to wait. Rather than make a scene with her at the bakery, Rich stood up as well. "Lucas, when you figure out what you're going to wear, call me."

Lucas tipped his head. "Sure thing."

Once outside, Claire looked ready to break into a run.

Rich grabbed her arm to prevent her from dashing away. "What's up?"

"I need to find out how Margaret's mother died."

Waiting for the medical examiner to call her back, Claire remembered something from when she had been working in Minneapolis—a natural death that had turned out to be something else.

She and her partner had answered a 911 call involving a death. When they arrived at the house in Bryn Mawr, the man was dead in bed, his wife grieving beside him. She was so distraught she wasn't able to make any decisions or even call the rest of the family. The wife explained that the man had a bad heart and they had known it was only a matter of time before he died. Claire called their family doctor, and he was going to sign the death certificiate. Then the son arrived and raised a stink. Over his mother's objections, he demanded an autopsy and got it.

A day later, the medical examiner told Claire the man had been consuming arsenic on a fairly regular basis and that the poison, rather than a heart attack, was what had finished him off.

Claire remembered the doctor handing her the findings and saying,

"I can't believe he lived as long as he did. But you do develop a tolerance to arsenic."

The wife had been turned over to homicide, but Claire heard later that she pleaded guilty and was sentenced to ten years for negligent homicide. Negligent, indeed.

The phone rang and pulled her away from her memories. Dr. Lord was on the line. "Yes, Claire?"

"I know it's Saturday. . . ."

"This sounds bad already."

"Could you check on a death certificate for a Florence Tilde?"

"I remember her."

"Did you sign her death certificate?"

"Nope. Her regular doctor did. Dr. Greenvald. Do you know him?"

"I don't think so."

"Geriatrics. Works out of the hospital. Probably out on the golf course today. What's the problem? She died last winter, didn't she?"

"Did she have an autopsy?"

"No need. Nursing home. Alzheimer's. She had been going downhill for several years."

"Could she have been killed?"

Dr. Lord cleared his throat. "Well, it's always a possibility. But I wouldn't suspect she was. Why bother?"

That stopped Claire. Why bother indeed?

"How long can someone live with Alzheimer's?"

"That depends on the individual. A few people go quickly, within a year of diagnosis, but most can last for five to ten years."

"So Florence could have lived another few years?"

"I really couldn't say, Claire. What's up?"

"I just have a suspicion. Might be all it is, but I want to check it out."

"Talk to Greenvald. He was her doctor. He could tell you more."

Two hours later, after Claire had left messages at several numbers, Greenvald finally called her back.

After she introduced herself, he asked, puzzled, "What can I do for you?"

"I'm looking into the cause of Florence Tilde's death."

He grunted. "Why?"

"Something has come up that has put it in question."

"No question in my mind. She had Alzheimer's and she died from it."

"How do people die from Alzheimer's?"

"That depends. Often just old age, something like pneumonia. With Florence, I think it was failure to thrive. She forgot to eat. She wasted away. When she died she weighed under ninety pounds. She went to sleep and didn't wake up. Probably heart failure brought on by her lungs filling up with fluid. Doesn't matter. Cause of death was Alzheimer's."

"But you couldn't say for sure."

"Ninety-nine percent."

"She could have died from suffocation or poisoning."

"Someone could have dropped her on her head too, I suppose. But that's not what happened. She was in a nursing home, for God's sake. She died. There was nothing mysterious or devious about it. And no one was unhappy. She was no longer really living."

Claire knew she wouldn't get much more from him. "Thanks for your time."

"You're welcome."

"Beatrice is playing bingo," the young nurse, Bonnie, told Claire.

Bingo? Claire thought. The poor woman must be getting desperate. Beatrice called bingo the stupid person's checkers, and she didn't think that much of checkers.

"I won't disturb her until it's over. If she knows I'm here, she might not finish the game."

Bonnie nodded.

Claire asked, "How do you think Beatrice is doing here?"

"Well, she knows what she wants. That actually helps a lot. She can get snippy, but she's never too mean. Not like some of them. She lets us know she'd rather be home, but that's understandable. I've seen a lot of progress in her. She's walking better."

"It must be nice to have someone who gets better."

"Oh, yes. So many people come here to die. They're sick when they arrive and then just go downhill. It can be discouraging to watch."

"Do you get many people with Alzheimer's here?"

"A few. They're the worst. Sometimes their behavior can get so bizarre and mean. And dangerous."

"Did you know Florence Tilde?"

"Sure. She wasn't any trouble. She was actually quite sweet. She wasn't here that long. I think she came before Christmas and was dead before Easter. I'd thought she might hang on for a while."

"Why's that?"

"Oh, I don't know. She was fully functioning. She didn't weigh much, but she walked the halls constantly. She was in remarkably good shape. Probably from all that walking. She didn't eat much, but we usually managed to get something down her every day. She liked sweets."

"I heard Patty Jo came to see her a lot."

"Yes, that was the nicest thing. They were old friends. Sometimes when people get Alzheimer's, no one comes to see them. All their old friends are too afraid, like they might get it themselves, and so they don't want to see what it's like."

"Do you know, by any chance, if Patty Jo was here the day she died?"

Bonnie shifted her weight and rolled her eyes back in her head, thinking. "I don't know. I came in the next morning. As I recall, she died on a Tuesday, and I have Tuesdays off."

"Who would have been working?"

"Well, Jolene always works Tuesdays, and she had Florence most days."

"Is she around today?"

"Yeah, I think she's calling out the bingo numbers."

Claire thanked Bonnie and walked down to the community room. She stood by the door and watched the small group of older people play bingo. She was glad to note that Patty Jo was not to be seen. Beatrice had three cards in front of her. That was one way of making the game more interesting. She also appeared to be helping the white-haired woman sitting next to her. It was a quarter to three. Claire figured she had fifteen minutes to wait. Jolene reached into the box and pulled out another number-and-letter combination. An older gentleman, one of the two men in the room, raised his long arm and waved it.

Jolene said, "Harry? What do you say?"

The old man stood up and said, "Betcha I got bingo."

Everyone clapped. Beatrice swept her three cards away. Jolene handed him a deck of cards. "Harry gets a nice deck of cards, donated by the Ellsworth Bank. They have their logo on it."

"That's my bank too," Harry said.

They started another round, the last. Beatrice won with a new card and was given a tissue-box cover. She didn't say much. Claire was relieved. Claire skirted the tables and approached Jolene as she was putting away the game.

"Jolene, I'm Claire Watkins."

"I've seen you here. You're related to Beatrice, aren't you?"

"Sort of. I'm actually here today for a different reason. I'm a deputy sheriff."

"I guessed that—you're in uniform."

"Right. Well, were you on duty the day that Florence Tilde died?"

"Yes, I was. I remember it well, because she got out of the Manor that day. She went for a little walk. But not far. I found her heading toward the lake."

"I heard she was a good walker."

"She was."

"Did Patty Jo come to visit her that day?"

Jolene thought back. "I think she did. I kinda remember her showing up after I got Florence back into her room. Patty Jo came by once or twice a week. It's hard to keep it straight."

"Did she ever bring Florence things to eat?"

"Oh, yes. We encouraged that. Florence had a sweet tooth."

"Might she have brought her something that day? Do you remember?"

"Well, I'm not sure if it was that day, but shortly before Florence died, she brought her some jelly. I think it was homemade. Crabapple or something like that."

"Jelly. Would anyone else have eaten it?"

"Oh, no. When people bring in some food for a patient, we mark it with their name and put it in the fridge."

Claire didn't dare hope. "Is there any chance that jelly might still be in the fridge?"

"I doubt it. We clean it out every few months. I could go check."

"That would be great."

Beatrice walked up as Jolene went off to look. "What're you doing here today? You already came this week."

"Just checking up on something."

"Me?"

"No. But it's nice to see you playing bingo."

"Want my prize?" Beatrice tried to give Claire the decorated tissue-box cover. It appeared to be covered with pieces of macaroni in a random pattern, then spray-painted gold.

"I wouldn't want to deprive you."

Beatrice started laughing. "I'll take it back to my room. See you later." She walked off.

Jolene came back shaking her head. "Sorry. It's not there. I seem to remember giving everything of Florence's to Margaret. I'm not sure, but I think I put the jelly with her stuff."

"Margaret might have it. I'll check with her. Please don't tell anyone about this," Claire asked Jolene.

Jolene's eyes widened. "Was something wrong with it? Do you think it had gone off?"

"It's a possibility."

Margaret was surprised to hear Claire Watkins's voice on the phone. Maybe she was calling about the goat. Claire had said something about buying it as a pet for her daughter. Margaret would love for the little goat to go to a good home.

After their initial hellos, Claire asked, "Margaret, do you still have the bag of your mother's belongings from the nursing home?"

"Not really. Why?"

"I'm checking on something. What do you mean, not really?"

"Well, I think I still have most of things that were in the bag, but I put them away."

"Was there a jar of jelly in the bag?"

Margaret couldn't figure out what the deputy wanted. Why was she asking about her mother's jelly? "Yes, I remember that."

"Where is that jar now?"

"I suppose I put it in the fridge."

"Would it still be there?"

"Let me check." Margaret set the phone down on the counter and walked over to the refrigerator. She could tell by Claire's tone of voice this was important, but she couldn't imagine why.

She looked into the fridge and didn't see the jar on the front of the shelves, so she bent over and dug in the darker recesses of the bottom shelf. Mark used peanut butter to bait traps for the mice in the house, and he would get down to the bottom of a jar and still put it back in the refrigerator. She was ashamed that she hadn't gotten around to cleaning it out since summer started. She took out two old jars of peanut butter and then found the jelly. Crabapple jelly. Neither she nor Mark cared for it—too sweet, the way her mother made it—but she hadn't been able to throw it away. She pulled it out and went back to the phone.

"It's here."

There was silence on the other end. Then Claire's voice said, "Great."

"Now are you going to tell me why this is important?"

"Yes, I'll be right over to explain. Set it on the counter and don't touch it. And, for God's sake, please don't eat any of it before I get there."

CHAPTER 24

Rat poison," Dale Peters, a lab tech from the Wisconsin Crime Bureau, told her over the phone.

"In the jelly? What does that do?"

"Poisons rats."

"What else?"

"The main ingredient is warfarin, the drug in Coumadin. You've heard of that?"

"A blood thinner, isn't it?"

"Yes. And when used in large enough doses, it might cause a hemorrhage. Makes people bleed out. Or animals—the rats eat the poison and go back to their holes and then slowly die of internal bleeding."

"Oh." Then Claire asked the important question. "Could this kill someone?"

"Absolutely. Fairly painlessly and without much of a sign. It might just look like they had a stroke."

Claire remembered searching the basement at the Tilde farm. There had been old, moldy mounds of bar bait around the floor. However, Patty Jo hadn't been living there when she might have poisoned Florence. At least, she didn't think Patty Jo had been living there. She should check with Margaret.

"Thanks."

"Did someone kill someone?" Dale asked.

"I think so. Now, I've got to prove it."

"Oh, the other thing you should be aware of is that the poison is only in the top portion of the jelly. In other words, it wasn't cooked into the product. It was added afterward."

"That's important to know. Thanks again."

"Good luck."

When Claire got off the phone, she called the district attorney's office. She'd need another search warrant. Mary Ann Jacobs wasn't there, so she left a message. Then she called her sister, Bridget.

"Rat poison," Claire said without a preamble.

"Give me a sec. I'm feeding Rachel. I need to get the cordless phone." Bridget was gone a minute than came back on the line. "Yeah, warfarin. What do you want to know?"

"Tell me everything."

"What's happened?"

"I think someone was poisoned with it."

"Rachel's decided puréed carrots aren't her favorite food." Claire could hear Bridget talking to Rachel, then she was back. "Poisoned. You mean like killed? Someone was killed with rat poison?"

"I think so. What can you tell me?"

"More than you want to know."

"You're an expert on rat poison?"

"I did my residency at the poison control center, remember? I had to read a lot about warfarin. You'd be interested to know where the name warfarin comes from—from our very own state. They discovered it when cows were dying from internal hemorrhages from eating newly mown hay that had been made into silage during a really hot summer. The silage was loaded with coumarin. This is about eighty years ago. So the Wisconsin Alumni Research Foundation sponsored the research. They took the first four letters to name the drug warfarin. Now it's one of the most common drugs prescribed. It's used to dissolve blood clots and for heart trouble."

"An easy poison, because it's so available."

"Yes. The other thing that would make it a good choice to poison someone is that it doesn't happen very fast. So you could give the poison and be long gone before they would die from it."

"How much would need to be administered?"

"I can't tell you the exact amounts off the top of my head, but I don't think it takes that much. I heard a story when I was at poison control of a woman who had to put out rat poison every week. Just from touching the bar bait, she absorbed enough through the skin to have a brain hemorrhage."

"The victim, in this case, was an older woman suffering from Alzheimer's. No one even suspected."

"How did you figure it out?"

Claire briefly filled Bridget in on Patty Jo Tilde's story.

"So you have the jelly? Is that enough proof?"

"I'd like to be able to link it with something in her house. I hope to get in to search the house today."

"Just in case you need to know, the antidote to warfarin is vitamin K."

"Thanks. How's everything?"

There was a pause, and then Bridget said, "Rachel and I are going out to eat with Chuck tonight."

"Is that good?"

"I think so."

"Then I'm glad. I'll talk to you later."

When Claire got off the phone with Bridget, she called Margaret. She didn't want to tell Margaret what she was looking into yet. No need to get her hopes up until Claire was more sure.

They exchanged pleasantries and then Claire said, "There's no easy way to ask this, but was your father living with Patty Jo before your mother died?"

Claire could almost hear Margaret squirm on the other end of the line. "I'm afraid so. She moved in about two months after Mother moved out. Dad said it was just to help Patty Jo out. He said he had all this room, she might as well save on rent. Who was I to argue? People have housekeepers."

"So when your mother died, Patty Jo was living with your father?"

"Yes, she was."

Claire had barely hung up the phone before it rang again. The district attorney was on the line. Claire told her she needed another search warrant for the Tildes' house.

"What are you looking for this time?"

"Jelly."

"That's all?"

"And rat poison."

When Claire and another deputy, Bill Peterson, drove up to Patty Jo Tilde's house, a Lexus SUV was parked in front of the house. Patty Jo's car was nowhere to be seen. Claire wondered if she had bought a new car.

"Who's here?" Bill asked. The two other deputies pulled up behind Claire's squad car. She had brought a bigger crew with her this time. She wanted to be thorough.

"Can't tell you that. But it's not Margaret or Mark. I don't recognize the car."

"I thought you had most everyone's car in the county down pat," Bill teased her. When she first moved down to Fort St. Antoine, Claire made a game out of memorizing all the vehicles, trying to catch up to the knowledge of the deputies who had grown up in the county.

Claire took a deep breath and stepped out of the car. A tall man she didn't recognize was standing in the porch, watching them.

Claire walked up the front steps, followed by three deputies. The man turned to look at them. His mouth stayed open while no words came out. He wasn't bad-looking—late forties, face a little too red, dressed in nice clothes.

Finally he asked, "Can I help you?"

"We're here to search the house."

He looked even more confused and shook his head. "We're not showing it yet. It's not really on the market."

Claire pulled out the search warrant. "We have a search warrant."

"I know nothing about that."

"I wouldn't expect you to. You don't have to leave, but we'll ask you to stay outside while we search the house. Is Patty Jo here?"

"No, she said she had someone to see. I expect her back shortly. I'm Sam Dante," he said, and handed her a card.

Edina Realty. Claire should have known. "She's not wasting any time," Claire said under her breath.

"She's got a nice piece of property here. I have told her she should get the field plowed under before we put it on the market. Those weeds look so messy."

"Good idea. If you'll excuse us, we have work to do."

"What are you looking for?" he asked.

Claire thought for a second. "Skeletons in the closet."

"Oh," he said, and walked down the steps and out to his car.

Claire turned to the last deputy. "Clark, would you stay out here and keep an eye on that guy?"

The house hadn't changed since the last time Claire had been there. That was good. It would have been a shame if Patty Jo had done any cleaning or thrown anything away.

She walked through the living room into the kitchen, still being trailed by two deputies. They all put on their gloves. "Bill, why don't you head downstairs? I know there's some old decomposing piles of bar bait down there. I saw them last time I was here. Bag at least a couple of them. See if you can find any unopened ones.

"Jim, you stay with me. We need to find some jelly." Claire had gone through the kitchen and thought she remembered some jars in the back corner of the pantry. She started pulling out jars from the second shelf: rhubarb jam, raspberry jam, gooseberry jam. The jars looked old, and Claire guessed they predated Patty Jo's residence at the

Tilde farm. Florence had made more jam than she and her husband could eat.

Claire pulled out twelve jars, but there was no crabapple jelly. The jars were a mishmash of used containers, none of them matching the one she had taken from the nursing home.

"Not a match," she said to Jim as she lined up the jars on the kitchen counter, feeling keen disappointment.

Maybe the handwriting would match. She knew a good handwriting analyst. They could prove something with all these jars. The labels appeared to be the same, but they were generic canning labels, probably used by most of the women in the area, and she didn't think they would prove much.

Jim opened the refrigerator and stuck his head in. "Let's keep looking."

Claire went back to the pantry and made a thorough search of every shelf. Nothing else, except a few cans of tomatoes and a small black plastic container of ant poison.

"I found a half-opened jar of something here," Jim said from the depths of the refrigerator.

Claire looked over.

He held out a glass jar. "Crabapple jelly," he said with a big smile on his face. "Always been my favorite."

"Great." Claire straightened up and felt a shiver of relief go through her. They would get Patty Jo. They would nail her to the wall. The jelly would link her to Florence's death even if it had no poison in it. In fact, Claire assumed it was not poisoned, since it had been sitting in Patty Jo's fridge. But it would still be enough.

How had Patty Jo mixed the warfarin in the jelly? Claire was having trouble seeing her grind up the bar bait. It would be hard to get that granular mess in the jelly. Then she remembered what Rich had told her about warfarin. He said that many of the farmers used a concentrate that they mixed with grain and scattered in the barns for the rats.

Claire could feel Jim watching her. "I want to look a little longer."

She started back through all the cupboards. Since Patty Jo did all the cooking, she wouldn't have had to worry about Walter finding the warfarin, but where might she hide it so he wouldn't stumble across it. Claire was looking through the baking shelf, which held flour and sugar and baking soda. Above that was the spice shelf. And in the back of the shelf, she saw a big aluminum tin with TEA written across the front of it. It looked like it belonged to one of those sets that had been so popular in the forties and fifties: flour, coffee, tea, sugar. Why was it in with the spices and why was it on its own? She lifted it down and opened it. An opened bag was stuffed into it, and when she lifted it out, she read WARFARIN CONCENTRATE written across the front of it.

She held it out for Jim to see. "Bingo."

"All right."

"We've got what we need. Now let's find Patty Jo and bring her in."

They walked out of the house and Claire went up to the Lexus and knocked on the window. The Realtor rolled it down.

"Where did you say Patty Jo went?"

He shrugged. "She said something about visiting someone in the nursing home. I think the name was Bea."

Claire froze. Beatrice.

Beatrice thought Claire was wrong about Patty Jo. Because of her job, Claire could be a bit of an alarmist.

Beatrice had liked Patty Jo from the first time they met. For one thing, Patty Jo couldn't believe Beatrice had even had a stroke. Patty Jo said she didn't act like a stroke victim. Beatrice hadn't liked the word *victim* and had corrected Patty Jo. The woman had taken that very well and said she couldn't have agreed more with Beatrice. Well, right there you knew the woman had good sense.

Beatrice had also been so impressed with Patty Jo's devotion to her aging husband. A couple of days ago, she and Patty Jo had been talking about their husbands, and Beatrice had mentioned seeing Patty Jo the night her husband died.

"I didn't know you then," she said, "but I remember you walking by. You must feel good about having been with him so close to his death. I was with my husband when he passed away."

Besides, Patty Jo was very agreeable and made it a point of helping her get to bingo. The days did get long at Lakeside Manor.

So Beatrice was happy when Patty Jo appeared and told her she had brought her a little treat. "I made some crabapple jelly the other night. Thought you might like a jar to go with your toast for breakfast."

Beatrice looked at the jelly that Patty Jo set on the rolling table next to her bed. It was a beautiful color, a jewel-like pink. Her mouth watered just looking at it. "That would be nice."

"Would you like to try some now?" Patty Jo asked, "I brought some butter and crackers."

"Sure."

Patty Jo took out four crackers, set them on a plate, spread butter on them, and put a large dollop of jelly on each one. Then she handed the plate to Beatrice.

Beatrice tasted the first one. The taste took her back to her marriage. She had learned how to make crabapple jelly to please her husband. She liked it because it had a little bite to it, the tartness of the apples coming through over all the sugar.

"Good," she told Patty Jo, who handed her another cracker. "Aren't you going to have some?"

"No, this is for you. I already tasted my fill when I made it."

Beatrice ate the three other crackers.

"How are you doing today?" asked Patty Jo.

"A little better, I guess. Hard to say. I walked up and down the hallway, but I get so sleepy."

"You seem discouraged."

"Yeah, I am. I want to be in my own home."

Patty Jo nodded in a knowing way. "I bet sometimes you wouldn't mind leaving this place any way you could."

"That's right." Beatrice was surprised again by how empathetic Patty Jo could be. She wasn't afraid to speak her mind, and Beatrice liked that about the woman.

"I have a feeling you'll be going soon," Patty Jo said with a smile.

CHAPTER 25

"Turn on the siren and head to Pepin," Claire told Bill as they jumped into the squad car, he in the driver's seat and she in the passenger's.

She got on the phone and asked the receptionist at the sheriff's department to put her through to Lakeside Manor. When Jolene answered the phone, Claire was glad to hear her familiar voice. "I'm calling for Beatrice."

"Oh, she has company. I think she's in her room. Let me go see." Claire could hear Jolene talking to someone else, and then the nurse came back on the line, "Yes, she's here with a visitor."

"Is it Patty Jo Tilde?"

The nurse said happily, "Yes, it is. She's such a dear."

Claire wasn't sure what she could ask the nurse to do. "Would you mind going and staying with Beatrice? I'm on my way there, and I'm concerned about her."

"Why? She seems fine."

"Just humor me. I'll be right there."

"Okay."

Bill was driving over sixty miles an hour and taking the curves tightly as the road wound around the farmland. Claire looked up and could see the lake before them. They were minutes out of town. She pulled air deep into her belly. Beatrice would be fine. What could Patty Jo do to her in the nursing home in broad daylight?

Claire answered her own question—just what she had done to her first husband, Florence Tilde, and possibly Walter Tilde. Poison her.

Patty Jo enjoyed every minute of the scene in the nursing home. The deputy came roaring in with her sidekick. They grabbed the jar of jelly. Handcuffed Patty Jo. Stuck her in the squad car.

Then an ambulance pulled up and Beatrice, despite all her objections, was hauled out of her room and to the ambulance. Patty Jo assumed they would take her to the hospital and pump her stomach.

Patty Jo couldn't help but let a little smile float across her mouth. Poor Beatrice! How foolish Claire Watkins would feel. There was nothing in the jar of jelly. Nothing at all but crabapples.

When Jolene had told her that the deputy was snooping around, asking about what had happened to Florence, she decided it was time to give her another scare. Maybe now she would leave her alone.

Patty Jo wouldn't mind this ride to the sheriff's department. She just hoped she'd be able to see Claire Watkins's face when she found out the jelly was untainted.

Through the window of the squad car she could watch everything happening. Claire Watkins was assuring Beatrice she would be okay, holding the old woman's hand as she was loaded into the ambulance. Too bad in a way that she hadn't given Beatrice some rat poison. Hard to watch someone with that much spunk be trapped in a life she didn't want anymore.

She had hated it when her first husband had been disabled. Then she came to hate him. It didn't take her too long to figure out a way to get them both out of the trap that life had set for them. Her husband, she knew, was glad to be released from his pitiful life. And she was glad to set him free.

After the ambulance pulled away, Patty Jo relaxed into the seat of the car.

The two deputies got into the front seat of the car. Claire Watkins turned around and asked Patty Jo what she thought she was up to.

"I thought Beatrice might like some jelly. I made it specially for her."

"You've just dug yourself a pretty big hole, Patty Jo. After what we found . . ."

"What you found? What do you mean?"

"Oh, I know how you like to have your lawyer close at hand. Let's just wait to talk about all this until we can get everyone rounded up. Then maybe everyone would like to have a cup of your tea."

Patty Jo felt her heart drop in her chest. Tea. She didn't like the sound of that.

With Patty Jo Tilde safely tucked in the backseat of the squad car, Claire felt she could relax and enjoy the ride back to the County Government Center in Durand, so she took the back route.

Approaching the Chippewa, Claire saw that the trees were starting to turn colors. The maples went first. Soft yellow, then dropping into sweet red-orange. A maple tree would surprise you on a hillside tucked into a stand of aspen. The hills were lovely in their early fall color. Claire hoped no rain or wind would come in the next few weeks to pull the leaves off the trees. It would be their last shot of color for about six months.

Bill sat next to her with the samples of rat poison and canister of tea at his feet. The crabapple jelly was in the other squad car. Jim had found it, and she was going to let him bring it in.

Patty Jo didn't appear to be enjoying the sights. She was leaning back in the seat, closing her eyes. Maybe she was praying.

Once they got to the sheriff's department, Claire led Patty Jo back to the interview room. She would let her sit there for a while. Soften her up. Patty Jo still hadn't asked her any questions when they left her there. She hadn't even asked for her lawyer. She seemed to have caved in.

Claire didn't quite trust her, but she also didn't see how Patty Jo could get out of this newest alleged crime. Murder. That's what it came down to. They would have to exhume Florence Tilde's body, but, thank goodness, she had not been cremated.

Claire went into the sheriff's office and told him what had happened. "She's here? You brought her in?"

"Yup. With some of Florence's homemade jelly. Jim's got it. He dug a half-eaten jar out of the refrigerator. But best of all, we found a bag of warfarin concentrate in a tea canister in the cupboard. I'm sure we'll find that it has Patty Jo's fingerprints all over it. Patty Jo probably poisoned Florence with her own jelly. I call that lazy and tacky."

"You've never cared for Patty Jo anyway. What does she have to say for herself?"

"Not much. I didn't ask her anything yet. I wanted you to be in on the whole thing. I told her we'd get her lawyer. But I'm in no hurry. Let her sit. Let her stew. She seems like she's in shock. Maybe she'll be more forthcoming this time."

"Good work, Claire."

"Thanks."

"What made you even suspect her of this?"

"There isn't much I'd put past her. She's a nasty person, out to get what she can get from everyone around her. If her sister is right and she'd already done away with one husband, I think it would have been easier the next time. I suspect she had a hand in the death of Walter Tilde, but I don't see any way of proving that, since he was cremated. Just like she cremated her first husband. Walter's death certificate reads stroke, and that's probably what he died from—just brought on a little early by rat poison."

"Impossible to prove?"

"I'm afraid so. Rich's mother saw Patty Jo visit her husband the night before he died, but I don't think we can make much of that." Claire stopped and added, "Unless she tells us about it."

The sheriff ordered some hamburgers from the café down in town. When the order arrived, the three deputies and Claire sat down with him to celebrate. Stupid jokes about rat poison were exchanged, among much laughter. Claire was glad to have Patty Jo back in custody. This time, Claire planned to keep her there.

When the sheriff and Claire got up to go talk to Patty Jo, Claire asked Jim to send the crabapple jelly off to the lab. Then she turned to the sheriff. "I suggest we book her on attempted assault and hold her until we get the lab results back. Unless she gives us more information."

"Sounds good to me. Let's go talk to her."

Patty Jo was sitting at the table with her hands folded in front of her. Any other person, Claire might have thought she was praying. With Patty Jo, she was certain it was a pose. Patty Jo was trying to scramble her way out of this latest fix.

Claire turned on the tape recorder and named the people in the room and the date.

"I don't think you can drag me back in here when I didn't do anything to your mother-in-law."

"Patty Jo, we don't know that yet. Besides, that isn't why you're here."

Patty Jo's head jerked up as if it were tied to a string the puppet master had just yanked. "What?"

"We searched your house again."

Patty Jo's eyes narrowed.

"This time we went looking for some particular jelly."

Patty Jo didn't say anything.

"I asked the nurse who worked the day that Florence died if you had been there. She told me she remembered that you had and that you generously brought in some jelly for her to eat. She even remembers you feeding it to Florence. Unfortunately for you, Margaret was given the jelly after her mother's death and stored it in her fridge. The lab was able to detect rat poison in the crabapple jelly you fed to Florence."

"I didn't bring her any jelly."

"We found a matching jar of jelly in your refrigerator. But I'm guessing it doesn't have rat poison in it." Claire waited two beats, then she said, "However, I did find a canister full of concentrated rat poison in your spice shelf. Not the place that a farmer like Walter would keep it. And I'm betting it has your fingerprints all over it."

Patty Jo ducked her head.

There was silence in the room. Claire signaled the sheriff to wait it out. She wanted to hear what Patty Jo would do with this new information.

Finally, Patty Jo breathed deeply. When her head lifted, there were tears on her face. "I'm glad you found out. I've hated carrying this burden with me. I'm not ashamed of what I did. I couldn't stand to see her suffer anymore."

What was this? Remorse? Claire shot a glance at the sheriff.

He looked back and rolled his eyes. He asked the next question. "Patty Jo, I want you to be clear about this. Are you saying that you admit that you gave Florence jelly with rat poison in it?"

Patty Jo nodded her head.

"You need to say something for the tape," Claire reminded her.

"Yes, I did it. I make no bones about it. I did it with Walter's blessing. He couldn't bring himself to feed her the jelly, but he asked me to do it. It was an act of kindness. She didn't have a life anymore, and we wanted to set her free."

CHAPTER 26

Claire drove up the winding road to Daniel Reiner's house. Ted Thompson sat next to her. She could see why Meg liked him. He had disgustingly long eyelashes, deep-blue eyes, and a great dimpled smile. He had been very quiet since she had picked him up from his house. His mother had asked Claire if she would take him over to the Reiners', since Claire had met Daniel.

"How's school going?" she asked him.

"Okay, I guess."

"Meg said you're reading about the Lewis and Clark expedition."

"Yeah, I like that. I'm not as good a reader as Meg. She sure is smart."

"She says you're a good hunter." Claire wished she could pull the words back. After all, his hunting skills were what had gotten him into this trouble.

Ted didn't seem to notice. He turned to her with the first flash of excitement she had seen on his face. "Did you know that Lewis and Clark had to catch everything they ate? They ate buffalo and deer and even bear."

"I didn't know that."

"I'd like to try bear sometime. This one book even has recipes for how to cook it."

"I'd like to try it too."

"Meg doesn't like hunting, does she?" he asked.

"Oh, Meg's got a soft heart. She doesn't like to see anything get hurt."

"I guess girls are like that."

"Some men are too."

"My dad says that you should be respectful to the animals you hunt. Never let a wounded deer go off into the woods. You have to track it down so it doesn't suffer."

"That sounds like a good rule."

"I'm sorry about the elk."

"I know you are."

"I'm glad he's better."

Claire pulled up in front of the Reiners' house. "Here we are."

"Is he going to yell at me?" Ted asked her anxiously.

"I doubt it."

They got out of the car and walked up to the Reiners' house. Daniel Reiner answered the doorbell and invited them in. Ted walked in slowly, obviously awed by the grandeur of the house.

Claire introduced them to each other and then looked down at Ted.

The boy reached into his pants pocket and pulled out a folded envelope. "Mr. Reiner, I'm sorry that I shot your elk. I didn't mean to hurt it. I just wanted to scare it so it would go away."

"That's understandable," Reiner said.

Ted held out the envelope. "Here's my allowance money for the month to pay you for the vet bills."

"Oh, I don't think that will be necessary."

"But my dad told me that I had to."

Reiner took the envelope. "Well, in that case, I'll buy the elk a bag of apples."

"I know he likes apples," Ted said. "Meg showed me how to feed him."

"Would you ever be interested in doing some work for me around here?" Reiner asked him.

"Work? Like what?" Ted looked up at him.

"Oh, I often need this or that done. Loading firewood or sweeping the patio."

"I could do that."

"Maybe even helping out with the elk?"

"I could try."

Reiner turned to Claire. "Think we'll ever find out who cut the fence?"

"I doubt it. Just one of those mysteries."

"I think I owe you again."

"Still waiting for that cherry pie."

Sitting at the kitchen table, Margaret looked down at her hands. They looked as old as any other part of her body. She worked them raw some days. They were often in water, and they had that crepey look old women's hands got with the veins standing up on the back. Her hands looked the way she remembered her mother's hands. Once in a while she thought to put cream on them at night, but often she was too tired to do anything but brush her teeth and dive into bed.

The phone rang. Margaret was afraid she knew who it was. She had talked to her lawyer earlier, and he had said he would call her back. But when they had first talked this morning, he had not sounded encouraging.

She picked the phone up on the third ring. At least Mark was out of the house right now. She could talk freely without him listening in.

Her lawyer said that, according to Wisconsin state law, Patty Jo would probably get the farm. "I'm sorry to say that even if Patty Jo is convicted or pleads guilty of killing your mother, it won't make any difference to her inheriting your father's estate. Only if she killed your father would that change."

"Patty Jo kills my mother so she can marry my father and inherit his farm and it doesn't matter?"

"If she killed your father, then she couldn't inherit from his estate, but killing your mother, which is still only alleged, won't matter. Yes, I know it's not fair."

Margaret was as close to speechless as she ever got, but she managed to conclude, "So there's nothing more we can do. She's going to inherit the farm and go to jail for the rest of her life."

"Listen, from the scuttlebutt I hear from the district attorney's office, I wouldn't be surprised if they don't end up plea-bargaining her. From what I hear, she'll probably get only fifteen to twenty years for killing your mom. She might easily live long enough to get out on parole. In the meantime she can go ahead with the sale of the farm, and the money will be held for her in escrow until she gets out of jail."

"What if she dies before then?"

"I assume she'll have her own will."

"So it's over."

"We'll see what the probate court judge does with the case, but I'm afraid it won't go your way. I'm so sorry, Margaret."

"Thanks for your help." Margaret hung up the phone before he told her he was sorry again. She wanted to lie down on the floor and weep, but she needed to get herself together before Mark came home.

This stupid, horrible woman had killed her mother, claiming she'd done it as a mercy killing—which was unadulterated bullshit—and she had inherited the family farm.

The baby goat looked up from the box by the fire and bleated at her.

"I know how you feel. The world isn't fair. Get used to it. I don't have a mom either." Margaret pulled a bottle out of the fridge, microwaved it, and then sank down on the floor and fed the little goat.

That was how Mark found her when he came back, almost asleep next to the baby goat. The first question out of his mouth was, "Did the lawyer call?"

Margaret thought of lying. She couldn't bear to see the damage in his eyes, the hopeless rage that would overtake him. But she knew it would only get worse the longer he had to wait. "Yes, he called. He said that she could still get the farm. It doesn't matter that she killed my mother. If she had killed my father, it would be a different story, but we have no proof."

"She kills your whole blasted family, torches our property, and she gets the farm?"

"I know, Mark." Margaret stood up and walked toward him to comfort him.

"Don't come near me."

She stopped, horrified. Worse than losing the farm was what the whole saga had done to him. "Mark," she entreated.

"I'm sorry. I don't want to hurt you. I'm so mad. I want to hit something. And I don't want it to be you."

"Mark, let me make you some lunch."

He started pacing back and forth in the kitchen, clenching his fists and raging. "Margie, I can't stand this. I can't seem to stop myself. I'm afraid of what I might do. When I thought we were going to lose the farm to that rich asshole from the Cities, Reiner, I decided to let all his elk go loose. Just to get back at him."

"You did that?" Margaret couldn't imagine Mark doing anything that might hurt an animal.

"I didn't shoot the elk; I just cut the fence line. They wouldn't have gone far. It was just something to relieve what I'm feeling." He picked up an old red bowl that her mother had given her and looked inside it as though there might be a secret there for him to read.

"She's going to be in court today. I saw it in the *Durand Daily.* Maybe I'll go down there and give them a piece of my mind."

He let the bowl fall from his hands. He didn't throw it, but it broke, nonetheless, in a rain of red shards all over the floor. He stormed out of the house, letting the door bang shut behind him. She called after him, but he didn't even turn around. He ran to his truck, jumped in, and drove out of the yard.

Margaret checked to make sure the baby goat hadn't been hurt by the shards. "I have to stop him."

She looked up a number and dialed it. When a operator answered at the sheriff's department, she asked for Claire Watkins. "I'll transfer you."

A moment later, Claire's voice came on the line. "Deputy Watkins."

"Claire, it's Margaret. I'm sorry to bother you. . . ."

"Oh, Margaret. I was going to call you. It's looking like Patty Jo might accept a plea bargain. She'll be in court this afternoon. Don't bother to come. It'll do you no good. I'll call when it's over."

"It's about Mark."

"Mark?"

"Well, he just stormed out of here as angry as anything, and he was talking about being at the courtroom when Patty Jo was there. I'm afraid of what he might do."

"Do you know if he took a gun?"

"I think he might have one in the truck. You gotta stop him."

"Don't worry. We'll get to him before he gets to the courtroom."

Margaret hung up. She didn't know what to do with herself. She thought of getting in her car and driving down to the government center, but she couldn't stand the thought of seeing what might happen to Mark. She'd be better off waiting at the house.

She stared at the old trunk sitting under the window. It was all she had left of her father and mother. At least she had that to remember them by.

Margaret went to the trunk and opened it. The faint smell of lavender floated out of it and took her back to her childhood, when this trunk had always been in her parents' bedroom.

Her father used to leave her surprises in a secret compartment that was tucked under the one drawer. Sometimes it was silver dollars, sometimes candy. Once he'd left her an arrowhead that he had found in the fields.

She opened up the drawer and then slid back the secret compartment. It was empty. Nothing from her father. She felt bitter disappointment. Then she realized that what she had thought was the lining was actually a piece of paper. She reached in and lifted it out. It was folded. When she opened it, she saw it was a letter from her father.

Dear Margaret,

If you are reading this, that probably means I'm dead. I always wanted to explain to you what happened with your mom. It was my fault, and I accept responsibility for it. When your mom got so sick, I didn't want her to live like that. You understand. I talked to Patty Jo about it, and she said she would help me release your mother from her illness. She killed your mom, but I helped her do it. After we married, she kept bringing it up and said if I didn't sign over everything to her in the will, she would tell what we had done. It was never my intention to hurt your mom. And I never wanted to hurt you. Please forgive me.

Your dad.

The letter was dated in the lower left-hand corner—five days before he had his stroke.

Margaret stood up and held the letter tightly in her hand. So Patty Jo had told the truth. Her father had helped Patty Jo kill her mother. Or rather he had known she was going to do it and hadn't stopped her. Hard to blame him. But this letter did prove that Patty Jo had coerced her father into writing a new will. This evidence might make all the difference. She had to stop Mark. Maybe her father had left her a way to get the farm.

Claire sat outside on the front steps of the government center in the autumn sun and watched as Mark pulled up in his Chevy truck. She knew his vehicle.

He stepped out of the truck and saw her sitting there. At first it looked like he was going to try to skirt around her, go in one of the other doors, but then he changed his mind and walked straight toward her.

"Hey, Claire. You taking a break?" he asked.

Claire stood up. She was between Mark and the door. She saw no reason to pretend. "Waiting for you. Margaret called me."

"Why'd she go and do that?"

"She doesn't want you to get hurt."

"I just wanted to check out what's going to happen to Patty Jo."

"I'll let you know."

He took a step closer, and Claire moved toward him. She was ready to get in his way if she needed to.

"What're you doing? It's a public building. I want to go in and watch."

"You going to let me pat you down?"

"Since when did that start happening here?"

"Since you might be carrying a weapon."

He looked chagrined.

"I think you should go home, Mark."

He slumped and turned toward the truck, then bolted. He ran toward the other door. But she was closer. She cut over the lawn and reached it before him.

She stood in front of the door and patted her gun. "Let me tell you how it is. There's two deputies stationed at the entrance to the courtroom. No way would you get by them. You're not getting by me. If you turn around now and get back in your truck, we forget this happened. If I have to pull my gun on you, you will be under arrest for not obeying an officer. If you are arrested, this will not be taken lightly."

"You think you have all the answers, but that woman is getting away with murder."

"I know. But you will only hurt yourself and Margaret if you try and stop this process. We all live under the law."

"It's fucked."

"It doesn't always work the way we want it to, but it's all we've got."

"But why do I have to play by the rules when she doesn't?"

Claire was fed up with him. "Mark, what is the matter with you? I'm sorry about all that's happened. Patty Jo can't mess up your life, but you can. If you don't pull yourself together right now, you will take one giant step toward destroying yourself. Then she will continue to win."

For a moment Claire thought she was getting through to Mark. He glanced down at the sidewalk and looked as though he was about to slink away. Then he grabbed her by the shoulders and started shaking her.

Claire couldn't get her arms free, so she kicked and connected with his knee. He screamed in pain but wouldn't let go of her. She slammed her head into his face and then he fell over, pulling her down with him.

He was on top of her, but he had let go of her shoulders and brought his hands up to his face. He was bleeding. She tried to scramble away from him, but he caught the belt of her pants, and she couldn't get away.

Just when she was ready to punch him again, she heard a scream. The next thing she knew, a woman had her arms around Mark's neck and was pulling him away from her. The woman was Margaret.

"Stop it," Margaret screamed. "Stop."

Mark quit fighting and put his face in his hands, sitting on the sidewalk.

Margaret stood over him, her hands on her hips, and yelled, "What's the matter with you? Do you want to ruin everything? You should be so ashamed, Mark. We're going to get our farm back from Patty Jo if you will just pull yourself together."

Claire dusted off her clothes and stood up. When she saw Margaret, she knew something had changed for the better, though she wasn't sure what it was. Margaret was yelling as though she had a new life. Her head was held high, and she was finally fighting for what was hers.

CHAPTER 27

Claire and Rich swayed around the dance floor in the old barn on Ruth and Jake's farm. It had been a perfect wedding: a crisp, bright, early November day, a large gathering of close friends, the woman pastor from Fort St. Antoine's Moravian Church doing the honors of uniting Ella and Edwin in holy matrimony. Meg's new goat had gaily pranced down the aisle by her side, both of them wearing crowns of flowers, although Poppy the goat had ended up eating hers during the ceremony.

Margaret and Mark danced close to them, and the two women smiled at each other. Margaret had told Claire the other day that Mark had gone to his first AA meeting in Wabasha. With the new evidence of Walter's letter, the court had decided that Patty Jo had used undue influence to force Walter to change his will in her favor.

Since the court had reversed its decision and given the farm to Margaret, she seemed so much happier. Claire realized she had never really known who Margaret was, having met her under such dire conditions. Also, Margaret had told Claire her hot flashes were finally subsiding.

Claire was glad that Patty Jo Tilde—she even hated that the

woman still carried the name of the man she had probably murdered—was out of the county for good. In a plea agreement she had been given twenty years for the murder of Florence Tilde, with possible parole after ten.

Someone started clinking a glass, and the whole room exploded with the sound of forks tapping wineglasses. Edwin and Ella stopped where they were on the dance floor and kissed. Cheers erupted. They looked so happy together. Ella had worn a lovely taupe silk dress, her hair in short white curls all over her head. Edwin had rented a tux. He looked like an English butler.

Stuart, Lucas, and Rich had all rented tuxedos. But Rich had insisted on wearing his cowboy boots. Claire had found a lovely rich claret silk dress at the thrift shop in Red Wing.

The wedding presents were in a pile by the cake. Claire could hardly wait for them to be opened. Rich and she had picked out a cream-colored hand-sewn quilt from the Amish Country store in Stockholm. She knew Ella would love it.

Claire looked around for Meg. Her daughter was dressed in a flowered dress that made her look like the teenager she would soon become. Claire was surprised to see her dance by with Ted. It looked like her daughter had her first boyfriend.

Even Beatrice seemed happy. She was sitting with two older women friends and had been talking away all evening. She was looking a little tired now, and Claire knew they'd have to get her back to the nursing home soon, but she seemed to have enjoyed herself. In another week or two, she was going home to her own apartment.

"Time to cut the cake," Ruth called out when the music ended.

Stuart had made a three-tiered cake and decorated it with lovely sculpted roses. Almost a shame to cut into it, but there was Ella brandishing a knife and ready to cut the first piece. Edwin circled her waist with his arm and then joined hands with her.

The cherry pie that Daniel Reiner had delivered yesterday was sitting next to the cake. He had left it with Rich, telling him that he owed Claire big-time and this was his way of thanking her. She could tell the pie had come from Le Pain Perdu, but it was the thought that counted. Maybe the guy had a chance of fitting into this community after all.

Claire felt Rich wrap her in his arms and kiss her on the neck as Ella and Edwin cut the cake.

"Are we going to have to wait that long?" Rich asked her, whispering in her ear.

"Till we're eighty? Maybe not."